Paperback: 978-0-578-74601-2
Lightning Source LLC, 14 Ingram Blvd
La Vergne, TN 37086

www.IngramSpark.com

The Otherside Chronicles
By Daniel Gerber

PART I

I

The twin traffic lights gleamed like the piercing eyes of a forlorn demon, watching over Bowie's shoulder intently as he walked down Keene road in the dark. The street lay empty beside him, and the night was silent and ominous. The brick walls and chain link fences that lined the streets returned eerie echoes in the cold night air. Bowie shivered in the frigid mist as he strode through the amber glow of the street lamps.

Bowie's shoes spattered the damp pavement rhythmically as he continued his long walk home from the warehouse. His hands were growing colder by the minute in the pockets of his black hoodie. He desperately wished that he had brought a thicker jacket and longed to be in a warm bed at that moment. More than the biting cold or the eerie dark, beyond anything he wished he hadn't agreed to work for Victor, the authoritative dick of a supervisor who had tricked him into taking a double shift.

He saw a figure moving up ahead, just on the edge of the glow from a streetlight. *It's one in the morning, who the hell would be up at this hour?* Bowie thought. From what he could tell at that distance, the figure was male. A chill ran up his spine and Bowie slowed his pace. The man continued his direction. Would he pass by? At first Bowie thought it was just a drunk wandering about in the fog, but that didn't seem likely. He was walking straight and upright. In that neighborhood, it was more likely somebody who was out to cause trouble. There had been an increase in gang activity over the last few years. A few months ago, there was even a shooting in the area on the news. Whoever he was, he walked with purpose in Bowie's direction. Feeling suddenly on edge and wary of the stranger, Bowie abruptly changed direction and crossed the empty street before the man could get much closer as a precaution. Whoever it was would have to cross to get to him and if it was just another stranger passing in the night then he would continue on his way.

Step by step they flanked the street across from one another. Bowie's heart beat faster. *Would he pass by? Would he keep going?* He hoped the man would just leave him alone. The last thing he needed was to get jumped. Another step. They were almost directly across the street from one another now. Bowie could see him more clearly out of the corner of his eye. The man was wearing a hoodie and jeans much like Bowie's, but he was hunched over and a grizzled, gray beard peeked out from the shadows beneath his hood. Another step. The man stopped and Bowie held his breath. *Keep walking,* Bowie begged, *Keep walking.*

The man knelt down to tie his shoelace. After a moment he got up and continued down the street away from Bowie, who continued forward with a heavy sigh of relief. His day had been bad enough. He didn't need an encounter with a psychopath to top it off.

As Bowie passed beneath another street lamp, he turned his head over his shoulder to take another look at the man in the hoodie. But as he turned a fierce grip seized his upper arm and spun him around. Bowie let out a cry of surprise and terror. *Holy Crap!* The old man stepped in close and slammed Bowie back against the light post. Bowie struggled to free his arm from the man's iron grip, reaching out with his other arm to push him away, but the old man's left shot out and pinned Bowie to the pole. He stepped in closer, breathing right in Bowie's face; his breath was thick and rancid like the stench of a dumpster. His gray, pinprick pupils pierced right through Bowie's eyes.

"Let me go!" Bowie panicked, struggling harder and harder, but in the old man's grip he couldn't move an inch. Bowie kicked up with his right knee to strike the old man in the groin but pain shot through Bowie's leg like he'd just kicked a solid brick wall. The old man didn't flinch or even budge, remaining ever intent on Bowie. "What do you want?" Bowie managed. Though he was terrified, Bowie tried to keep his voice as calm as he could to show that he wasn't afraid.

The old man leaned in even closer until he was only a few inches from Bowie's face. Bowie could hear a faint but chilling pipe organ playing from a pair of earphones nestled in the old man's ears. "Things are going to change." The old man whispered over the muted sound of the lilting organ.

"Yeah, sure. Okay. Whatever you say, man. Just let me go, okay?" Bowie struggled and pleaded.

"Remember to use iron, solid iron. It must be iron, or steel. Nothing else will hurt them!" The old man insisted.

"What? What the heck is that supposed to mean?"

"You'll figure it out when the time comes." The old man let go of his grip and started walking the other way. It was all Bowie could do to not collapse.

"What the hell..." Bowie started to say as he clambered back onto his feet.

"There's no time. No time for conversation. Things are already moving, Bowie Swift." The stranger said over his shoulder. "You should hurry home and get some rest. You're going to need it!"

"How do you know my name?" Bowie yelled after him, but the old man did not answer. He simply walked away to the rhythm of the pipe organ.

Bowie quickly snapped his phone out of his pocket and dialed 911. But when he put it to his ear all he heard was static. "What the... Come on, come on." He pleaded with the phone. He tried again to no avail. His phone showed good reception, but when it connected all he got was white noise.

When he looked up again to see where the old man had gone, there was no one. The street was empty again. There were no side roads, no exits near this part of Keene road. The sidewalks were flanked by chain link fencing and brick walls. He hadn't heard the clinking of fences. The old man couldn't have hopped over them. He was simply gone. Gone from the silent street in the chilling night. *What the hell was that all about?* Bowie thought. He clenched his jaw and massaged his knee.

The eyes of the traffic light, now red in the distance, still watched him. Bowie put his phone back in his pocket and ran home. His pulse was racing and, more than anything, he wanted to be someplace safe and warm.

When Bowie reached his small apartment, he locked the door and shoved the old brown leather couch against it. He placed his aluminum bat on the counter in the kitchen next to the bathroom and took a long warm shower.

A gray dawn cracked through the blinds and down on Bowie's face as he rubbed his eyes in the agony of morning. He flailed his hand around on the alarm clock until the incessant buzzing ceased and silence reigned once more in the small bedroom. He slid his legs from beneath the faded blue sheets and onto the carpet floor.

Bowie's bedroom was a sparse one. A twin bed sat in the corner beside a plywood nightstand he'd made himself. There was a desk lamp and an old hotel alarm clock on the nightstand. Aside from that, the white walled room was barren.

He tossed aside the sweats he'd slept in and threw on an old gray Steelers shirt, a pair of blue jeans and some socks. He fixed himself a bowl of Corn Flakes and a glass of orange juice and sat quietly at the small oak table that stood lonely against the far wall in the living room. Today was going to be another long day.

After breakfast he went into the cramped bathroom to shave. His lids drooped lazily over his pale blue eyes as he ran the razor over his chin. He drew his fingers once through his mid-length straight brown hair to comb it, brushed his teeth, splashed a handful of water on his face and finished dressing. Once he got his steel-toed work boots on and the black hoodie over his shoulders he dragged the leather couch away from his door and stepped outside to begin the long trek to work.

Bowie rarely looked forward to work. Echo City was large and home to over 150,000 citizens. The commute was ten minutes by bus, but Bowie usually walked to work even in the cold just to avoid the smell of cigarettes and the ugly faces of the wary passengers that stared at him when he boarded.

He spent his days working for a big box store called Fleischer Home and Garden that supplied people with all the hardware and gardening supplies they could possibly want. Bowie had been hired for a position in freight management at the nearby warehouse that sat a hundred yards away from the actual hardware store. The warehouse was a large expanse of concrete surrounded by walls covered in aluminum siding. Each wall was bedecked with steel h-frame racking and stacked nearly to the ceiling with pallets of drywall, lumber and customer orders. Aisle after aisle of sundry goods filled the center of the warehouse leaving only enough space for a fifty-foot square expanse of pallets stacked two or three high and various shipments set loosely on the ground with no real care. A small corner room by the time clock served as an office for important personnel, namely the manager, Victor.

Bowie's job was to supervise the freight crew and also find out how many items were in stock based on reports given him by other employees, determine how much would be needed and then order what needed to be ordered. His co-workers rarely complete their responsibilities on time, and more often than not Bowie was behind in his work. The freight crew was always slammed trying to get everything in and out of the warehouse. He had stayed late the previous night for that reason, counting items himself and getting his totals in line.

The cement floor felt even harder on his feet than usual as Bowie slid the paper punch card into the time clock.

"Glad to see you're up." Came a cocky baritone voice from over his shoulder. Bowie didn't even have to look to know the immense smirk that had spread across Victor's face. "I hope you weren't kept too late last night."

Bowie turned and looked past his overweight manager, ignoring the comment. He shrugged his shoulders, walked past, making sure to avoid eye contact. A rough hand grabbed him by the forearm.

"I don't want to have any attitude from you today. Got it?" Victor said. Victor was two hundred pounds and about five and a half feet tall. He wore a bulging gray shirt and a strained pair of khaki slacks. His face was very round, bedecked with a pair of large steel rimmed glasses, and topped with short slate gray hair. He stood a few inches below Bowie, who was convinced the difference in height only served to make Victor more spiteful.

"Whatever you say, Victor." Bowie mumbled.

Victor squeezed his arm and jerked him around so that Bowie was looking directly into his face. "Like that. You need to learn to show some respect, Swift. How do you expect to get ahead in this world if you don't know proper etiquette?"

"I haven't done anything. Please let go of my arm." Bowie sighed. Work was always like this.

Victor looked Bowie up and down before releasing his arm. "You haven't been drinking, have you?"

Bowie knew that Victor was only looking for an excuse to make life even worse than it was. *I wish I had. Then you could fire me and I wouldn't have to stare at your disgusting fat face all day.* Bowie thought. "I'm just tired. I had a long night last night."

"How late did you stay?" The corners of Victor's mouth curled up with pleasure.

Bowie had had enough conversation. "Late." He said simply as he walked away. Victor didn't follow.

"Man, my boss is a douche," Bowie mumbled to himself later that day as he walked his fingers through the folders of a gray filing cabinet in the cramped beige office in the corner of the warehouse. The day was passing slowly, and Bowie had managed to keep his cool so far but work was starting to take its toll.

"Hey man," came another familiar voice as Bowie stepped out of the office and let the heavy door swing shut behind him. Eduardo was a burly man from a big Hispanic family. He kept his head shaved and sported what could only be generously described as a ratty mustache. He was wearing what he typically wore: a too-long pair of worn blue-jeans with holes forming in the seat and the legs, a brown hand-me-down tee-shirt. A pair of faded white Reeboks completed his outfit. "Victor says he wants me to show you how to file something, man. He wants to make sure you know how to put your report into the computer."

"Don't bother, Ed. I already know how to do that. Vic's just being a dick."

"You sure, man? He might get mad if you don't go through it again." Eduardo knew Bowie could do it, and he also hated it when Victor was in a bad mood just as much as Bowie did, which was most of the time.

"Victor can go screw himself," Bowie snapped.

"Whoa! Hey. Come on. Take it easy man; you still got half your shift left. Don't let the boss man get to you like that."

"Sorry, Ed. I'm just tired," Bowie yawned, "I stayed late last night because Victor needed a recount, and I got jumped by some crazy old guy on the way home."

Ed's eyes widened.

Bowie didn't pay it any mind. The last thing he wanted to do was talk about a near mugging and get lectured on walking home alone at night. "I'm gonna go finish the count on the nails. Just tell Vic you walked me through it, alright?"

"Okay. But if he finds out…"

"Yeah, I know. Look, if he gets his pants in a twist, what's he going to do, fire me?"

"He might. Hours have been kinda slim here." Eduardo kicked the heel of his shoe on the cement floor. "Hey, did you ever talk to that cashier with the ponytail? The one you were talking about a couple days ago." Eduardo nudged Bowie and gave him a devious smile.

"No. Not yet. I'm not good at that kind of stuff anyway. Sheesh."

"Huh? Come on, man. What's the problem?" Eduardo continued.

"Dude, she doesn't even know me. What am I supposed to do? Walk up and say 'hey, let's go on a date?' She'd say no."

"Hey, it doesn't hurt to try, man. You never know. Maybe she'll say yes." Ed gave him one of those 'you-won't-know-until-you-try' looks. "I heard she likes scary movies. Totally hot, man." He wiggled his eyebrows.

"I don't think so."

"Whatever." Eduardo sat down on a pallet of rolled insulation. "That's called giving up."

"Did Vic mention anything besides inputting data in the computer?" Bowie asked.

"I think he was talking about going through the store today and double checking everything."

"Crap. Really?" Bowie sighed.

"Yeah man. I don't think he's been too happy about the last few inventory counts. Corporate keeps walking his warehouse lately. You better be careful. You could get fired."

"I really don't care if I do. The better for me," Bowie replied. "I'm sick of Vic and all his petty bullshit."

"Hey man, why you still working here, then?" Eduardo raised an eyebrow.

The comment struck Bowie dumb.

"You started working here like two years ago, but all I ever see is you complaining about how much you hate it," Eduardo pushed.

"Look, I don't have another job just waiting for me, okay? This is the only source of income I have. If I quit, I'm on the street."

"I'm just saying. You complain a lot about this job but you never leave. And besides, quitting and getting fired is the same thing. You'd still be out of a job."

"It's not that simple. Besides, you think Victor is just as much of an…" Bowie dropped his voice suddenly as he saw Victor out of the corner of his eye inspecting a pile of lumber Bowie had just put into inventory. "You know what I mean."

"Yeah I know what you mean. But you don't see me complaining, man. I do my job. I respect my job." Eduardo's face grew redder as he continued. "You're lucky to have a job. I had to scrape my way into this. This is what I have to do to support my family. But I choose to do it."

"Well I don't have a family, Ed," Bowie said.

"Sorry man. I'm just sayin' you don't have to do this if you don't like it." Eduardo stood up. "Grow some cojones man. But don't complain to me. You should be grateful you have a place to work!"

"Sorry. I'm sorry, man." Bowie hushed his friend. "I didn't mean it like that."

"If your job ain't going anywhere, leave." Eduardo practically spat the words on Bowie's shoes. "Spend your time off looking for something else. I'm sure there's something you would rather do than work here."

"I don't know," Bowie trailed off.

One of Eduardo's powerful arms gently grabbed Bowie by the shoulder. "I know it's hard. I've been there too, man. I used to blow all my money drinking and stuff and didn't care what I was doing with myself. I guess somewhere I decided I wanted a family, you know? I'm just saying nobody knows what they want to do with themselves when they're your age. You'll figure it out." He leaned down and looked right into Bowie's eyes. "Just take care of yourself. All right?"

"Yeah." Bowie shrugged.

"I'll pretend we went through the computer stuff again but don't make Vic madder than he already is."

"Yeah, I'll do that. Thanks." Eduardo released his grip and Bowie headed off to take stock of the palletized screws and nails boxes.

Bowie saw Victor writing some things down on his clipboard and decided that he should hurry up and submit his monthly report before Victor asked him to re-do the whole thing.

"Swift!" Victor bellowed from the other side of the warehouse tapping his foot. He stood beside the steel shelves housing a myriad of assorted tubes. "Swift!" He shouted again as Bowie slid outside of the gray door to the office. Bowie had made it at last to the end of his eight-hour shift. Once he was off the clock he was done. In one quick fluid motion, Bowie grabbed his yellow time card, slid it into the time-clock, and placed it back in one of the tin slots on the wall before Victor could get to him. Bowie casually turned around to face Victor who had since moved quickly to catch Bowie before he could leave.

"What's up?" He asked disinterestedly as he pulled his black hoodie over his shoulders.

"Did you just clock out?" Victor's voice hissed like a broken steam pipe.

"Yeah," Bowie shrugged, "Shifts over; I'll see you tomorrow." *And I'm not putting up with you anymore today.*

"Clock back in, I need you to work another double shift. You need to re-do the report in lumber."

"I double checked lumber last night when I did the report. The numbers were wrong, and I corrected them. Besides, the report has already been filed. I'll take a look at it tomorrow."

"Swift, I asked you to clock back in. You need to fix it." A cruel smile spread over Victor's face. Victor always knew when he had Bowie on the ropes. Bowie needed this job to pay his rent, and Victor could cut his hours or fire him as he wished.

Bowie halted his escape a yard from Victor, turned on his heel and faced Victor. Bowie could almost feel the tension rising up through the room like steam. "Sorry, I can't. I have a prior engagement." Bowie lied.

"Like what?" Victor prodded.

"It's personal."

"Like what?" Victor's voice rose in agitation.

"It's personal." Bowie's voice rose to match.

"What could possibly be so important that you're refusing a shift?"

Bowie assumed a calm emotionless tone as he answered. "That's not any of your business. I'm sorry. I'll see you tomorrow."

"Don't take that attitude with me." Victor threatened.

"I'm not. I'm simply stating the facts." Bowie lied again. There was nothing Victor could do to force Bowie to come in for a shift at the last minute that he hadn't agreed to previously. Of course, that didn't stop him.

"Don't get snippy with me."

"I'm off the clock, Vic." When Bowie used the nickname, Victor gave him something resembling a snarl. "I've got to go."

Victor's round face grew crimson like an enormous cherry. Bowie didn't wait around to hear what Victor had to say. He slipped out the door and onto the cold sidewalk outside. Two employees were standing by the building, smoking. As the steel door behind him closed he coughed and waved the clouds of smoke out of his eyes.

His hands curled into fists as he skipped over the parking lot curb. The damp grass sagged beneath his shoes as he crossed the short lawn separating the lot and the sidewalk. What did he care if the warehouse struggled? It wasn't like his work was appreciated anyway. He was just so tired of it all...

15

II

Ed's right. Why do I stay? Bowie wondered as he walked back to his apartment. *I can't leave. I wouldn't have a job, and without an income I can't even afford my rent. I have to stick it out. But for how long? When is enough enough? Maybe I should just quit. But where would I go? Dammit! Why can't my life just function for once?* He kicked a small rock down the street as he crossed an intersection. *What the hell kind of world lets guys like Victor become managers? I mean, come on!* He was passing a suburb on his left and paying no mind to the passing traffic that whipped by. *How am I supposed to do anything with myself if I can't leave my stupid job? And what would I do even if I could? Nothing!* He realized all too simply. *I'm not anything. I'm nobody.*

It was after five o'clock, but Bowie was still furious, so he took a quick detour down Blue Jay Avenue into the worn-out suburb to blow off some steam. The houses had been around for decades and most of them looked it. The paint was faded and many of the lawns were dead in the winter months. Each house Bowie passed became a painful reminder of the life he was living.

A German shepherd barked out viciously as it rushed the chain link fence separating Bowie from an old brown one story house with simple garden tools leaned up next to the doorstep. Something about the dog got to him.

"Shut up!" Bowie yelled at the beast as he kicked the fence. The dog kept barking and Bowie got angrier and angrier. He shouted again and the dog only barked louder. His rage got the better of him and he grabbed a beat-up steel garbage can from the curb and hurled it against the fence as hard as he could. "I HATE this!" He shouted. "SHUT UP!" he screamed at the dog. He stomped down on the garbage in rage as it spilled onto the sidewalk and kicked it against the fence again and again. He wound up and booted it as hard as he could down the sidewalk and watched in his fury as it clattered down the street several yards. He gnashed his teeth, and spat, and cursed again and again at the dog and the can; again and again at his job and his life.

As he turned to continue his walk, he noticed someone standing on the half-dead lawn of the house across the street. It was a man, about six feet tall with a medium build. He was wearing a red flannel shirt and light blue faded jeans. He stood staring at Bowie, never blinking.

"What?!" Bowie spat angrily, trying hard not to be embarrassed.

The man didn't say anything.

Bowie walked over to the can and set it right side up again. "I was just leaving, anyway. Sorry about the mess." He had started to walk back toward his usual route home when the man in the flannel shirt started walking toward him. Bowie didn't really feel like getting into a confrontation, so he picked up the pace and started to run.

The man rushed forward in a mad dash and tackled Bowie in his mid-section. The two went down in a heap. Bowie scrambled furiously to get away but the man was on top of him. He scraped and kicked his way out from beneath the man and regained his footing. The man stood up and came at him again, still saying nothing.

"Hey, man! I'm sorry. Just leave me alone!" Bowie shouted at him. But his words didn't seem to matter. "Hey! I said I'm sorry! Take it easy!"

The man swung a heavy fist into Bowie's face, which sent him stumbling back a few feet to the curb. Bowie was pissed. "Fine! You wanna go?" he shouted,

"Let's go!" He lunged at the man and started pummeling his chest and head. The man didn't flinch or seem to feel anything. He just stood there and took it.

The dog in the yard began whimpering and backing away from the fence.

Bowie danced a few feet back, and when the man came at him again, he aimed a kick straight at his groin. It was a direct hit, but it didn't stop the man from slamming his arms down on Bowie's shoulders. Bowie grunted and nearly crumbled under the force of the blow. He grabbed the man by the arms and the two began grappling with each other. To Bowie it was like wrestling with a horse. No matter how hard he tried, the man was stronger and wouldn't budge. With a false step backward, Bowie toppled over the curb and into the adjoining dirt yard, dirt smearing on his face.

The man ended up on Bowie's other side during the tussle, by the chain link fence. The whimpering dog behind the fence backed up even further and hid behind the corner of the house.

Bowie got up and rushed to tackle the stranger, shoving him as hard as he could face-first into the chain-link fence. There was an audible hiss, and the man convulsed and shook in Bowie's grasp. Bowie let go in surprise and stepped back a few paces.

Bowie's eyes went wide as the man peeled his singed and distorted face from the fence, looking angrily at Bowie. Where the chain link had touched his skin, the man was covered in black puckered burns and oozed black ichor. As Bowie took a few steps back in horror the man rushed him and slammed a fist hard into Bowie's gut. Bowie flew through the air nearly ten feet and crashed into the side of the house near the doorstep, knocking the wind right out of him. When he struck the wall the garden tools leaning by the door fell down in a pile on top of him.

Desperately he struggled to get out from beneath the pile.

The man was still coming at him. He frantically searched the pile for something to use to defend himself. There was a rusted shovel with a long wooden handle still leaned up against the doorjamb of the house. Bowie snatched it up as the man rushed him and, using the full length of the shovel, slapped the man in the face with the flat of the spade. To his surprise the man spun around and lost his balance. He stumbled over his own feet till he was standing just in front of the chain link fence while Bowie took the opportunity to get between his adversary and the street. He should have run, but by then Bowie was lost in the fury of combat. Using the spade like a spear, Bowie gnashed his teeth and charged the stranger, driving its tip into the man's chest.

The flannel shirt ripped and the man was pushed back against the chain fence. Steam hissed from the wound and his body shook violently as Bowie pressed the shovel harder and harder into the wound. With a sudden stillness and release, the shovel went through the man and clinked against the chain link as the man's chest grew black and bubbling like crude oil. Then his arms, waist, head and legs all melted into the same black goo and slopped and dripped over Bowie's shovel before splattering on the hard dirt.

Bowie dropped the shovel in shock and looked down at the thick puddle. It began flowing over the dirt, across the curb and then to the center of the street. As he watched it go the pavement sank suddenly into a gaping sinkhole and the black sludge poured over the side and out of sight.

Bowie stared in disbelief. *What had just happened?* He waited a moment before going cautiously over to the hole to look down. From where he stood, he could not see the bottom even though the sun was still high in the sky. It seemed to stretch endlessly down into the dark pits of the earth.

Bowie's body was shaking as he raced towards his apartment. *What the hell just happened? Did I just kill someone? What the hell!* Bowie flipped out his cell phone as he ran to call the police but the screen read 'no signal'. All he could think of was to get home and lock the door. He needed to sit down and make sense of things. *Who would believe me anyway? I need to calm down. I need figure out what just happened. I just killed someone!* The thought made Bowie sick. *Or something...*

It wasn't until Bowie reached his apartment that his hysteria subsided. He snapped the lock and leaned his back against the door and took a moment to breathe.

"What was that?" Bowie mumbled to himself. Even as he said the words the old man's voice echoed in Bowie's mind. *"... Use iron, solid iron. It must be iron, or steel. Nothing else will hurt them!"* Bowie went into his bedroom and hefted a black wooden storage box from his closet floor and set it on his dining table. It was full of keepsakes he'd taken from his old house when his father had passed away. After he opened the dusty lid, he dug through the various odds and ends. There were photographs from when he was younger, pictures of his father as well as an old silver piccolo his father used to play before he passed away, still inside its case. He set those things aside and found what he was looking for: an old knife.

The knife had been handed down to him by his father, and from his father's father who had carried it in World War II. It was made by Bowie's great grandfather and his friends in the railroad company before the war had started. He'd been told that his great grandfather's friends had helped him forge the weapon from an old steel leaf-spring they'd got from an abandoned Buick. The blade was two inches wide and ten inches long, shaped like a Civil War era Bowie knife. The blade was tarnished and worn but still sharp despite its use. The handle was long with a dark leather grip, inlaid with copper bands. The handle was capped where it met the blade by a bronze oval disc that serve as a guard. It weighed over a pound but felt light in Bowie's hands.

Bowie's grandfather had wanted something to use in place of the standard issue army machete that, after an hour of hacking through dense undergrowth of the South Pacific, would grow the dull. The knife seldom needed re-sharpening, and Bowie's grandfather had never needed a replacement.

Bowie had always looked up to his grandfather though he had only really known him for a few years. When he was eight his parents had broken the news that his grandfather's house had burned down with him still inside. They never did recover the remains but the authorities believed it was a suicide. Archer Swift had been battling depression for decades after his time in the war. Since his death, Bowie had held on to the knife as a keepsake.

The weapon felt good in Bowie's hands as he removed it from its hard leather sheathe. He ran his belt through the loop in the leather and re-sheathed the knife. He wanted to have it on hand, he was sure. Until he could make sense of things, he wanted to feel safe.

Maybe this is all just in my head. Bowie's mind started racing. *Oh, God. I'll get arrested for murder! But they can't prove it. He turned to sludge, didn't he? He went down that hole... I drove the shovel right through... Oh god. I'm gonna be sick.* He clutched at his stomach and put a hand to his mouth to suppress the urge to vomit.

I should call the police. It was self-defense. He attacked me first. Maybe if I turn myself in, they'll go easy on me.
It's the right thing to do.
He picked up his phone once more and tried to dial out but again the screen flashed 'no signal.' He'd have to go to the police station himself if he was going to get anything resolved. He wavered. Had somebody seen him? Someone could have been watching the fight through the windows. After all, he had made quite a racket in the quiet neighborhood. With a deep sigh he put on his beaten brown leather jacket over his hoodie. It was getting colder outside, and by the time he returned from the police station (if he returned), it would be very dark and below freezing.

He locked up his apartment and walked to the Conoco station on Keene Road, partly because he was avoiding the uncomfortable inevitability of talking to the police and partly because he was still a little spooked.

The cold air was prickly as Bowie crossed the empty space between gas pumps and a breeze kicked an old candy wrapper across his worn boots. Bowie entered the station through the glass door and a cheap alarm bell announced his presence. He passed down an aisle where the emergency supplies were displayed. He took a moment to scan the shelves before he grabbed a flashlight from the shelf and a can of Pepsi from the cooler. His blood sugar would run low before the night was through, and he was sick of walking home in the dark. He heard the alarm bell and the sliding door behind him. He glanced over his shoulder and almost jumped.

A mechanic in navy blue coveralls standing just inside the door was staring right at him. Bowie stared back. It was just another customer. He was probably just grouchy from a hard day at work. The balding stranger had a rugged face belonging to a man in his late forties.

Bowie thought he'd seen the man before, but he couldn't be sure where.

Deciding he was harmless, Bowie carefully walked down the aisle to the gray counter in the middle of the store to pay for his things. He kept his gaze on the stranger who hadn't moved and still kept his gaze on Bowie. Bowie placed his items on the counter and turned his attention to where the cashier should have been standing.

However, there was no friendly face waiting for him. He looked left and right but he didn't see an attendant anywhere. About ready to call out for assistance, Bowie's gaze happened to drop just below counter level where a small splatter of blood glistened on the gray cabinets. He leaned over the counter and saw a bearded overweight man in a Conoco uniform slumped against the cabinets with his skull bashed in. Bowie's eyes widened and he stumbled back a step. He quickly turned to leave through the main entrance.

The mechanic didn't say a word. He simply stood in Bowie's way blocking the exit. "Excuse me," Bowie said as he took a courageous step forward. The mechanic didn't move. He didn't speak. He stood, never blinking, staring at Bowie. "Excuse me." He said again.

The mechanic said nothing.

"Please. Move." Bowie said. It was becoming clearer by the moment that this man wasn't going to move. Losing his grip, Bowie panicked. He needed to get to the police station. Bowie drew his grandfather's knife and pointed it at the man. "Get out of my way."

The mechanic looked dully at the knife, and then back up to Bowie. Bowie took another step toward the door, keeping the blade trained on the man. Suddenly, the mechanic rushed Bowie and tried to mash his fist into Bowie's skull. Bowie wasn't ready for the sudden assault and took the hit hard. As he stumbled back, he took a swipe at the mechanic and hit the man's arm.

The swipe connected with flesh and a spray of black peppered the air but the man made no sign of pain or distress. Instead, the mechanic took another swing. This time Bowie was ready. He dodged the hit and grabbed the mechanic by the collar. He plunged the knife into the man's stomach. The mechanic clutched at the black gushing wound looking up at Bowie with hardly an expression as his face melted away and his clothes and body became another black puddle on the tile floor. A chill ran through Bowie's body. *This isn't real,* he thought. *This can't be real...*

The goo ran over the floor with a will of its own, forced its way through the crack beneath the door and out onto the asphalt. Bowie quickly pushed through the door and followed it. It slithered its way to the curb that bordered the station. As it did, a chunk of the sidewalk suddenly crumbled, a gaping hole opened up to a deep abyss, and the black sludge vanished over the edge. Bowie raced back into the store, stuffed the goods into his pockets and hurried back outside.

The darkening streets were empty, and a chill wind was picking up as Bowie hurried toward the police station. The buildings seemed to leer down at him as his hollow footsteps echoed in the night. It was almost a twenty-minute walk from the Conoco to the downtown police station. It felt like the longest twenty minutes he'd ever experienced.

As he rounded the corner of a drug store onto Blackwell Street, he stopped abruptly. Across the street on the sidewalk was a young, blonde, college woman in a short skirt and heavy jacket accompanied by a balding attorney in a suit and tie. The unlikely pair were staring at

Bowie and stood eerily still. Bowie wasn't sure if they would turn out to be monsters like the mechanic. He wasn't terribly inclined to find out.

Bowie still had a long way to go. The buses weren't running, and Bowie hadn't seen a single car on the road since he left his apartment. It was as if the streets had been cleared for his own personal judgment day. Calling a cab would be out of the question, and besides, his cell phone still had no signal. He had little choice but to proceed on foot.

The pair didn't remain stationary for long. The woman walked toward him while the attorney began circling around to block his escape route.

This can't be happening. Bowie thought. He turned and ran down the sidewalk, made a sharp turn into an alley, hurtled over a stack of cardboard boxes and kept running. He could tell they were following close behind but at least they could only come at him from one direction in the alley. The alleyway veered sharply around a corner and Bowie followed it. He ran fast and hard, and when he'd reached the next street, he continued across the street and right into another alleyway. Footsteps pattered behind like heavy rainfall. As he glanced over his shoulder, he could see a teeming mass of shadows blocking out the small amount of evening light that clawed its way into the alley.

Their numbers were growing.

He passed an empty dumpster that stood at an angle along the alley wall. Bowie skidded to a halt, thrust his weight at the jutting end and forced the dumpster sideways into the alley until it blocked the route through. It wouldn't stop them but at least it would buy him some time to get away. He turned and ran for all he was worth. The shadows slowed and convened in silent communion before the dumpster.

He continued through the labyrinth of alleyways, his heart pounding, until at last he stumbled into a pool of flickering light from a street lamp. His steamy breath billowed out into the night air and for a moment he thought he was safe.

His respite was cut short. He heard a scuffle and grunts and wheezes from somewhere nearby. He hurried past a concrete loading ramp and around another corner before he found the source of the disturbance. A trio of thugs, each clad in black jackets, jeans and chains were pounding a huddled mass against a cinder-block wall. Ordinarily, Bowie would have left them alone, but he knew the victim. It was the old man from the night before. His haggard voice cried out as he endured their blows.

"Hey! Leave him alone!" Bowie shouted as he sped across the asphalt and struck the body of the first of the thugs with his shoulder. Bowie rebounded and grabbed his shoulder in pain. He backed up a few steps, and the skinhead thug turned to see what had struck his side.

Bowie made a split-second decision. It was either him and the old man, or the thugs. He unsheathed his knife and rushed in again before the skinhead thug could react. Bowie thrust the knife forcefully and black ooze erupted from the thug's chest.

The other two thugs turned away from the old man. Bowie held the knife in his right hand and kept his left arm up at the ready. However, instead of simply rushing Bowie, like he had anticipated, the one sporting a Mohawk reached into his pant pocket and pulled out a bone-handled stone knife.

Mohawk lunged. There wasn't enough time to dodge out of the way, but Bowie swung his knife down at the thrusting arm. The slash severed the arm and Mohawk's forearm slopped to the ground. The stone knife struck Bowie in the sternum, which stung sharply, but otherwise hadn't done much damage. Bowie clutched his chest with his free hand as he pointed the knife at his enemy. Mohawk stared at his arm stump with little more than curiosity, and dissolved into a puddle. Bowie let the bubbling mass slip its way to a sink hole that rapidly formed a few yards away. Instead, his attention turned to the last punk who turned and ran. As Bowie watched him run, a cloud of smoke enveloped his body and he vanished without a trace.

Bowie was speechless. "What the hell was that?" He wondered aloud. The old man picked himself up off the ground. "Did you do that?" Bowie said between breaths.

"No, that was not me." The old man began. "But there's no time to explain now. I see you've brought iron. Good. There's more I require of you."

"What do you mean more? This is bullshit! What the hell are those things?" Bowie growled. "You owe me an explanation!"

The ancient figure staggered close to Bowie and tightly held the sides of Bowie's head. "There is no time!" He said angrily. "Weren't you listening? You must pay attention and do exactly as I say. My time here is limited. You must meet me at the sewage plant north of the city in exactly one hour, and you must bring with you a mirror. A mirror and a brass ring. Don't forget either, and don't forget the iron weapon you brought with you." The old man's gnarled fingers pointed at the knife in Bowie's hands. "It is critical."

"What do I need all that stuff for?"

"I told you my time is limited. I can't hold on here much longer." And with another cloud of smoke the old man vanished too.

"Dammit!" Bowie shouted to the night air as he kicked the brick wall. "The hell is going on!" He let himself cool off for a moment until his racing heartbeat slowed.

His gut told him the old man was right, that he didn't have much time. He slipped down the alleyway and onto Blackwell Street. An hour was pushing it. He didn't have time to run home to get a mirror or a brass ring, even if he could find something like that in his apartment. Most stores were closing soon and lay in the opposite direction. He knew where the old man wanted him to go. It would take him an hour just to get to the sewage plant. He knew there was a pawn shop about a block away. Maybe if he was lucky, they'd have a mirror there. He just hoped he wouldn't run into any more creatures along the way.

The run-down pawn shop was dark and the door was locked. None of the lights from the neighboring properties were on. The only illumination came from the unhealthy glow of a street lamp further down the street. Bowie had often walked by, but he had never ventured inside.

Bowie looked down the street to make sure no one was watching before returning his attention to the door. "I've come this far." He grimaced. He took his grandfather's knife and rammed the butt into the window, shattering it. Careful of the glass, Bowie reached his hand inside, snapped the deadbolt, wrenched the door open and slipped inside. Grabbing the flashlight out of his pocket, Bowie began searching through the display cases of odds and ends to find what he was looking for.

He paused the light on the cool calming surface of an ornate silver mirror. The mirror was about the size of a ping pong paddle and would just barely fit inside the pocket of his hoodie. No doubt it had once been a family heirloom. Now it seemed only a reminder of hard times. He smashed the glass case that contained it and stuffed it in his pocket.

Now for the brass ring. He didn't bother breaking the other jewelry cases open. He knew there would only be gold and silver rings or cheap replicas within and he couldn't be certain the cheap ones were brass. More likely they were painted pot metal. He hopped behind the counter and rummaged around hoping to find a brass key ring. There were none on the cluttered shelves, but something else had caught his eye. In the corner Bowie had noticed a worn copper pipe emerging out of the wall and angling upwards towards the ceiling. Two feet above the angle was a shutoff valve connected with brass coupling rings. *Would that work?* He wondered. With a grunt and a hard twist, Bowie shut the valve. *But how to get the ring off?* Bowie glanced out the window to make certain there were no visitors outside. Only shadows played on the windows.

He searched around the store for a few minutes, looking for anything that might help him get what he needed. On the back wall, Bowie found a beat-up Leatherman in a wooden box labeled 'tools'. Using it, Bowie disconnected the upper pipe from the valve. Stagnant water spilled out, spattering the front of his shirt but he paid it no mind. He put the Leatherman in his pocket absently in order to grip the coupler with both hands, turning it as hard as he could. It was a strain before the coupler suddenly gave and came loose. He had his brass ring. He only hoped that it would suffice. Now all he had to do was get back to Keene Road and head north to the sewage treatment plant that lay to the north of Echo City.

Bowie started for the door but hesitated, his heart pounding. He'd already encountered more than a handful of the strange creatures that had attacked him, and he was bound to run into more. The bus line didn't go near the sewage plant and if he had to walk there, he wasn't going to make it in time. He checked his watch and silently cursed to himself. By the door he spotted an old bicycle in the display window. "Nice." He grabbed it off its display and rolled it outside. Looking down the street to his right he saw moving shadows in the sickly glow of the street lamps. He didn't have time to waste. Bowie quickly swung a leg up over the seat, placed his feet on the pedals and sped off down the street.

He'd sped past anyone and everyone he'd seen on the streets and hadn't stopped even once to catch his breath. The hammering of footsteps behind him had died off long before he reached his destination. If Bowie was lucky, they wouldn't know to find him here. If those creatures were going to get him, they'd have to catch him first.

Bowie turned onto the gravel road leading to the sewage plant. A "No Trespassing" sign staked to the right of the entrance was nearly hidden and overgrown by tall grass. The only light on that backwater road came from the nearby suburb and a single lamp post a hundred yards ahead. The sewage plant itself was nestled among the branches of Russian olive trees and hidden from the main road that led to it. The ill-used dirt path and largely overgrown weeds surrounding the road told him that only sewage plant employees ever came this way.

He got off the bike and rolled it up to the open gate. *Okay. I'm here.* Bowie thought. *Now what?*

Past a large aluminum-sided structure which sat quietly in the pale glow of the plant's flood lamps, there were two large rectangular pools on either side of an overgrown dirt path that led from one end of the facility to the other.

The sound of shifting gravel brought Bowie's attention to the corner of the building. Around the corner came the old man. He seemed tired, as if the old man struggled just to keep upright as he walked. Bowie could hardly blame him. Those thugs or creatures or whatever they were had given the man quite a beating. Bowie moved forward and stood before the him once more. This time the man was smiling.

"You've brought everything. Good." The old man nodded.

"Can you *please* tell me what's going on?!" Bowie demanded. "What were those things?"

"There's no time." He said as he led Bowie down the path between the two pools. "I can only maintain this puppet for a few minutes at most."

"Of course, there's time." Bowie insisted.

The old man shook his head and pointed. "You have company."

Bowie looked where the man was pointing and went pale. Coming through the gates he could see a throng of men, women and children walking toward them with vacant expressions.

"The mirror!" snapped the old man.

Bowie took the mirror out of his jacket pocket. The old man placed it on the ground. "The ring!" He grabbed at Bowie's hands even before they had left his pockets. The old man set the brass ring on the mirror, held the ring down with two fingers and with his other hand, forcefully pounded the ring down once, cracking the mirror into a spider web of fractures. The only portion of the mirror that remained whole was the surface on the inside of the ring. "Your blood. Quickly." The old man hurried.

"What!" Bowie said, appalled.

"Trust me!" The old man held out his hand for Bowie's.

The crowd was quickly nearing. Some of them had broken into a run.

"In the center of the ring. Hurry!"

"Okay!" Bowie clipped his finger with his grandfather's knife and a single drop of blood fell into the center of the brass ring and onto the broken mirror beneath.

Suddenly the very world around him buckled and swam, tearing to ribbons, replacing itself with shifting shapes and blurs. He lost focus and his stomach heaved violently. Lightheadedness took him and he reeled and struggled to keep his balance. He turned desperately to face the oncoming horde, but they too blurred and shifted like rain in a hurricane. At last the visions settled, the cacophony of thundering feet was silenced and Bowie passed out.

III

When he regained consciousness, Bowie looked up at the old man but saw only a stranger. His grungy street clothes were replaced with furs and tribal feathers. His hair was no longer gray and mangled. In its place were crystalline shards that melted into his wrinkled skin. In his hands was an old wooden grinding organ with peeling red paint and a cracked leather strap that hung from his neck. Though it somehow seemed perfectly healthy, the old man's skin was translucent. A crystalline skeleton lay beneath, hazy and indistinct. Bowie's eyes went wide. The old man reached out a gnarled hand to help Bowie up off the ground.

"Welcome to Otherside, Mr. Swift."

Bowie tried to stand up, but found it difficult and fell quickly to the ground. The very ground beneath his feet seemed to blur as if torrential winds tore at it. The air seemed ragged before his eyes and the trees that had surrounded the sewage plant were broken and jagged, as if some monstrous creature had dashed each one to crooked splinters. The few colors he could see were muted and dead. Only the wet blood on the tip of his finger seemed to hold any real color. When Bowie looked up, he was relieved to see that the sky was still dark as it had been before. It was the world beneath, however, that had been transformed into a broken reflection of its former self.

"What is this place?" Bowie's head was swimming.

"Otherside." The old man repeated.

"Where?"

"Otherside. This place you are in, it isn't your world." The old man stopped himself at that and allowed Bowie to take everything in.

"I don't understand." Bowie said.

"You are not in the world you used to know any longer. You are in a different world. The last one of your kind to come here called it 'Otherside'."

"Where is here? Where is Otherside? I don't get it." Bowie finally managed to position his body over his legs and stood hunched and breathing hard.

"Otherside is not part of the world you live in. It exists next to it."

"Like another dimension?"

"You could say that."

"So, what is this world then?"

"It's like a reflection of your world. A mirror, in a way."

"This world doesn't look anything like my world." Bowie said dryly, looking at the surroundings. "Hell, you don't even look anything like *yourself*."

"I know, but please, let me explain. Ask what you wish while we have a few moments, and I will do what I can to bring light to the matter." Bowie nodded, and so the old man continued. "Otherside is a reflection of your world, but not in the same sense you would imagine a reflection to be."

"Why is that?" Bowie asked.

"A mirror would show you exactly what was in front of it. But if a mirror were broken the image would become distorted."

"I don't follow. Are you saying your world is broken?"

"No. I'm saying it's a broken reflection. It's not a true reflection of your world."

"So, you look different now because your reflection is distorted."

"Yes. It's not exactly that simple but, in a way, you perceive me as you do because of that distortion, which would not exist in your world. But don't make the mistake of assuming that I come from your world. I don't. Are you feeling alright? You look ill." The man said, placing a comforting hand on Bowie's shoulder.

"Yeah. Just a little…" Bowie heaved a little before he took a moment to steady himself. "Just give me a minute." After a while he felt a little better. "So, where do you come from? Are you a spirit or something?"

"I come from here. I'm an Effigy, a reflection of another being in your world. Here I was born, and therefore my natural state would seem to you a distortion."

The old man started leading Bowie toward the entrance to the sewage plant, his fur coat billowing behind him as he headed toward the path between the two pools

"You're a reflection of someone?"

The old man chuckled. "Everyone in Otherside is a reflection of someone else in your world."

"So, everyone in my world has a reflection?"

"No."

Bowie cocked his head at an angle in weary confusion. "Huh? Slow down. This is all a little..."

"Your world is not dependent on mine, but mine is dependent on yours." The old man explained, cutting Bowie off. "Everyone here is a reflection of people from your world, but not everyone in your world has a reflection in this one."

"What? Why not?"

"Because when my people die, your people may not. We're not human. That's what your people call themselves, isn't it? Human?" Bowie nodded. "We are Others. That's how you would translate it, anyway. I am someone else's Other self. And somewhere in this world, you have an Other self as well."

"So, who are you?"

"In your world there is a man known as Geoffrey Vogel. I am his reflection."

"What do you call yourself?" Bowie tilted his head forward to get a more direct answer.

"I prefer Halloran, in our native tongue."

Bowie gave him an odd look. "How about Hal? Can I call you Hal?"

The old man seemed amused. "Whatever suits you."

"Wait, earlier you said that someone else came here. Who?"

"It was many years ago. A man much like yourself was the first visitor to arrive. You are the second to come here Your predecessor's arrival was quite by accident."

"But you brought me here on purpose." Bowie stated.

"It was you who brought the knife and the mirror and the ring. It was you who cut your finger. You are responsible for your arrival, not I." Halloran pointed out.

"If I hadn't, I would have died! And it was you that told me about all that stuff."

"Yes, it is quite confusing. To be honest, the whole setup has become quite unbalanced since your predecessor's arrival. Until he came here, we had no knowledge of your world." The old man shrugged and began to grind the same lilting tune Bowie had heard during their encounter on Keene Road.

This old man is nuts, Bowie thought. Halloran was certainly strange and the more he talked the less Bowie understood.

"You should consider yourself lucky, to some degree." Hal said.

"Why's that?" Bowie stopped following as his attention switched to the two pools that flanked the gravel path. Each pool was bone dry. Cracks ran through the white earth like a dried-up lake bed.

"If your duplicate dies, you won't." Hal kept walking. Bowie turned and trotted to keep up.

"So, we're not that closely linked?"

"On the contrary, we are very closely linked to your kind. If you die, so does your duplicate."

"Wait. What? Why?"

"Think of yourself like the sun. The light from your sun is what makes the moon shine bright. If the sun were to die, the moon's light would fade as well. But if the moon were to disappear, the sun would still shine. After all, the moon is simply a mirror for the sun."

"So, you're like a mirror for humans?" The wheels in Bowie's head started spinning.

"That's right."

"A broken mirror. That's why you look so different."

"I suppose that could be true. We've looked like this for quite some time now."

The pair continued walking in silence past a concrete foundation where the aluminum sided building had been. Bowie absorbed every image he could. When he got near the gate he looked to where he had set the bicycle down. It was still there, but the frame was separated and twisted up, like it had been sheared clean through and mangled. He was so distracted with it that he tripped over a stone and stumbled to Hal's side.

"Why is it I can see perfectly well, and yet it's pitch-black outside?" Bowie noted as he took a look at his own hands and then at Halloran.

"Your eyes don't see light like ours do here. To you the light plays tricks. And besides, I wouldn't call this night in the traditional sense. Look above you. Do you see a moon anywhere?

Bowie scanned the skies but saw nothing above. The sky seemed empty, as if someone had taken something precious from the night.

"There are no mirrors here in Otherside." Halloran explained quickly as they passed the carrion and continued down the gravel path towards the woods. "That includes the moon."

Bowie hadn't even looked to see if the broken mirror he'd stolen was still laying on the path. "Hal…" Bowie began, "Why is all this happening? Why did you tell me about the iron? Why did you bring me here?"

Halloran said nothing for a minute or so as they continued down the gravel path. The only sound was the echoing crackle of the gravel beneath their feet. He seemed lost in thought, trying to make sense of it himself. "Like the moon and mirrors we have no iron. It is death to us. As to why I asked you, I don't think you'll quite grasp the situation without witnessing it firsthand."

"What! What do you mean, 'firsthand'? I almost got killed back there!"

Hal nodded in sympathy. "The Eidolon puppets you encountered are part of a larger problem. You've only seen the symptoms of a far more complicated issue."

"What does that even mean?"

"You cannot diagnose a dead patient simply by noting that he died. You must learn about his symptoms or how he contracted the disease."

"What are you talking about?"

"I was speaking metaphorically." Halloran explained.

"What is this all about then?!" Bowie threw up his hands in exasperation.

"You will see. Please. Follow me, and make less noise." Hal stopped grinding his organ. "Occasionally, the Hellion prowl these woods."

"The Hellion? What is a Hellion?"

"You'll understand soon enough," was all Halloran said as they continued on the long trek back towards the 'Other' Echo City.

IV

The city was vast and hollow. A few stone husks of buildings stood as sentinels at its center, while the rest of the buildings were reduced to little more than their concrete foundations. The Echo City Federal Building was the largest structure at its center, towering over the entirety of the city like a foreboding monolith. Bowie could see the great sentinel even from the edge of the city as he and Halloran emerged from the woods.

Bowie's pace slowed as he neared the first block of the shelter-less suburbs. Each concrete foundation lay in the ground with no real structure above to give it purpose. Only copper pipes and door frames stood above the cold and barren concrete. However, that is not why Bowie stopped. On each concrete pad, a motionless family stood. Bowie pointed them out as they continued on. "Why are they just standing there?"

He could see them more clearly now. The nearest group consisted of a young boy, a short thin blonde woman, and a taller heavily built man with a crew cut. They looked to him like they were posing for a family portrait on the concrete.

"Those are Eidolon," Hal cut in, "they're usually harmless. Pay them no mind."

"Usually?" Bowie piped in.

The family's' expressions were vacant and hollow. Truly hollow. Bowie cringed as he realized that their eyes were completely missing. Only empty sockets, black and ominous, stared straight ahead. Their jaws were relaxed and hung loosely from their skulls. Like Halloran, their skin was pale and somewhat translucent. A hazy white indication of a skeleton was visible through the skin, but the clothes they wore were modern clothing like from his own world. The family had no life, no soul. Just empty expressions and the image of a family.

As he passed each foundation, Bowie was certain that he had seen some of their faces before. They had gone to church with him, back when he went to church. Bowie waved, but they took no notice. Bowie took a detour from the road, leaving Hal behind, and passed through an empty door frame to get a closer look. "What's wrong with them? They're just standing there. Are these Effigies too?"

"They are duplicates as well, but not like me. As I said, those are Eidolon. You've encountered them before, don't you remember?" Hal took a few steps toward the house but remained on the lawn.

"Before?" Was Hal talking about his attackers in the real world? "Why are they so different?" Bowie wondered.

Halloran cleared his throat. "There are people in your world who don't care. They simply want to live out their lives, and die without any hassle. They are apathetic and dead inside. They simply live to end up at some end they don't bother to imagine. In Otherside their reflection manifests itself like that."

"Even the kids?"

"Well, you know. Kids always emulate their parents, don't they?"

"Huh." Bowie started to reach out as if to touch one. "Do they ever do anything?"

"They walk out of their homes through Other Echo for a while and then return when the sun sets."

"The sun?"

Hal chuckled to himself as he walked past the family and through the streets. Bowie followed quickly behind. "We may not have a moon, but the sun exists here as well. It should rise shortly."

"Good." Bowie rubbed his eyes. How long had it been since he'd slept? His muscles ached and he felt exhausted.

Hal turned sharply on his heel and grabbed Bowie by the shoulders. "No, it's not good. Once that sun rises the Hellion will be out to prowl the streets. They're looking for us."

"What would they want with me?"

"A meal." Halloran let go of Bowie and turned briskly to continue on. "To them you're good sport, my boy." Halloran pointed toward the federal building. "We need to get there before they start their hunting parties. We'll be safe there. Hurry now. Hurry." Halloran took off at a jog, and Bowie followed shortly after.

The pair hurried past block after block of empty foundations and Eidolon families with void expressions. Their number surprised Bowie with each passing house. He opened his mouth to ask why but the sun's light shot out over the horizon and into his eyes. "That's not good."

"No." Hal said. "It most definitely is not."

"How many Eidolon are there exactly?" He asked in between breaths.

"I can't give you an exact number. It's a sadly large number, though. With the loss of effigy lives, the Eidolon outnumber both the Hellion and the Effigy population."

Bowie's jaw dropped. "How can people live like that?"

"You tell me." Hal said over his shoulder as he started picking up speed towards the Federal Building. "Hurry! We won't make it if they catch us in the open."

As Bowie and Halloran darted into the shadows of the gray cement husks of downtown's older buildings, something started stirring in the alleyways.

The pair stopped dead in the alley between two concrete structures.

"Are we gonna make it in time?" Bowie's eyes darted from one shadow to the next.

Hal pawed absently at Bowie as he kept his eyes on the street. "Get out your knife, boy. It's the only defense you have."

"From what?"

"The Hellion."

"You still haven't told me what they are!"

"Shhhh!" Halloran held out a hand as he glanced nervously back and forth. "Don't make any sudden moves," he whispered, "we only need to make it a little further."

Bowie slowly unsheathed the knife as quietly as he could for fear he might alert the creatures hiding in the shadows. His throat felt tight as he tried to swallow.

The strange old being started moving toward the street. Following his lead, Bowie kept close as they cautiously made their way across the vast road. As they approached, Bowie got a good look at their destination. Were it not for his fear of what lay in the shadows he might have appreciated it more for what it was. And what it was not.

The Federal Building was nothing like the concrete monolith Bowie remembered from his own world.

It was a fortress. Literally.

The outer walls were made of large pale stone, cracked and worn with the signs of siege, interrupted only by the occasional window that was barred and covered with strong lumber. Surrounding the front entrance were fortifications with stone spikes and concrete barriers as if in preparation for a frontal assault. Or D-day. The building looked as if it could withstand anything short of carpet bombing and still hold its structure. Behind the surrounding fortifications a massive stone door towered over the entry path. It was all at once inspiring and terrifying in size, as if warning those without of the power held by those within. It almost seemed to pass judgment on Bowie as he and Halloran crept up the steps of the ponderous refuge.

"Now what?" Bowie whispered to Halloran as he stood before the door, waiting for it to open.

"Patience." Halloran held his hand up. "It will take a few moments for them to get the gate open."

Just then the sound of splitting concrete rang out from the streets and the hollow buildings. Shadows and nightmares began peering out around corners and up through the sewage holes as the sun destroyed the concealing darkness they had hidden themselves in.

A block away a pack of three hunched figures pounded across the pavement like rabid dogs, wild and excited as they caught sight of their quarry. Each one emaciated in sickly brown skin that covered only a portion of their distorted bodies. The rest was left for all to see, raw and gleaming wet in the sun. Their faces, though almost human, had hungry burning eyes that sat above a mouth too large for any human. The lower jawbone was separated down the middle and only held together by a stretchy membrane across the bottom that formed a funnel into an exposed crimson gullet that ran from beneath the jaw to a large sac held within an exposed bristling rib cage. They had no stomachs, just twisted muscles that curved around an empty pit. Their shoulders and backs were studded with thin bone spikes protruding like needles from their naked skin. Their arms and legs were far too long, ending in clawed fingers the length of a man's forearm. Their feet split apart more like hands, and a toothy claw curved out of the back of each heel. They ran on all fours as they moved leaving scratches and score marks on the asphalt.

Bowie's shook in terror as he saw the horrid beasts. "We don't have a few moments!" Bowie turned and panicked as he pounded his fists on the cold rock. "Let us in!" He pleaded. "Please, for the love of God!" He nearly screamed.

Halloran put a hand on the young man's shoulder "Remain calm. You must first deal with the problem at hand." With a firm grip, the old man spun Bowie around to face the nightmares racing down the street.

"I ain't gonna fight those!" Bowie protested as he looked everywhere for an escape route.

"Then you will die." Halloran said with a voice suddenly full of authority and command.

"Ahhhh! Come on!" He pleaded.

Eidolon had been one thing. Fighting the inky emotionless creatures had been difficult for him. They were like fighting a brick wall that you had to hit in just the right place to knock it down while it tried to beat the hell out of you. He didn't want to even imagine what it would be like to tangle with something far more agile and horrifying. Yet, here he was and there were three charging right at him.

Bowie fumbled at his belt for his knife and held it up in front of him. As he tried to steel himself for the oncoming assault everything seemed to slow down. The Hellion at the front of the pack leaped high into the air to come down on Bowie from above. He tried to lift his arms to block the attack but he wasn't quick enough. The creature brought both arms downward with closed fists and slammed Bowie into the cement landing like a rag doll. Blood spattered out his nose as his vision blurred. He cried out in a mixture of panic and pain as the impact shot lightning through his nerves. The creature lifted his arms to start clawing at Bowie when Bowie started flailing around wildly with the knife. His desperate attempt did little more than manage to nick one of its arms.

The creature leaped back a few paces howling in pain as black sludge began pouring down its arm.

At the same time the second Hellion leaped into the fray, but as it lurched forward something shot through its left hand and pinned it fast to the street as it let out an unearthly howl. Before it could free its hand two more streaks shot through the air and pierced its right shoulder and pinned its left ankle to the ground.

Bowie was too preoccupied to notice from where the shots had been fired. The beast he'd wounded with his knife had recomposed itself. The monster's gaping mouth slathered as it cocked its head at Bowie, its needle-like teeth ready to take a fresh bite. Bowie scrambled upright and held the knife at the ready.

The beast took a few steps forward, making itself look as large as it could. With a deep breath Bowie rushed forward with his shoulder and, with both hands on the knife, tried to ram the blade into its gut. The creature brought up an arm to deflect the blow and swatted Bowie aside effortlessly. Bowie let out a yelp as concrete and stone dug into Bowie's body as he tumbled toward a stone barricade. The Hellion did not relent, but rushed Bowie and lashed out with its jaw to bite out Bowie's throat. Bowie screamed and panicked, thrusting the knife forward blindly in desperation. When he opened his eyes, his arms were inside the throat of the Hellion who had frozen in place. The neck of the creature began bubbling and shaking. With a last shudder its head sloughed off from its shoulders and the writhing mass fell to the ground where it lay unmoving.

Bowie's victory was all too short lived as four more Hellion sprang out of the alley ways and charged the entrance.

The old man had been holding his own against one of the creatures somehow and now joined his companion. When he saw the four Hellion pounding across the pavement, he swiftly positioned himself between Bowie and the creatures and began furiously turning the crank on his grinding organ. The old wood wheezed into life and chilling pipe music rolled into the air like a frothing tide. As the music came to life the sound seemed to strike the very core of the creatures. With each turn of the crank, the Hellion clutched at their skulls with their bony clawed hands and fell to the ground, desperately trying to keep the agonizing waltz from tearing their heads asunder.

Another arrow shaft flew through the air and caught one of the monsters right in the neck. It squealed and crumpled to the ground awkwardly, injured but not incapacitated. It snarled and glared up at the top of the tower. Scrambling upright, it fled down the street and ran as fast as it could back to whence it had come. The remaining three followed suit and soon they were lost from sight.

"Get in!" A sharp voice sounded from above.

The gargantuan stone gate groaned as it swung slowly inward allowing passage for those who waited outside. Halloran and Bowie did not waste any time. They darted inside and helped the group of Effigies at the front gate push it closed with a heavy slam.

A great sigh whispered out of Bowie as he gave himself a moment to breathe. It was over. They had arrived. He found the wall near the gate and leaned against it, his head tilted back, his eyes closed, and there he spent a minute or two thinking of nothing. Not the black ichor staining his clothes, or the hellish creatures called Hellion or anything. He just breathed. Once his body had stopped shaking, he opened his eyes and took a look at what lay around him.

On the inside, the Federal building was much the same as Bowie knew it in his own world the few times he'd been there. It was large and had high ceilings, pale beige walls with half paneling and rail, black and white marble tiled floors and wide hallways large enough to fit at least eight men abreast. However, the hallways were empty and ill-lit. The building seemed all too vast and empty. And quiet. Effigies stood around him in silence, waiting.

Hal stood nearby, patiently waiting for Bowie to recover. He smiled when he met Bowie's gaze and nodded in approval. "You're safe now. You can relax. They haven't penetrated this fortress since it came to be and today was no different." Hal put a comforting hand on Bowie's shoulder. "Come. We should meet the others."

As he followed along, Bowie wondered. "What the hell were those things?"

Halloran's expression became distant, saddened somehow, as if he regretted some great folly. "Those were Hellion."

"What are Hellion? Why do their faces look like people?"

Halloran stopped in the hall and turned to Bowie. "They are people." He said quietly. He spoke slowly as he explained. "They are the reflections of those in your world most dedicated to their own appetites. They are the product of selfishness and hatred grown to maturation. Here they manifest as the monsters they truly are. Here they gain form that shows them how truly terrifying they should be, but in your world such differences are hard to notice. They thrive on misery and seek personal gain with no respect to the well-being of others. Those creatures are the real image of those who would destroy your societies, your happiness."

"There were so many. We... I couldn't fight them..."

"You did just fine. You're safe here now, that's what matters."

"How many more of those creatures are there?" Bowie wondered as he inspected his damp clothes.

"More than I care to think." Halloran sighed.

"Are there really so many? I didn't think there were so many people like that."

"They grow in number as the years go on." Hal said disinterestedly as he led Bowie down a hall. "Here, they wage war upon us. It brings them some twisted form of satisfaction. We do our best to survive, but I'm afraid a defensive war is the only battle we can manage to fight."

Bowie nodded. This war Halloran spoke of seemed far more complicated than he wanted to know. He decided instead to change the subject. "Why does this place look normal on the inside?" Bowie asked as they walked to the far corner to a stairway.

"Some things in your world have a very functional purpose. People attach very little to them. Thus, the reflection is more near to the original. We also appreciate its functionality here. I always felt that the two similar views were the cause for the more precise duplication, but that's just a guess."

"Do your kind live here?"

"We stay here, yes. It's one of our few remaining refuges." Hal smiled as they reached the stairway. "There have been rumors of other settlements here and there, but they are *only* rumors and we haven't had the strength to search for them."

The stairway was an arduous climb. There were ten floors and twenty flights before they led to the roof. The stairway was dimly lit from strangely unseen sources, but at last daylight pierced through the doorway at the top.

The rooftop battlements were crowded with Effigies representing all walks of life. Each had crystal either jutting or flowing from their heads like hair. They wore similar furs and feathers but it was clear that some had either more wealth or more rank based on the extravagance of the clothing each wore. Bowie wondered from what creatures the feathers might have come from.

"So, this is him?" Came a female voice. A woman hopped down from a stone ledge and onto the gravel roof. She was slender and athletic, somewhere around Bowie's age. Her deep blue eyes watched him keenly as she approached. Her hair, if you could call it that, flowed down her head to just above her shoulders like water. The elegance of her features was striking in her ornate feathered dress, but the arrow she had notched on the long-bow she carried abruptly stopped Bowie's wandering eyes.

The bow was made of white bone and wood with an ornate leather grip. In her hands it almost seemed out of place, but the ferocity in her eyes cautioned Bowie that she was dangerous.

"Why did you bring him here?" She demanded.

The rest of the Effigies formed a half circle around Bowie, staring at the newcomer with their hands at the weapons they carried.

"You have no need to fear." Hal assured them. "He's here under my protection, Varela." He told the woman with the bow. His steady glance warned Varela to be wary of her actions.

Varela stopped her advance a few paces short of the young man. "And what exactly warrants such protection? He's an original. He doesn't belong here, and this will only make it easier for Arsen to do what he wants to do."

"I will not condone murder here, in this place." Hal said gravely.

"It's not murder, it's suicide!" Varela snapped loud enough for all to hear. A startling silence followed.

Bowie shifted uneasily. "What are you talking about?" He asked.

Halloran spoke over him. "He isn't committing suicide."

"He is and you know it!" She bellowed. "Everyone knows it! You can't keep pretending not to see the truth."

"We need the boy if we're going to resolve this." Hal pointed out. "Without Arsen getting himself killed." He added.

"He is weak." She snapped. "This is only going to make matters worse."

Halloran sighed. "If I recall, you were once traveling down the same path. Do not forget what it felt like to be in those shoes."

"Well, I'm not going to risk the life of an original. He's going back." She said, lifting her head high. "Seize him." She commanded.

The crowd of Effigies began closing in on Bowie.

"When last I checked, it was I who reigned chief of our people, not you." Halloran tapped his fingers on the lever of the grinding organ and the Effigies stopped cold. "The boy is necessary until I say otherwise."

"What are you *talking* about?" Bowie interrupted angrily "Can someone please tell me what is going on? I'm not going to commit suicide."

"This doesn't concern you." Varela silenced him, her attention still on Hal.

"The hell it doesn't!" Bowie shouted. "I nearly got killed by Hellion and messed up ink monster things just to get here. I meet this weirdo" he tilted his thumb at Hal "and then suddenly I'm being attacked by Eidolon and running for my life and risking everything just to get through your bloody front door! So YEAH, it concerns me."

"Varela, please." Halloran held his hand up to silence her before she could respond to Bowie's outburst. "He came here of his own free will. He deserves some leniency after all he's been through." He turned his attention from Varela, who seemed nearly boiling over with rage. "Tell me Mr. Swift. Who do you find to be conspicuously absent from our present company?" Halloran gestured to the silent mass of Effigies.

Bowie scanned each of their faces briefly. "How the hell should I know? I don't even know you people."

"Haven't you wondered about your own duplicate?"

Bowie stood dumbfounded.

"Surely you've been curious ever since I told you about this world and its nature." Hal suggested.

Bowie shook his head slightly.

The old Effigy began pacing slightly, gesturing as he spoke in a playful, whimsical way. "Is your other self one of us? Or one of the Eidolon? Or perhaps even worse. Perhaps your reflection is one of the Hellion?"

"Get to the point," Bowie urged.

"You have a duplicate, an Effigy. A close to perfect duplicate, like myself. But you will not find his face among our ranks tonight. The reason you were brought here and the reason for your duplicate's absence are one in the same." Bowie half listened, but his eyes were watching the dark expressions of the other Effigies as each gaze seemed to pierce right through him like he was the enemy. "Your Other, Mr. Swift," Continued Hal, "an Effigy known as Arsen, has left us, and we don't know why."

"We know why!" Varela snapped. "He turned traitor. He has forsaken our laws."

"Varela, please. You don't know that for certain." Halloran held his hand up, but to no avail. She continued speaking over him.

"I should put an arrow through the boy right now and end this whole mess." She raised her weapon and brought the arrow back to a full draw.

"I didn't do anything!" Bowie yelled. He felt like nothing he said was getting through to these people. The assembly erupted into shouts and accusations. Some Effigies were pointing toward Halloran, demanding the old Effigy's words be heeded while the rest were moving behind Varela, eager to fight on her side. The more Effigies joined in, the louder the din became before the whole mass of people were raising arms and bellowing out challenges to one another.

Amid the uproar Halloran gripped the handle of the grinding organ, raised his other hand up, and snapped his fingers. The sound was so sharp and loud it echoed out over the city below and nearly deafened all those present.

The mass fell silent.

There was a brief moment where no one spoke, but before Halloran could say anything Varela cut in, "You had little business saving him. He's more trouble than he's worth."

Halloran ignored the comment and addressed Bowie once more. "You see, Bowie. The reason you were attacked by the Eidolon, or 'ink monsters' as you put it, is because someone was controlling them. Eidolon do little of their own accord. They have to be directed to step outside the bounds of normalcy. Many of us believe that your Effigy is trying to kill you."

"What? Why? I don't want to die." Bowie insisted. "Why would I try… or my duplicate… try to kill me?"

Halloran shook his head. "If he is trying to kill you, there is only one reasonable explanation."

"He's trying to kill himself through you. Suicide by Proxy," Varela interjected.

"Huh?" Bowie's head swam.

"Suicide is taboo here," Halloran clarified, "As the defensive side of an endless war we can't afford such losses or else the war will tip in favor of the Hellion." Hal gestured for Varela to lower her bow. "We don't know for certain that suicide is his aim." He glared at Varela. "It is possible that there is another reason. One never can tell. We can't be sure until we find him, and until then we can't afford to lose you either."

Varela slowly released the tension on the bow and lowered the arrow tip toward the ground. "The chances it's something else are slim."

"How many of you are there?" Bowie asked. "I doubt one loss means all that much."

"This is the remainder of our allied forces." Varela stated. "That's the bottom line. You see, when we die, there are none to replace us, save for the newly born and it is difficult to get to them before the Hellion do."

"The Hellion kill newborns?" Bowie asked, disgusted.

"The Hellion consume them. As they would us. Newborns are necessary to our survival because they replenish our numbers. When a new person enters your world, one appears here and we have to retrieve it before it is taken. And so, we kill the Hellion, the Hellion kill everything and we do what we can to survive. But, like a plant feeds off the sun, we cannot survive without you. We live off the essence that our counterpart provides. And, as the saying goes, you are what you eat." Varela sighed and begrudgingly placed the arrow back into the quiver over her shoulder. She took a step away to cool off and Hal continued for her.

"There are some of us who are a more perfect likeness to our original counterpart. Like myself and a few others. More perfect duplicates possess greater power. Power that could turn the tide of this war. That's why we are so desperate to retrieve your counterpart. We need every advantage we can get."

"So, bad people have Hellion counterparts? That's pretty bleak." Bowie's expression was one of disgust. "The numbers seem pretty skewed."

"I wish that things were different," Hal shook his head sadly. "Things have grown out of balance. It didn't used to be that way. Our legends tell of times years ago when things were better."

Bowie looked over at Varela who stared ahead far into the distance, lost in thought. "The Hellion. Why do they look the way they do?"

"In your world, people hide who they are. They seem all smiles and compassionate but behind that mask some people are only concerned with themselves and their own desires. In this world, there is no mask. Their true nature is fully exposed and so they appear as they truly are."

55

Bowie watched the sun as it rose overhead. It was broken and dim, like he was looking through cracked sun glasses. "So how did they end up trying to kill me?"

Hal sighed. "They didn't. It takes a great deal of effort to create the puppets that attacked you. Those were Eidolon, not Hellion. It takes an even greater effort to create and maintain the form of an *intelligent* representation of one of us in your world; thus, why my appearance was so short."

"What do you mean by puppets?" Bowie interrupted.

"The only presence we can have in your world," Hal explained, "is a kind of puppet form that we control from here. We do not employ these lightly as they consume our energy considerably and they risk creating a kind of panic in your world. Eidolon have no reason to project themselves into your world. They do very little beside wander around sometimes. Why target you at all? The Eidolon do not care. That is their nature."

Bowie absently massaged his bruises. "But they did show up in my world. You were there, you saw them."

Hal nodded. "You are right. So, the conclusion we reach is that someone made them do it. As far as we know the Hellion have no means to project themselves into your world and it is doubtful they even know how. If it wasn't the Eidolon or the Hellion, it must be one of us."

"He's gone rogue." Varela interjected from her position at the edge of the roof."

Halloran shook his head with a frown. "We think Arsen is directing the Eidolon to create puppets in your world in order to kill you."

"But why would he do that?"

"To kill himself by killing you. Thus, circumventing the taboo." Varela replied.

"We're not sure." Hal corrected. "There's no real way to tell unless we can find him. All that can be said for certain is that we cannot afford to lose you or him."

"Do the Hellion use the Eidolon like that?" Bowie asked.

Varela came back over to join in the conversation. "Sometimes. But they don't know of your world like we do. They mostly use them to get the upper hand during a skirmish by outnumbering us."

Hal sighed, "We are a dying breed, Bowie. We need all the help we can get."

Bowie nodded. "Okay, then what now? What is my part in all this?"

"Well, we are hoping we can learn why Arsen left us in the first place while we still have you under our protection." Hal said hopefully. "We will wait until the sun sets. With it gone there will be less Hellion on the prowl, and you will have a brief window to locate your Effigy, and with any luck persuade him to return to us."

"Why do I have to be the one to do it? Can't you convince him yourselves?"

"Because, boy," Varela said angrily, "he's you, and you're him. If anyone can understand and get through that thick skull, it's you. If we were able to come to settle this ourselves, he wouldn't have left in the first place. You should rest up before the sun sets. It's going to be a long night."

Halloran nodded and showed Bowie to a room a few floors down where he could rest and then disappeared to the levels below.

The room was sparsely decorated with primitive beads and feathers as well as basic furniture. It had a makeshift bed that was little more than a mattress tossed into a corner. Bowie tried to get comfortable and sat in thought for a long while, pondering his enigmatic double.

Bowie had never even contemplated suicide. None of it made sense. Though he could understand why Arsen might up and leave. An endless war would be taxing on anyone. Bowie wouldn't have stayed to fight it out either. He just wanted to live his life and not worry about who was going to die and if he was going to be next.

When Bowie's stomach began to growl, he gave up trying to figure out his other self and wandered through the Federal building's rooftop fortifications to clear his mind. The edges of each side of the rooftop were patrolled by two Effigies armed with bows similar to Varela's. Undoubtedly, it was their marksmanship that had kept him alive down below on the street. One of them caught his gaze and he nodded with respect. He couldn't think of anything to say so he left it at that. He was grateful. He only wished he knew how to express it to the strange crystalline Effigies.

"Where can I find something to eat?" Bowie asked as Halloran surfaced from below. The strange old man had started talking to a younger looking Effigy who looked like he might have been a professor in Bowie's world.

Halloran raised an eyebrow. "What do you mean?"

"Uh..." Bowie didn't know where to start. "Don't you guys eat food around here? I'm starving. I haven't eaten in like a day."

Halloran shook his head. "Like I told you, we feed off the energy of the people in your world. Whatever it is that you eat we do not have. I'm sorry I cannot be of more help."

As his stomach rumbled in protest Bowie remembered the can of Pepsi still in his pocket. He didn't particularly like the thought of a single can of soda to keep him until nightfall, but it was all he had. He popped the tab and sipped it but it gave him no satisfaction. "Next time tell me to find a mirror, ring, and a sandwich," he muttered as he retreated through the roof access to return to his room.

V

A sharp poke in the ribs from Varela's foot woke him, and he grumbled as he climbed up from his mattress. He steadied himself with a hand on the wall.

"It's nightfall. We're going now," Varela said coldly.

"Where's Hal?" Bowie asked.

"I'll be your escort. The hunting party is waiting downstairs. Halloran will be staying here."

"Why can't he come with us?" Bowie asked, disappointed.

"Because. From now on you'll take orders from me. Now move. We have a lot of ground to cover." She commanded. Bowie could not help but follow. She was clearly a seasoned warrior and used to a position of authority. Bowie noticed a small scar clipped through her right eyebrow, but decided it better not to ask about it.

"How are we supposed to find him, anyway?" He asked. "He could be anywhere."

"We'll find him." She said simply, as if that were the natural answer.

Bowie sighed and the pair descended the stairs through the old Federal Building and emerged through the massive stone doors. The night was cold and Bowie held his arms together to keep warm.

"Duplicates and their counterparts have an innate bond with each other. I'm not like you so there's very little I can tell you about it. I just know it can be done. You have to trust yourself to know where he'll be." She said as if it explained everything.

Bowie was skeptical. None of it really made any sense to him. "Ooooookaaaayyyy… Is there something I'm supposed to say to him when we meet? Like 'hey, I'd really appreciate it if you didn't try to murder me'?"

Varela rolled her eyes. "You know him better than any of us. What we need you to do is convince him to stop. This has gone on long enough."

"And if I can't?" Bowie asked.

"Then you'll die." She said simply.

"You don't care much for me, do you?" Bowie asked.

Varela didn't say anything for a few moments. "I try to keep my relationships strictly professional. A good warrior never gets close to anyone." She avoided eye contact with him. "The rest of our hunting party is just up ahead. They'll be keeping you alive should we get ambushed by any Hellion so stay close. Now please, focus. Reach out and try to figure out where he is."

Bowie shook his head. *Great.* He thought.

* * *

The hunting party was a group of ten, each dressed in similar tribal garments and armed with various weaponry. Most had bows. Some had stone tipped spears or pikes. After an hour's march they stopped to make camp while Bowie tried to get his bearings.

"What do you make your bows out of?" Bowie asked Varela as she ran some sort of wax over her bowstring.

"Hellion bones." She replied disinterestedly. "Now, take a deep breath. Clear your thoughts. If you were walking through a night like this, where would you start walking to? Relax and try to picture it in your mind." Varela instructed.

Bowie frowned and shook his head. He looked down the way towards where his apartment complex should be. "That's where I would go."

He began walking, impulsively at first, but as he continued his steps felt more and more directed, as though he had walked that way before, even though he'd never really spent any time in that neighborhood.

"Hey, man. You know how to use that thing?" Came the deep voice of a Burly Effigy with crusted bits of crystal growing on his upper lip.

"What?" Bowie asked.

"The knife. You know how to wield it?" The Burly Effigy continued, pointing at Bowie's hip as he followed from behind.

"Not really." Bowie slowed so the big Effigy could catch up.

"Here let me show you." The Effigy drew a stone knife from his own sheathe and held it at the ready. "Always hold it this way." He demonstrated. "I'm Reuel, by the way."

"Bowie." Bowie drew his own knife and mimicked Reuel. He noticed as he did that the knife in Reuel's hand was similar in design to the one the Eidolon thug had in the alley when Bowie had helped Halloran escape their abuse.

"Never rush an opponent with a knife." Reuel said sternly. "The blade is way too small. All they have to do is dodge to the side and hit you in the back or gut and you're finished. Let them come at you and strike when you can reach their torso. Move in when they raise their arms to attack and strike. That'll take them out quick."

It was something in Reuel's voice and mannerisms that seemed familiar and after a moment Bowie realize he was talking to a good friend. Or at least his Effigy. At work, Eduardo was always talking about how he lived life to help others. That was the only thing that made Eduardo happy. Bowie remembered the time when Eduardo was walking him through how to operate a propane powered forklift. He had used the same conversational tones, the same direct manner of speech. Bowie smiled.

"What is it?" Reuel's voice brought back Bowie's focus back to the present.

"You. Er… You remind me of a friend."

"Oh." Reuel shrugged. "Okay, so when an opponent comes at you with a swipe from the left dodge like this." Reuel demonstrated how to dodge. "Okay, I'm gonna come at you real slow now. I want you to dodge and then without stabbing me, touch me in the gut."

"You sure you don't want me to stab you?" Bowie joked.

Reuel laughed. "Hey man. I don't need any more holes, you know?"

"Shouldn't we keep moving. We need to find Arsen." Bowie pointed out as he noticed Varela and some others giving him looks.

Reuel nodded. "This will only take a few minutes, and you might need it in case we run into something out here. Okay?"

"Alright."

The pair practiced a few simple maneuvers until Reuel felt that Bowie had the hang of things. "You're gonna have to do this a lot faster, without knowing where your opponent is going to strike from." Reuel warned. "You have to rely on your instinct."

"Okay."

"And Bowie." Reuel said gravely. "That knife is death to our kind. Iron causes more harm to us than anything else. If you can strike a vital area, the Hellion will die quickly. If you cut through their arms or feet and maim them, they'll most likely retreat. Remember, Hellion value themselves more than anything else."

Bowie nodded.

Reuel looked curiously at Bowie. "You know my other self, don't you?"

"Yeah," Bowie confirmed.

"Is he as good looking as me?" Reuel grinned.

"He's a good man," Bowie assured.

"I know he is," said Reuel. Then he struck a pose and joked. "But is he as handsome?"

Bowie would have laughed but for a sudden awareness, like the tremors of a pulse echoing through him. He turned and held up a hand. He looked in the direction he felt it emanating from. "Hey, hold on." He said quietly.

The company's attention was drawn to him and the Effigies watched with apprehension.

"I think I can sense him." Bowie announced. He began walking toward the source of the sensation. Varela followed closely behind, an arrow at the ready with the rest of the group behind. Steadily they made the long journey toward Keene Road.

Their own footsteps echoed over the streets as they ventured through an endless sea of motionless Eidolon. Each expressionless family stood on their own concrete pad, facing the streets like an audience ready to witness the events to come. In his own way, Bowie started to understand the void in their expressions. It was an empty life they were living. Pointless. They were alive, sure, but to what end?

"It's easier for people to become Hellion, isn't it?" Bowie said after a minute as they continued through the haunting suburbs.

Varela stopped momentarily as Bowie continued on. "What do you mean?" She asked before resuming her step.

"Hellion are basically people who do whatever they want and don't care about other people, right? It seems so simple. Just do whatever you want."

Varela shared a glance with Bowie. "Men fall quickly to wicked ways. Not all of us are prepared to overcome the challenge."

Her answer seemed somewhat cryptic to Bowie. What challenge? He hadn't ever given it much thought. He didn't know what he should say, so he kept quiet and decided to focus his mind on locating the source of the disturbance he felt.

The feeling he had grew stronger by the minute as he continued, but at times he couldn't tell if he should alter course to the left or right, or just keep walking in the same direction. It was as though whatever pulled him onward was moving.

Ahead of him the vacant eyes of the traffic light peered down the empty stretch of Keene Road. Street lamps, twisted and pale, lined the street like a demented rib cage. The distorted world seemed a dark caricature of the city he knew. The brick walls and fences that lined the road appeared tattered and ill formed as if they had been chewed and torn up. He was getting closer, but there was something else that nagged at the back of his mind.

With each step he grew more aware of the presence of others. Figures began emerging from the shadows of the walls and fences that lined the street, clambering over them. They moved sluggishly, and Bowie could tell right away that they were Eidolon. They moved with little speed or urgency over the fences and walls and where some had managed to get over. Their behavior was so unusual, Bowie couldn't help but think that they were being directed toward him.

Bowie kept moving down the street, ignoring the Eidolon. He could feel it in his bones. His other self was near.

Varela broke the silence, causing Bowie to jump. "They should be in their homes," She trained her bow on the nearest Eidolon. "Something is wrong here."

Looking back, Bowie realized that the Eidolon had been moving to surround them. A large group had formed behind the Effigy expedition and was closing in. With every step the Eidolon moved closer, closing the gaps and making escape impossible. They formed a large circle around them and closed in until they were about ten yards away. The air hummed with tension as Bowie gripped the handle of his knife. There were at least a hundred of them, outnumbering the Effigies ten to one. If the Eidolon decided to make their move, they would be quickly overwhelmed.

The Eidolon suddenly stopped and became motionless.

Strolling through the silent crowd of Eidolon, a strange man cloaked in red feathers and shifting shadows approached. His cloak billowed behind him as the Eidolon parted before him. His crystalline hair was wild and spiked and his eyes were startlingly red as he stared angrily from beneath his furrowed brow.

"Arsen..." Bowie heard Reuel whisper.

"You worthless piece of trash," Arsen shook his head slowly from side to side as he gritted his teeth. "Though I'll give you credit, you've lasted a lot longer than I expected."

"Arsen, enough! This stops now," Varela demanded as she stepped forward to protect Bowie.

"Oh, no. It starts now. Don't you see, you've made this so much easier by bring him to me. I should be thanking you."

"Wait. You're my duplicate?" Bowie asked incredulously. The stranger seemed to have his father's jaw and mother's eyes but that was where the similarity ended. Their facial features looked almost nothing alike, to say nothing of the vengeful demeanor Arsen held himself with.

"You don't have to do this, Arsen," Varela chided, "It's forbidden for a reason. You can't commit suicide this way."

"I'm not. I'm committing murder. The taboo doesn't hold." He said calmly as he clenched and unclenched his fists.

Varela took a step forward "That's not... This is insane, Arsen!"

"You think you're going to stop me? You'll have to kill me first. Either way, I win. Now please," he smiled sadly, the sound of regret hidden within his voice, "get out of the way. This doesn't concern you." Arsen swept aside his feathered cloak and reached for a stone knife sheathed on his hip.

"ENOUGH!" Varela's voice roared louder than humanly possible, nearly deafening Bowie and echoing out over the city like thunder. Even as she spoke, she pulled her bow taught and pointed an arrow at Arsen. "Stop this nonsense," she commanded.

"This isn't any of your business!" Arsen barked back, "this is between me and him."

As he watched the two teetering on the edge of violent confrontation, Bowie was struck with a realization. He quickly stepped in between them and held up his arms to shield Varela. "He's right. This is between him and me."

Arsen watched silently, his eyes locked on Bowie's. Varela opened her mouth to challenge Bowie's decision but Reuel put a firm hand on her shoulder and gave her a grave look.

"Well this should be interesting," mumbled Arsen.

Bowie took in a deep breath. "I get what you're trying to do, but it won't work." He tried to explain. Even in his own head it didn't seem to make a lot of sense. "In my world, doing something that will definitely get you killed, is called suicidal. What you're doing is suicide, no matter how you try to dress it. Even if it is by proxy."

"So, what?" Arsen shot back, "you deserve it just as much as I desire it."

That was enough to cause Bowie to raise an eyebrow. "What did I do? Huh? What the hell did I do to deserve death?!" Bowie shouted at Arsen, "I haven't done anything to you."

"You've done plenty." Arsen spat. His eyes started to become bloodshot as they filled with tears. "Can't you see?"

"What are you even talking about? I've never seen you before. I've never even been in this world before. Don't go acting like I ruined your life."

Varela whispered from behind him. "We are mirrors of your world, remember? Without ever having been here you can cause significant change to your other self."

"So, what? I'm not… there's nothing wrong with me. I didn't screw him up or anything."

"Idiot!" Arsen yelled. "Don't you get it? The more you wallow in your stagnant life, wasting away, the more I become like them!" He thrust his finger at the motionless Eidolon. Even as he spoke his eyes suddenly lost all color and sank deeper into his head becoming little more than shadows.

Bowie was speechless.

"Killing him won't solve any of your problems, Arsen," Varela pointed out.

Arsen gritted his teeth. "If he dies, I die, and this ends. I don't care about the consequences anymore."

"Why don't you just kill *yourself* then? Huh?" Bowie shot at him. "Or just go and sit on a corner and wait for the Hellion to come and kill you? Problem solved, end of story. Just leave me out of it!"

Arsen's voice seemed to lose its emotion as he replied. "That's just what I'd expect of you. Let someone else deal with the problem. It saves you the trouble, after all." Arsen drew his knife and took a step forward. "If I go, I'm taking you with me."

"Then stop commanding these Eidolon to do it like a coward," barked Varela. "Act like a real warrior for once instead of skulking around in the shadows."

Bowie furrowed his brow as he realized something about himself. "Hold on," he said. "If you're really supposed to be my other self, then I know you wouldn't do something to get yourself killed!"

"Because you don't have the guts!" Arsen shouted. "That's your problem. You're a spineless waste of life!"

The insult was the last straw. Something broke inside and Bowie growled and rushed Arsen, tackling him clumsily onto the ground. The pair began beating and tearing at one another.

Bowie had already drawn his knife. With each swipe he made in the chaotic grapple he could hear a hissing sound as his blade bit pieces out of his other self.

Arsen roared and writhed in pain, lashing out with his own knife, cutting and scratching his opponent, doing everything he could to force Bowie to drop the knife. He craned his head as he held the knife at bay and took a bite into Bowie's forearm. Bowie roared in agony as he tried to wrench his arm free but Arsen wouldn't let go so long as Bowie still had the knife.

Decisively, Bowie slapped Arsen across the face several times with the back of his hand before taking control and rolling on top of Arsen, pinning him face first into the ground. He dug his knee into Arsen's back and quickly grabbed him by the hair and held the knife under his throat. The other Effigies gasped and drew their weapons, ready to strike Bowie down where he was. Keene Road went silent.

Bowie glanced nervously around, panting heavily.

"Bowie, you need to let go, man." Reuel warned. "We didn't come here to kill him."

Bowie wasn't sure what he should do.

"He won't listen," Arsen said hoarsely, "he's already given up on me. Just like he's already given up on life."

As those words finally hit home, a tear rolled down Bowie's cheek. He hated it so much, but Arsen was right. "I haven't given up!" He said through clenched teeth. "There's more to it than that. I have to survive. I can't just leave or... and what would you know about it? Huh?" He threw Arsen's head down and backed away.

"If I had known this… If I had known that you were here, with all these people… I would have... I would have done something, you know? It gives me a choice. Just like it gave you a choice." He dropped the knife to the ground. The cold sound of metal on asphalt echoed down the street. "But you wanted out. You wanted to leave all this but you couldn't. It was taboo."

Bowie looked at the saddened faces of the Effigies. "So, you found a way to do it. You made that choice. You would rather die than... than become one of them." He pointed to the Eidolon.

"But I don't want to die." Bowie wiped the salty tears from his face. "And maybe if I knew that, life wouldn't be so damn hard. I... I need to change all this." His plea seemed so pathetic when he finished speaking. What did these people care about how difficult his life had become? They were fighting every day just to survive.

"Then prove it." Arsen said as he pushed himself up off the ground.

An unearthly howl ripped through the quiet street suddenly.

"What do you mean?" Bowie asked as he looked around wildly for the source of the noise.

"Hellion," Varela said as fitted an arrow on her bowstring. With a resounding boom, she let off a shot into the darkness, and a howl rang out in that direction. "Ready yourselves! We have incoming!" She shouted.

VI

"Where are they coming from?" Bowie could already hear the scratching of claws on pavement from every direction.

"All around us, mostly from there." Varela pointed east down Keene Road.

Bowie fumbled for his flashlight and flicked it on, pointing it down the road. Just faintly he could make out the gleam of dozens of sinister eyes in the dark closing in quickly.

"We're screwed, aren't we?" Bowie said dryly. To his surprise, Arsen grinned.

"Have a little more faith," Arsen said eagerly.

The battle broke like the crashing of a wave. The Hellion charged and the Eidolon under Arsen's command suddenly rushed out in front to meet them. The Eidolon's listless efforts, however, hardly slowed the Hellion down. The monsters tore through the emotionless husks in a torrent of ichor and frenzied roars.

"Form a perimeter!" Varela barked. "Reuel, help me cover our flanks! The rest of you, focus your attacks to the front." She loosed another arrow and took down a screeching Hellion as it climbed over the nearby stone wall along the road.

They were outnumbered. Bowie soon realized he was in the middle of a losing battle. He caught sight of his Effigy as he struggled to figure out what to do.

Arsen glanced sideways at Bowie and nodded before rushing out to meet the wave of Hellion. He quickly drew the knife from his hip. The blade was similar in shape to Bowie's but in the dark it glowed white and orange as if made solely of flame. With a yell he hurled the knife at one of the oncoming Hellion, and the knife stuck squarely in its gullet. The creature screamed and burst into a yellow flame as it rolled in agony on the ground. Bowie watched as, with a flick of his wrist, the knife flew back to Arsen's hand as though pulled by a cord. Arsen quickly turned to slash at another Hellion that had tried to come at him from the side, but the Hellion was too quick. The tackle sent Arsen tumbling to the ground. With cries of excitement, several more Hellion joined in like descending hounds and Arsen was lost in a whirlwind of claws and flame.

Bowie tore his eyes from the carnage just in time to see a massive Hellion leap up into the air over a line of Eidolon and come down between him and Arsen.

As it snarled and coiled its muscles to pounce, Bowie recognized the plump face of Victor. The fact that the Hellion was larger than the others, with its split jaws, too-long nails and visible ribcage, Victor's duplicate was downright terrifying. Bowie's nerve broke and he did the only thing he could think to: he turned and ran.

With an excited cry, Hellion Victor gave chase, drool spattering the ground behind him as he went.

"Varela!" Bowie screamed.

"I'm Busy! You're on your own!" Varela barked as she loosed arrow after arrow at a cluster of Hellion charging towards her. Victor quickly caught up with Bowie and raked his claws at his left calf. Nails bit flesh and Bowie fell to the ground in agony, scrambling forward only to find stone walls along the road blocking his escape. With an expression of ecstasy Victor slashed downward with both claws to rend trenches in Bowie's flesh. Bowie threw himself to the side to avoid the attack, but one of the claws struck home and tore down his left side. Bowie screamed in pain and turned to face the Hellion. He began crawling away on his back, holding the up the knife awkwardly in one hand as he pulled himself along with the other. Victor smiled cruelly, his mouth a nest of needle teeth ready to rip Bowie apart. He stalked closer and closer, savoring each step that brought him closer to his prey. Unable to resist the thrill of hunt, Victor rushed forward, rising up to descend for the kill. In the height of his wild excitement, an arrow shot through his left shoulder and he reeled backward, losing his balance.

"Bowie, get back!" Varela shouted from down the street. She had only managed to let off a single shot as a brief lull in the action gave her time to fire in his direction.

Seizing the opportunity, Bowie got to his feet, using the brick wall as a brace, and hobbled back toward his comrades clutching his bleeding wounds.

Victor howled and tore the arrow from his shoulder before twisting himself upright and searching for his lost prey.

Bowie hadn't managed to get more than a few yards away and was completely exposed against the wall. Even if he could run, he would never reach his comrades in time. The only choice he had was to fight. He swallowed his fear and bit down, turning to face Hellion Victor once again. Bowie raised his knife and prepared for the onslaught.

Victor bound across the asphalt at Bowie and swiped at his head. Bowie ducked and the claws tore into brick beside him, sending a spray of stone powder over the sidewalk. He countered with the knife, slashing at Victor's mid-section, but the searing pain in his calf slowed his effort and the attack missed. Victor slammed an open palm into Bowie's shoulder, knocking him to the ground. He slashed his claws at Bowie, but Bowie quickly rolled away, gritting his teeth as bits of rock dug into his wounds. He swiped up a handful of gravel and hurled it at Victor's face, hoping to blind the walking nightmare.

The Hellion staggered back, clutching at its face. While it was distracted Bowie got up. He remembered what Reuel had showed him. *Dodge, then strike.* Bowie told himself.

Hellion Victor charged once again, snarling and thrusting out with his claws to spear Bowie through the chest. Bowie dodged right, using his free hand to brush the Hellion's arm slightly to the side. As the creature narrowly missed, Bowie grabbed its arm and brought the knife down, severing the arm in a spraying hiss of black ichor. While the Hellion recoiled in pain, Bowie ducked down and swiped at Victor's gut. The blade left a shallow gash and Hellion Victor howled. The creature hopped back several paces before it turned and leaped over the wall, retreating into the night.

As soon as Victor left, the remaining Hellion fled, leaving those still standing alone in the middle of the street.

Holding his side, Bowie looked around him. The Effigy forces lay scattered on the ground in a mess of black ichor and crystalline carnage. The Eidolon force had been completely wiped out. Only a handful of Effigies were still standing and they were haggard and heavily injured. Bowie gritted his teeth through the pain and looked around in sorrow at the sea of bodies around him. The pain in his side and leg was growing and he could barely stand. He took in a labored breath and let out a sigh of relief as he fell to his knees.

Reuel had managed to survive. There was ichor dripping down the Effigy's front, but he stood proudly. When he noticed Bowie kneeling in pain, he hurried over and offered Bowie a hand. "You did good, Bowie. Real good."

Bowie took his hand and got to his feet. He could see the gash in Reuel's shoulder and a few minor scrapes. Other than that, Reuel seemed to have made it through the battle intact. Some of the others had fared far worse.

Arsen stood nearby panting as he glanced at Bowie from atop a pile of smoldering Hellion. He was oozing black ichor from a dozen wounds and holding his hand over his left side, searing a weeping gash closed with his palm.

"Holy crap, Arsen!" Bowie hobbled as fast as he could to his duplicate's side. Reuel slowed him down and held him to keep him upright.

"He'll be alright if we can get him back to the tower." Valera sighed as she plucked an arrow from a Hellion corpse. She had managed through the fight relatively unharmed. "It's you I'm concerned for."

"What do you mean?"

"Arsen knows Otherside and he's seen far more battles than this one. With that injured leg you're going to slow us down, and you can bet the Hellion will be back when they smell those wounds. You won't survive if they regroup and attack. Besides, your blood smells much stronger than ours."

"I can't smell anything," Bowie said.

"Trust me. They can." Varela offered her shoulder for Arsen to lean on. "We have to get you back to your world. The sooner the better. Arsen, do you think you can return him?"

"Wait." Bowie tried to protest but the others didn't hear him.

"You've taken quite a beating. Are you up to it?" Varela said quietly to Arsen.

"Why can't you do it?" Bowie asked Varela.

"The only person who can return you to your own world is your Effigy."

Bowie raised his eyebrows. "Wait. You mean if he had died, I would have been stuck here?"

Varela gave Bowie a look that made him realize just how much had been risked in the last battle.

"I can do it," Arsen coughed, "give us some space."

The remaining Effigies moved off to give them some room. Arsen winced as he walked over to face his counterpart, still clutching at his side.

"Nice job," Arsen said.

"Huh?" Bowie said.

"I was wrong. You're willing to fight. That means there's hope. You did a good job out there. I saw how you stood up to that Hellion. You fought for yourself, which is honestly more than I thought you were capable of."

"Gee, thanks," Bowie snorted.

"And you showed me how foolish I was. I'd given up just like you. But you're willing to stand and fight, and that's enough." Arsen nodded in respect and he and Bowie shared an awkward silence.

"That's an impressive weapon you have," Arsen motioned towards Bowie's knife.

"Yeah, it's my Grandfathers."

"Promise me one thing," Arsen offered his hand.

"What's that?" Bowie took it.

"Promise me you won't just lie down and die the slow death." Arsen nodded to the butchered Eidolon. "I don't want to end up like them."

"I promise." Bowie said quietly.

Arsen nodded. He put a hand on Bowie's shoulder and looked him in the eye. "Let that promise be a fire. Let it burn and become the source of your strength."

Bowie nodded, feeling somehow that he understood. "Am I always this corny?" He asked with a half-grin.

"Always." His Effigy returned the same smile. "You've lost a lot of blood. I'm sending you home. I can't let you die here." He put his hand on Bowie's shoulder. "One of us needs to make it."

"Wait, what?!"

Before he could get an answer Arsen lifted his own knife high into the air. The glowing light from the weapon condensed, moving along the edge of the weapon until it coalesced at the tip of the blade. A rush of sound and light blinded Bowie's senses. The last thing he saw there was Reuel nodding in respect and Varela looking curiously at him. He collapsed on the pavement as the world turned black.

When he came to, Bowie was sore and groggy. His wounds throbbed and his skin felt like needles. He lay there for a few moments in the middle of Keene Road. His clothes were ripped and blood was soaking through. Bowie shivered. It was dark, silent and cold, but there was a full moon shining on him. The twisted signs of Otherside were gone. He slowly became aware of the sound of an approaching car. Bowie staggered upright and saw a jeep driving toward him. Its horn blared and the vehicle veered left as Bowie stumbled over to the sidewalk. The jeep drove on and he was left alone again in silence and the light of the street lamps. His vision began to blur. Bowie realized that if he didn't get help soon, he would bleed out. He slumped down with his back against the light post and put as much pressure as he could on his leg with his hands. Seeing how little his hands could do he unfastened his belt and tied it around his thigh. The effort was exhausting and he leaned back breathing heavily.

It wasn't long before an old sedan drove up and stopped in front of Bowie. The door opened and someone climbed out. Bowie looked up and saw a dark blur in the pale light. He couldn't make out the stranger's features.

"Are you alright?" Came a familiar woman's voice. "Oh my god, you're bleeding! You need to get to the hospital."

After she finished calling for an ambulance Bowie's vision began to clear, he thought he recognized her face. He noticed a little scar through her right eyebrow.

For a moment Bowie was very confused. "Varela?"

"Who?" She said not recognizing the name.

"Do I know you?" Bowie asked in a daze.

"No. Well, I just started a few weeks ago."

"Huh? Started where?"

"The hardware store. I'm cashiering there. I'm Amy, by the way. I saw you leaving yesterday. You looked pretty mad."

"Yeah." Bowie had all but forgotten about the incident at work with Victor. He cast his eyes at the ground while he recalled what had happened.

"So, what happened to you? You're all torn up."

You wouldn't believe me if I told you. Bowie thought. "I got attacked by a... mean piece of work." He grimaced. "Uh, a dog got out nearby. It got the better of me and then ran off."

She nodded and stood there next to him while they waited for the ambulance. "Must have been one hell of a dog." She said, looking at his wounds.

"Say, would you hang on to this for me." Bowie said as he took his grandfather's knife and sheath and handed them to Amy. "It's an heirloom and I don't think they'll let me have it at the hospital. I don't want to lose it."

"Sure." She said casually. When she realized it was a knife, she gave him a curious expression. "Why were you wearing it?"

"It's a little complicated. I got jumped the other night, so I kept it on me just in case it happened again."

"Did it help? You know, with the dog?" She asked, wondering if anything in his story was true.

"No." He shook his head. "Well... I guess it did. He still got away though."

"You have some pretty bad luck." She chuckled a little. "Yeah, I'll hold on to it." Amy smiled and took the knife.

The paramedics arrived soon and started working over Bowie.

"I never caught your name." Amy called over the paramedics.

"Bowie."

"Since I'm holding on to this, would you mind if I dropped by the hospital tomorrow to see how you're doing?" She asked, smiling with her hands behind her back.

"Uh, yeah." Bowie blushed. "That would be good... er, nice... Yes. Nice."

"Do you have any family here? I could call them for you if you'd like."

"I have family," Bowie smiled to himself, "just not here, they're in Otherside- the other side of town. Don't worry about it." He said, gesturing off in the distance.

"Okay, well I'll see you tomorrow." She smiled at him as she went back to her car.

"Hey." Bowie called after her.

She turned as she walked away. "Yeah?"

"Thanks."

PART II

VII

Cold water ran down his face and dripped quietly into the small pool in the sink. Bowie stared blankly at the mirror in front of him. Deep circles hung beneath his eyes and his mouth felt dry. He gazed into the depths of his own pale blue eyes yet he saw nothing of himself there. Just the splattered carnage of Keene Road.

His nostrils still tingled with the stench as he remembered standing amidst the broken pieces of those who had fought beside him. No, not just beside him. For him. They had fought and died *for* him. They'd been torn to ribbons, their bodies ripped and gnawed and broken into glistening bits of ichor, meat and bone. He remembered each of their lifeless eyes as they lay strewn over the asphalt forever staring across ebony pools at their comrades, their crystalline hair chipped and fragmented. He shuddered.

The muffled noises of talking and lift equipment buzzed through the bathroom door as he splashed water on his face one more time. He had been staring at himself for quite a while.

It had just been a dream. A horrible nightmare. It would fade in a few days and he'd forget all about it. The trick was not to think about it. None of it had happened. Of course, it hadn't. It was all just something he'd imagined a few nights ago. That's what he told himself, anyway.

He'd only just turned to go when his leg flared up with pain. He gritted his teeth and winced.

The physician had stitched him up, dressed the wound and told him to take it easy for a while. The lacerations weren't too deep. The biggest thing was not to open them up again. Of course, the physician had also insisted he stay off it for a few days and only after that could he return to work provided he had a crutch or cane to take the weight off his leg.

Bowie couldn't afford to miss work. The injury wasn't deemed serious enough by Fleischer to warrant a leave of absence. Only reasonable accommodation. Since his job didn't officially require he lift anything heavier than a clip board he was cleared to return to the warehouse to perform his duties as normal with a few extra breaks to get him off his feet for a while.

It was agony.

Bowie grabbed the aluminum crutch from where it leaned by the door and limped his way out of the small restroom.

The warehouse was in full swing as he stepped out onto the floor. Eduardo was busy guiding one of the newer associates on a forklift carrying a bunk of sheet rock, and most of the other employees were busy unloading two full sized trailers full of mixed pallets.

Bowie hobbled his way across the floor, each step its own fresh burst of pain. Even with the insoles he'd bought the concrete was unforgiving.

From across the way he saw one of his subordinates approaching with a piece of paper hanging from her hand. Her name was Jennifer, but everyone called her Jen. She was young and attractive, with the sculpted body of a track and field athlete, long blond hair pulled back in a pony tail, and a pair of hazel eyes tucked behind a cute pair of steel rimmed glasses. She was also just above four foot eight inches. The expression on her face gave Bowie the impression that she was trying to look positive and happy but secretly she was about ready to strangle someone with piano wire.

"Bowie." She called out to him as she got closer. "I'm not going to be able to finish the cycle counts for department eighty. I finished everything but the appliances, so at least what's left should be easy to get caught up on."

"Alright." Bowie nodded back. "Thank you. Are you going on vacation this weekend?"

She gave him a cute and bouncy shrug. "I'm heading up to Alaska to visit my boyfriend."

"Ah. Okay."

"You alright?" She noticed as Bowie tenderly set his foot down as he came to a stop.

"Yeah. I'll be okay. A dog attacked me the other day. It's gonna take a while to heal."

"Are you going to be able to finish the counts?"

Something in her voice told Bowie she was more concerned with her own work getting done than with his well-being, but he decided not to mention it. "I'll get it taken care of. Have a good weekend." He tried to muster a smile. It came out half a smile and half a wince as the pain in his leg suddenly flared.

She handed him the report and turned to leave.

"I don't suppose you have any pain killers?" He asked.

She shrugged. "Nope. Sorry. I think Ted might have some."

"Alright. I'll have to ask him, then."

She continued on her way with the same bounce in her step.

Bowie knew she could have finished the work already but was probably too preoccupied texting her friends about her upcoming trip. He sighed.

As Jen was leaving Bowie could see Victor on the approach. He seemed even more bloated than usual. When Bowie caught his gaze, he raised a finger silently and increased his pace.

"Damnit..." Bowie muttered under his breath.

"Mr. Swift. I need to borrow you for a moment." Victor said as he got closer.

"Sure." Bowie nodded. He expected to get chewed out again, but the cruelty normally present in Victor's voice was strangely absent.

Victor gestured for Bowie to follow and led him to the corner office. Skirting around the small desk, he sat down in his computer chair and gestured for Bowie to take a seat.

Bowie considered remaining standing just to spite him but he was grateful to take the weight off his feet. He sat down and looked to Victor. "What's up?" He asked.

"Well, we're getting to that time of the year where we focus more on performance management, and it's time to have a check-in with everyone. I just want to ask you some questions about my performance as a manager over the last six months and I'd like you to answer as honestly as you can."

Everything in Bowie screamed *It's a trap!* But what choice did he have? "Okay. Fire away."

First, Victor asked him about how he felt the warehouse was operating in terms of efficiency. Bowie simply told him everything was good. He kept his answers generic and tried to give Victor answers he thought he wanted to hear. The questions seemed fairly routine but Bowie could sense where the conversation would go once they got away from measurable details.

"This next question is with regard to my performance as your manager. What can I do to help improve your job?"

Bowie shifted uneasily in his chair as he considered the question. He wanted to answer passively and get it over with as soon as possible but he remembered his promise. He was going to be present in his own life. This was it. He had a choice. He could say that nothing was wrong, or he could be honest. If he said nothing, nothing would change. Victor would continue being the overbearing tyrant he had always been and everyone else in the warehouse would continue to suffer. He also knew where honesty would lead him.

"Well... I don't know..." Bowie started.

"Please." Victor encouraged. "Be honest. I need this feedback if I'm going to make any improvements."

Bowie wondered if Victor's superiors had put pressure on Victor to go through this sort of exercise. He chuckled to himself. Victor was busy leaning his elbow on the arm of his chair and straightening the pencils on his desk. Bowie wondered if Victor was really paying attention. He was about to tell Victor that nothing was wrong when he stopped himself.

Dream or otherwise, Arsen had taught Bowie that he needed to take charge of his life, instead of simply going through the motions. He felt he owed it to Arsen and the others to take action. Even if it hadn't been real.

He sighed, sat up straight and spoke.

"The thing I think you could do that would help improve everyone's job is to stop getting in everyone's face when they make mistakes." Bowie said in as diplomatic a tone as he could. He immediately regretted his choice of words but it was too late.

Victor's elbow slipped and he sat upright. He didn't say anything, but it was clear Bowie had struck a nerve.

"You know, everyone here has a pretty difficult job," Bowie continued, unable to stop himself, "and we're bound to make mistakes. It happens. I'm not saying we shouldn't be held accountable, but there's a line between coaching people and berating them when they do something wrong."

"What do you mean?"

Bowie could hear the anger rising in Victor's voice, but he continued. "Every time someone screws up, you raise your voice and immediately tell them what they did wrong. Then you ask them why they did what they did and it sounds like you're accusing them. I get that you need to manage your people, but when you talk to us about things like that it feels like you're attacking us."

He had barely finished his last word when Victor broke in. "I'm not attacking anyone." He insisted. "As your manager I need to know why someone did something so I can fix the problem."

Bowie couldn't stop himself. "You may perceive it that way but that's not the way it comes across. You don't even give people a chance. You assume that they did it wrong on purpose and then immediately start assigning blame."

"I do not. Why would you think that?" Victor shot back.

"See? You start focusing the attention on the person instead of on the problem."

"Well if people did things right the first time I wouldn't have to." Victor leaned forward.

"People make mistakes." Bowie pointed out.

"A lot of mistakes." Victor agreed. "Maybe instead of focusing on what *I'm* doing, you should be spending more time focusing on your job." He said, his voice growing louder with each word.

"You called me in here to talk about your performance," Bowie tried to remind him, "not criticize my work ethic."

"That's beside the point. You clearly have no idea what management is all about. I brought you in here to discuss what I can do to improve my job but it's clear that there's a deficiency in your own performance and it's clear that you aren't going to treat this with respect!"

Bowie stood up, pushing the chair back behind him and placed his hands on the desk. He took a deep breath, kept his eyes on the desk for a moment, then looked up at Victor and told him in a quiet tone. "If you want to do something to improve my job and the jobs of all the people who work for you, you need to listen to us instead of berating us. You are not perfect. Frankly, you're awful. You wanted my opinion. There it is. So, get off my case!" He practically threw the words at Victor before he turned and left the small office.

Bowie hobbled quickly down the aisles, his heart racing, before ducking around a corner. There he took in a deep breath and let it out slowly. His hands had started shaking and he felt lightheaded.

He had done it! He had finally stood up to that monster and if felt great!

It was the first time in years Bowie had felt like he'd stood up for himself. Victor was awful. It was a wonder the man hadn't been fired years ago. The turnover rate for employees at his warehouse was the highest in the region. Sure, the numbers were met, but morale was in the gutter and there was really only one person to blame.

Bowie calmed down and returned to work. He didn't see Victor on the floor for the rest of his shift. He started wondering if maybe he had gotten through to him somehow. He doubted it, but who could say.

Sometime around four Eduardo took him aside by the receiving dock.

"What's up?" Bowie asked as he stacked some fallen boxes back on a hand cart.

"Nothing man. I was just wondering if you had seen Victor lately?" Ed seemed a little uneasy.

"Not since earlier today. Why?"

Ed shrugged. "I don't know. I guess I'm just used to him running around shouting all the time." He laughed.

"Yeah. I don't know. We kind of got into it in the office."

Ed raised an eyebrow. "What happened?"

Bowie shrugged. "I'll tell you after work."

"Hey, that reminds me." Ed pushed a flat cart out of the way as another employee started hoisting the rolling door up with a chain. "I'm having a barbeque tonight with the family. You wanna come?"

"Yeah. Sure. That sounds awesome. Isn't it a little cold though?"

Ed gave Bowie a fiendish smile. "Nah, man. This is the best time; you know what I'm saying?" He wiggled his eyebrows up and down.

Bowie laughed and shook his head. "Yeah. I'll definitely be there. What time?"

"About seven."

"Do I need to bring anything."

Eduardo shrugged. "Bring whatever you want. My wife won't let me drink anymore so if you want some beers or something, you'll have to bring your own."

Bowie chuckled and nodded. "Alright. I got the hint. Hey, let's get out of the way. Looks like we have another truck coming in."

Ed and Bowie returned to the floor and finished out the day. The shift ended with little fuss and Bowie was free to return to his home.

VIII

Bowie arrived at Eduardo's house later than he had intended that night. He had accidentally gone the long way home again, taking a detour through the neighboring suburb. What started as a short walk had turned into a long one as thoughts of Otherside rose to the surface.

When he finally got home and saw what time it was, he changed his clothes, downed some pain killers and headed right back out the door. He picked up a six pack of beers at the convenience store. He figured Ed had been craving a brew for quite some time and it'd give the poor guy a chance to sneak one. He was reluctant to spend that much money on something he didn't need but his friend was worth it. Ed had always been there for him and since he'd injured his leg, he somehow felt closer to his coworker.

He got off at the bus stop a block from Ed's house and hobbled the rest of the way. He had only been over a handful of times since the two had started working together, but he remembered the place well. Unlike the other well-kept lawns that sat neat and trim on either side of the property, Ed's lawn was reminiscent of a yard sale without tables or "for sale" signs. The lawn had grown yellow in the winter chill and children's toys and household projects disguised it well. The garage door had been left open and two of Ed's kids ran screaming out of it onto the lawn as Bowie came up the walkway that divided the yard in two. The yellow siding on the house was old and chipping in a few places, but otherwise Ed had kept his house in decent shape. In Bowie's opinion it was a miracle he kept up maintenance against the weather and the full-blown hurricane of raising five children.

One of the kids dropped a broom handle he had been using as a sword and ran to Bowie just before he got to the front door. The second child followed suit and soon Bowie was being assaulted with cheers and shouts and excited questions.

Bowie laughed and was about to ask the kids where their father was when the front door opened.

"Hey, man. You made it!" Ed said jovially. He opened his arms to give Bowie a big hug.

"I brought you something." Bowie lifted the six pack once Ed had released his grip. "I figured you could use a tall one."

Ed took Bowie with an arm around the shoulder and led Bowie away from kids and the front door and toward the garage.

"Oh, man. You don't even know how much. Come on. Let's break into them before Anissa finds out."

Ed took a seat on a couple of two-by-fours resting on some boxes that he had been using as a makeshift sawhorse. Bowie carefully stepped over the mess and found a seat on a small stool. "Hey, I don't mean to be mean or anything, but your garage... It's kind of a mess."

"Yeah." Ed agreed as he took out his pocket knife to pop the top off his beer. "I don't really know what happened. I had it all cleaned up yesterday... My wife's got a list, you know" He looked around at the war zone and sighed. "Man. That's what I get for having more kids."

The two laughed and joked as Ed downed the first bottle. He offered the next one to Bowie but Bowie raised a hand in protest. "I'm not really feeling up to a drink. I've had a lot on my mind, you know?"

"Yeah, man. What's going on with you? I didn't want to say anything at work, but you're different. Something good happen?"

Bowie shrugged. "I guess so. I'm not really sure how to put it. I'm just... more awake than I've been for a while, you know?"

"You mean the ladies are keeping you up at night, right?" Ed laughed as he tilted his beer to Bowie.

Bowie laughed and shook his head.

"Well, that's good. You know. If you don't see your life for what it is, it gets away from you. I used to be like that. Then I had kids." He opened his arms wide to indicate the entire garage.

"Dude, I don't even know how you deal with them all and keep your house in order on top of having a job. What's your secret, man?"

Ed leaned over closer to Bowie, his expression suddenly very serious. "Duct tape."

"Repairs that bad, huh?"

Ed shook his head. "No. For the kids."

Bowie burst out laughing. "What, you just tape their mouths closed."

"No, man. You have to tape them down in bed when you want them to sleep. With five kids, nothing else works."

Bowie shook his head again. "Man, you're crazy."

It was Ed's turn to shrug. "I'm just messing with you. But seriously. Duct tape. It fixes everything." Ed got off his seat and took a good long swig from his beer. "So, does you being different have anything to do with what happened to your leg?"

The question caught Bowie off guard. He looked down at his leg, a little uncomfortably.

Ed noticed. "Hey, man. You all right?"

"Yeah..." Bowie started to say.

"What happened, anyway? Everyone at work is talking about it. You're limping around like an old man."

For a moment Bowie considered grabbing a beer. He really didn't want to talk about it. However, when he looked up at Ed, he saw a friend who deserved at least some kind of explanation and felt bad.

"I got attacked by a dog on the way home." He lied, more to himself than to Ed. "I took a detour through the houses over by my apartment and there was this dog that got out. I tried to run but I wasn't fast enough."

"Oh man." Eduardo raised his brow, impressed. "That's crazy. What happened?"

"Well, I kept running until it caught up with me." Bowie explained. "I fell on the concrete pretty hard. Then this car drove up and must have scared it off. It was pretty dark, so I think the lights spooked it."

"What kind of dog was it?"

"It was kind of hard to see," Bowie stalled. "A German shepherd, I think. Or a German shepherd mix or something." Bowie rubbed his shoulder absently. He remembered the barking dog behind the chain link fence when the Eidolon had attacked him. He could still hear the sizzle as the chain link fence had melted through the creature's face.

"If I ever get a dog, I'm gonna get a chihuahua." Ed said thoughtfully. "That way it's too small to do any real damage."

Bowie was grateful for the change in topic. He gave a half smile. "Yeah, but those things are so small. They're like a little football with legs, just waiting for you to punt one across the street."

Ed grinned and nodded. "That's true. Actually, it's my wife who wants one. I like bulldogs. They're way better as pets, you know. A lot less health problems."

"Do you even know anything about bulldogs?" Bowie gave his friend a look.

"No," Ed confessed. "I just think they look cool. They're so adorable with their big floppy faces, you know?"

"Yeah. I hear you." He couldn't help but agree. They were kind of adorable. "Maybe you could get a half-bulldog half-shih tzu. Then you can call it a Bull-shit."

Ed burst out laughing and Bowie joined in. Ed finished his drink while Bowie sat enjoying his friend's company. When he was done and tossed the bottle over to a rubber trash can in the corner, Bowie spoke up. "Hey. I was wondering if I could ask you something."

Ed nodded.

"I need to find another job. You were right. I'm pretty miserable. I need to leave. The problem is I don't know where to begin. I mean, there's like a million freaking jobs out there. Where do I even start?

Ed thought on it for a moment and got up from his seat. "Come on, we'd better join the party before my wife gets suspicious." He gestured to the back door leading out of the garage and into a small but quaint backyard.

Unlike the front yard, the back was well kept. There was a concrete patio with a curved edge bordered by some retaining rocks and flower beds. Beyond was a lawn somewhat smaller than the front yard. A barbeque was going full tilt, covered with hamburgers patties, franks and billowing out white smoke. Someone Bowie didn't recognize was fanning the smoke away with their hand and ducking their head down to check on the meat beneath. A few other guys were lounging on lawn chairs and talking in Spanish.

"I think you can find a job; you just have to know where to look. What kind of work do you want to do?"

The question caught Bowie off guard. He found a quiet space next to the sliding glass door. "Well, that's a problem. I don't know what I want to do." He said.

"There's got to be something."

Bowie shook his head and leaned against the aluminum siding. "Just not this." He said. "I just need to do something else. I don't know what I want to be. That's the problem. There's so much out there. Where do I start?"

"Oh. I see." It took Ed a minute to think of what next to say. "Well, if you don't know what you want to do, then I guess it doesn't really matter where you start. Hey. You know what my cousin did? She took a phone book and went through the yellow pages one at a time and circled anything that sounded good."

"How'd that work out?" Bowie asked.

Ed's brows furrowed as he tried to remember. "I think she's working at Walmart."

Bowie gave him a dead look.

"Or you could go and just ride through town on the bus and whenever you see someplace that looks like you might want to work there, write it down and give them a call. That's what my brother did."

"Where's he working?"

"Simplot, I think. Look, man. You just have to start. It doesn't matter where. Once you get started, you'll get a feel for where is hiring and where isn't, but if you don't start somewhere, you'll never get there, you know?"

The grill started smoking even worse and the backyard was suddenly hazy white as Ed and his family scrambled to get the fire under control.

Bowie got out of the way and decided to wander back out to the front yard. He started collecting some of the toys to clean up the mess Ed's kids had left. He was leaning down to grab a big wheel by the handlebars when he felt the hairs on the back of his neck stand up. He noticed someone standing across the street.

The man was thin, dressed in jeans and a black leather jacket. He stood on the sidewalk next to a street lamp, a cigarette burning in his hand. He looked somewhere in his thirties and had unshaven stubble in a patchwork on his chin. He lifted the cigarette to his lips and took a drag as he stared calmly at Bowie.

The stranger was almost eerily still as he continued staring. Bowie stood up straight, the big wheel dangling from his hand. He tried to say something but words escaped him. *What's up? What's your problem?* He thought. The man continued to stare and it became unsettling and awkward. He was starting to feel uncomfortable so Bowie carried the big wheel to the garage and set it next to some other toys the kids had left out. When he turned back to the yard, the man was still there, still staring.

Flashes of the motionless Eidolon passed before Bowie's eyes as he remembered the streets of Otherside. He had seen people just like that. They had followed him, attacked him, tried to kill him. Was this one too? Or was this just some stranger with nothing better to do? Bowie returned to the toys and continued picking them up. When he had a few foam noodles bundled under his arm he looked up at the stranger. "Hey." He said casually as a greeting.

The stranger didn't say anything. He just tilted his head slightly in a nod as the cigarette between his lips flared.

"Hey, man." A hand grabbed hold of Bowie's shoulder.

Bowie jumped. "Geez. You scared the crap out of me!"

"Food's ready. It's a bit smoky, though." Ed informed him. "What are you doing out here?" He asked, looking at the toys in Bowie's arms.

"I thought I'd clean up the front yard a bit while you guys dealt with the grill." Bowie said, turning around. "Sorry. The smoke was pretty bad."

Eduardo laughed a little. "Man, you didn't have to do that. But thanks anyway. Come on, let's go get a bite to eat."

"Alright, alright." Bowie agreed. He turned to follow Ed into the house. "Hey, is he one of your neighbors?" Bowie asked.

"Who?"

"That guy over there." Bowie thumbed over his shoulder.

Ed shook his head. "What guy?"

Bowie turned back to point out the stranger but he was gone. "Uh... Huh. Never mind. He must have gone around the corner." Bowie pretended to shrug it off. He couldn't help but take a last look back to where the man had been as he went in through the front door.

They went to the back yard and enjoyed a cold night of barbequed pork and potato salad with his friend's family for the rest of the evening.

IX

The next day after he woke up, Bowie dug out his phone book and began flipping through the yellow pages like Ed had suggested. He had the day off for a change and decided to make the most of it. After about a half an hour of scanning though the pages and half a dozen phone calls, Bowie was convinced that most of the jobs available required special training or a degree. The few that weren't were looking for people for hard manual labor. He didn't feel too good about most of the businesses. They just didn't seem like the right fit. He decided to call Kaiser Steel on a lark and see if he could figure out what positions might be open. The woman who answered the phone was polite, but when he asked if there were any positions open, she asked him what kind of work he was looking for. He told her the truth. He was interested in anything, but with his education and work experience, unless it was a supervisor position, he needed an entry level job for someone with a high school education. She told him that she could only help him find something specific so he thanked her and hung up. He tossed the phone book on the dining table with a sigh and grabbed his jacket.

He needed to get on his feet and go do something, maybe talk to someone face to face. He was feeling restless so he left his apartment and hopped on the bus. Maybe getting out of the apartment would help him focus more.

The bus was almost empty. There was an old woman in a green coat huddled in the back corner and a young blonde girl in her teens sitting up near the driver but that was it. Bowie was somewhat relieved. He didn't feel like talking to anyone. He just needed to get out and see what there was to see.

He transferred a few times to get to the heart of the city but spent the majority of his afternoon riding from stop to stop, noting anywhere that had a 'Now Hiring' sign in the window. From what he could tell, Echo City wasn't hiring. Most of the shops or businesses looked cold and uninviting and the few hiring signs he'd seen were for run down stores and often had "part-timers wanted" written on a sign. Bowie needed a full-time job. That was the only way he could manage on his own. Part-time just wasn't going to cut it.

Around three in the afternoon, Bowie got tired of riding the bus so he got off at the next available stop.

He stepped out onto the sidewalk next to the greyhound station. A few blocks East was the train yard. He heard the blare of a train's horn in the chilly afternoon sun.

The Echo City train yard was perhaps one of the oldest yet most influential businesses in the city. The shipping industry had been the foundation of the now sprawling population center and was responsible for most of the commerce that occurred within city limits. When the town had originally been founded, it was at a crossroads between two major shipping lines. Naturally, a town was erected surrounding the now massive train yard, and from there the city had grown over the years. Echo City had spread mostly Westward from the train yards, spanning across the wide rivers that cut through the center of the city.

Bowie had never been there himself, though he'd seen it in passing on the bus or occasionally when he'd left town for a family vacation back when his father was still around. He'd never considered the rail industry as a source of employment and he was nearly certain he'd need some sort of degree or contact within the company to get a job at Echo City Rail, but he started walking in that direction anyway. Maybe he'd get lucky.

He had just passed a large warehouse with steel siding when his phone went off. He pulled it from his pocket and flipped it open. He didn't recognize the number. "Hello?"

"Hello, Mr. Swift. This is Victor." Came the voice on the other end.

Bowie considered throwing the phone onto the ground and stomping on it for a few seconds. "Hi, Victor." He said, doing his best to keep the contempt out of his voice.

"I need someone to come in for a few hours today to help move some freight. One of my associates was a no call, no show and the another called out. Can you come in today around four?"

Bowie looked at his watch. It was almost three-thirty. He looked up just in time to see the next bus pull out of the station in the distance. It would be at least half an hour before the next one, and he wasn't wearing the right clothes for work. "As long as it won't aggravate my injury, I can get there by five thirty. Will that work?"

"I need you here by four." Victor insisted.

Bowie mimed breaking the phone in half. He shook his head and repeated "I can get there by five thirty. I'm not at home right now. I'll have to get back and get changed before I can come in."

"Where are you right now?"

Bowie remained silent for a few moments. He smiled to himself mockingly before he spoke again. "I'm out running an errand. Again, I can come in for the extra shift, but I can't get there until five thirty. Will that work?"

The line remained quiet for almost ten seconds before Victor responded. "Fine. Yeah. That will work. Just get here and clock in as soon as you can."

"Alright. I'll be there by five thirty."

"Okay. See you then." Victor said before he hung up.

"I'll be there when I freaking get there, asshole." Bowie sighed as he put the phone back in his pocket. He looked over at the ECR building. Something in the back of his mind made him want to go take a look, but he needed to get to work before Victor had a meltdown. He turned back and walked over to the bus station to wait. Eventually the bus arrived and he headed back home.

Once he'd gotten into his work boots and a collared shirt, he headed back to Fleischer Home and Garden.

.

The warehouse floor was a mess and what few people were present were scrambling to clear a space large enough to accommodate two full trucks worth of freight. Victor was shouting orders left and right as one of the receiving associates tried to maneuver a pallet that had been stacked too high out of the semi and in through the low receiving door.

Bowie didn't bother announcing his presence. He got clocked in over by the office and immediately started pitching in by moving pallets out of the way.

An hour later things had calmed down and the crew at the warehouse took a quick five-minute break. Almost everyone was exhausted. Bowie did his best to steer clear of Victor, but it didn't last long. He was almost done with his short break when Victor marched around the corner barking orders for everyone to get back to work. Bowie got up off the crate he'd been sitting on to rest his leg to return to work with the rest of the crew but Victor stopped him short.

"I need you to come with me to the office." Victor said simply. His tone had no malice in it, but Bowie got the feeling it wasn't good news.

He followed his manager to the cramped corner office and waited for Victor to sit down. Victor went behind his desk and put his hands down on the table to support his heavy frame as he leaned forward. He kept his eyes downcast and seemed to be moving his lips as if toying with a piece of gum in his mouth as he tried to formulate his speech in his head.

"What's up?" Bowie asked, eager to break the silence, finish talking, and get back to work.

Victor stood up just enough to look at Bowie and left only his fingertips on the desk. He narrowed his eyes. "I've spoken with HR on this and they've come to a decision."

"Spoken to HR about what?" Bowie asked. If Victor was still mad about what Bowie had said to him during their last row, he made no indication of it.

"I've informed them of your behavior over the last few months and the poor work ethic you've demonstrated and they've decided to make a personal trip to assess your merit as an employee of this company."

"Oh. Okay." He played it off casually but it was certainly unusual. What kind of manager goes up to corporate to assess their own employee, he wondered.

"When they arrive," Victor continued, "they are going to look at your work, your behavior as well as my formal review of your performance. If I were you, I'd start looking for another job."

The suggestion was intended to be a threat, but Bowie had already had it with Victor.

So, with a certain amount of malicious joy, he ran with it.

"Oh, man. Way ahead of you, Vic."

Victor was so surprised by the remark he didn't notice that Bowie had used the nickname he hated.

"I was actually already looking for other employment."

"Were you now?" Victor eyed him suspiciously.

"Yeah. I mean. This is a great job and everything, but you've made it clear to me that you're not going to make any effort to work together with me or the rest of the employees here, so I figured I'd get ahead of the curve and find a job I like before you end up firing everyone."

Victor's face turned beat red with rage.

"Did you have anything else, or can I head back to the floor?"

Victor was speechless. His anger was so immense it blocked his windpipe and it was all Victor could do to mouth the words "Get out".

Bowie nodded in acknowledgment, backed out of the office and went back to work as if nothing had happened. His pulse was racing and he felt great. That fat bastard deserved everything he got. Victor had been on his high horse so long, Bowie was thrilled for the chance to knock him down a peg. He smiled as he reached the mountain of freight and greeted his co-workers. Somewhere deep down, his smile only served to mask the fear of what might come next, but in that moment he didn't care. He was going to find a job one way or another. He was sick of living life passively. He was going to fight tooth and nail every step of the way and nobody, especially not Victor, was going to stop him. Even if it cost him his job.

The rest of the shift went smoothly, or at least it seemed to. His co-workers could sense that something was up, but nobody said anything about it.

By the time Bowie clocked out it was nearly nine o'clock and a gentle fog had settled over Echo City. Bowie headed home on foot and for the most part his trek was uneventful. He laughed aloud to himself, his voice echoing over the asphalt. "Screw you, asshole!" He shouted, lifting a middle finger behind him in the direction of the warehouse, his heart pumping spiteful anger through his veins.

The following day he had precious few hours to hit the streets before a one o'clock shift. He grabbed a handful of applications from a couple of fast food restaurants and local businesses before heading down toward Echo City Rail. He was surprised when he got on the bus to find a familiar face sitting on one of the seats facing the main aisle.

"Amy? Hey."

"Oh, hey Bowie!" She smiled at him and gestured to the empty seat next to her.

"I didn't expect to see you here. What's up?" He slid into the seat as the bus hissed into motion.

She shrugged. "I'm going to visit a friend of mine."

"Why the bus? I thought you had a car." He noted.

She began digging through her purse. "Yeah. My car is broke... Some asshole decided running a red light was a good idea." She pulled her phone from the purse and began tapping the screen. "See." She held up the phone for him to see the photo. What was left of the Ford sedan was mangled on the driver side corner. "Can you believe that?"

"Oh my god." Bowie leaned in closer to get a better look. "What happened?"

"It was a green light, so I went. It was green for like two or three seconds and I was already most of the way out into the intersection and then this truck just barrels through and hits me on the corner." She frowned.

"If it had been a half second later, he would have hit the driver's seat. You could be dead. Are you okay?"

"Yeah. I'm fine. My neck is a little sore, but otherwise I'm alright. The car spun around a bit, but I wasn't going that fast. He was going like fifty-five in a thirty zone though. The worst part is the guy just drove off. The cops showed up and took down my information but that's it."

Bowie shook his head and leaned back against his seat. "That sucks. Why would someone just hit and run like that?"

"Maybe he was uninsured. Or an illegal or something. Who knows? I took it to the shop yesterday and I'm supposed to pick it up tomorrow morning but for now I have to ride the bus." She put the phone back in her purse. "So, what are you up to?"

"I'm trying to find a different job." Bowie said dryly.

"Ah." She said, a little sorry she asked. "How's that working out?"

Shaking his head, Bowie slumped down in his seat. "Not so well. I can't seem to find any leads. Nobody is hiring. At least, that's what it seems like. What really pisses me off is that I keep hearing that there's 'tons of jobs out there'." He made air quotations with his fingers, "but there's not. Not for a guy like me anyway. Everyone wants a degree *and* experience in the job itself. I don't know about you, but I think it's pretty stupid to require job experience when the only way to get that job experience is to have the job in the first place, you know?"

Amy laughed. "Yeah. I know what you mean. I guess you have to get promoted or know someone before you can go work someplace else, you know? So where are you headed?"

"I wanted to check out Echo City Rail, actually."

She raised her eyebrows, impressed. "I never thought of working for them. I wonder if you need a certification or something."

He shrugged a shoulder. "Only one way to find out. I figured I'd go and at least ask. Pick up an application. You know?"

"Why didn't you just call them?"

Bowie took out his cell phone to check the screen. "My signal's been kind of off lately. I'll be in the middle of downtown and suddenly it's like 'no signal'."

"Really?" She asked.

"Yeah. Sure. I mean look at this." He held his phone out in front of her. A warning at the top read 'no signal'. "It keeps going off and on like that. Almost like I'm being stalked by bad reception."

"Well, that is kind of weird. Hey. This is my stop coming up. I'll catch you later, okay?" She reached up and pulled on the stop cable. "Good luck with the job hunt. I hope you find something."

"Thanks." He said as she got up from her seat. "I'll see you later."

Bowie remained on the bus until it reached a transfer station near ECR. Bowie could see the train yard in the distance. He was determined to get there this time. If Victor called, he told himself, he was not going to answer. He decided he was 'unavailable due to personal circumstances' if anyone asked. He wasn't about to let his boss dictate when he could or could not find other employment.

He was just a few blocks from the station, in front of an empty lot of brown cheat grass when he noticed the stranger from before. The man he'd seen at Ed's.

This time standing right in his path, staring at him intensely. The hairs on the back of Bowie's neck stood on end and it was all he could do to keep his nerve. He stiffened and waited, refusing to take his eyes off the strange man. The cold gleam in his eyes, the detached way he stood there eagerly, patiently, was enough to make Bowie want to turn around and run the other way.

Sure, it could just be some nut case walking the streets. Bowie told himself over and over in his head that it was just some punk out to cause trouble.

Bowie had just opened his mouth to say something when his phone rang. He jumped.

He fumbled around and took the phone out of his pocket and checked the screen. Victor was calling.

He hit the silence button and shoved it back in his pocket. When he returned his attention to the street it was empty. There was no one.

Bowie suddenly felt lightheaded. There were no nearby fences, no cars or other hiding places. Just a dying field of cheat grass. He went over to where the stranger had stood and looked around, but there was nothing to indicate where he had gone.

He wondered if he was just seeing things; that maybe there hadn't been anyone there in the first place. In his gut he knew what he'd seen but he didn't want to believe it. It was just some creep. Someone was stalking him or something. That's what Bowie decided. Everything inside him told him he was wrong, but he pushed those thoughts from his mind. He didn't have time to deal with that right now.

Somewhat shaken by the encounter, he took a deep breath and tried to give himself some encouragement before he continued heading toward Echo City Rail.

X

Echo City Rail's main office was a modest building, two stories at one end, with a slanted roof at the other, covered in pebble concrete siding. Large tinted windows made up the main front of the building. The parking lot was nearly vacant. There was only a white company van sitting silently next to a crimson Camaro with a chipping coat of paint. As Bowie approached, he could barely see the empty lobby and the vague shape of a front desk.

He swung the front door open and peered inside for a moment. There didn't seem to be anyone inside and it was dead quiet. He felt awkward in the empty room but he decided to continue over to the front desk anyway. He was here to get a job. He wasn't going to be dissuaded by an empty room. The desk had a small bell on the counter, so he rang it and waited.

He heard distant footsteps and soon he was greeted by a wiry, middle-aged man who appeared from around a corner. The man had short thinning hair combed to one side and a large pair of glasses that sat on his nose. He reminded Bowie of some of the old 1980's scientists he'd seen in movies.

"Hello. Can I help you?" The man said uneasily.

Bowie felt severely out of place. He started to think about what to say and the words didn't quite come to him quick enough, causing an awkward silence to fill the large lobby. "Uh. Well. I um..." He took in a deep breath to compose himself. "I was looking for work and I was wondering if Echo City Rail had any job openings."

The man rubbed his chin for a moment. "Well. I don't know, to be honest. Tell you what. Sit tight for a minute and I'll see if I can get a hold of someone."

"Alright." Bowie said.

The man turned and left the way he had come, leaving Bowie alone in the painfully silent lobby. Nearly ten minutes passed and Bowie was about ready to leave when the man reappeared with a single sheet of paper in his hand.

"Here's an application."

"Oh. Thanks." Bowie waited for a moment for the man to add something but he seemed eager to return to his own work. "Is this where I'll need to turn it in?" Bowie asked.

"Uh. Yes. Yeah, just bring it back here when you get it filled out." The man nodded.

Bowie offered his hand. "Thank you." He said.

The man shook his hand quickly and then disappeared around the corner once more without so much as a goodbye.

Bowie looked at the paper in his hand and shook his head. It was one of those generic applications most businesses didn't use anymore. There was even a place at the top to write in the company's name. He had been hopeful to get a better reception when he came in. He had a sinking feeling in his gut that this would turn out to be a waste of his time.

He sighed and started for the door. He had been standing in the lobby so long that his leg had started to ache and he was glad he'd be able to sit down on the bus ride to work. He checked the time on his phone. He'd have to run when he got off the bus but he'd have just enough time to make the one o'clock shift.

Outside, the world seemed all the more cold and empty. His footsteps echoed out over the asphalt as he limped his way to the bus station. He was glad he didn't pass the same stranger on the way back. Bowie'd had enough stress and strangeness for one day.

His leg started to feel a little better the more he moved and he was hobbling less and less. It was likely the cold weather was doing his leg some good. The chill numbed the pain and when he got moving his circulation picked up. It was still hurting, but the pain had grown to more of a dull ache.

The walk to the station went by slowly but when the bus pulled in, he was relieved to get some warmth and take a seat. The ride seemed a lot longer than it should have as he mulled over all of the applications he'd picked up. Most of the places he'd visited he didn't really want to work for. They all had an almost aggressively polite attitude toward him at first but once they handed him an application, they seemed all too eager to return to their own work. He leafed through the applications. What a pain. He'd be up all night filling in the same information over and over again.

He stopped at the application for Echo City Rail. He was almost tempted to throw it away, it seemed like such a joke. The chance they'd even look at it was pretty slim. He started to crumple it in his hand but stopped himself. He had to at least give it a shot. Giving up before he even started didn't seem like the kind of life he wanted to live. He folded it into quarters and stuffed it in his pocket with the rest of the applications.

When he arrived at the bus stop nearest to Fleischer it was already one o'clock.

"Crap." He muttered under his breath.

He disembarked and made a dash for it. He had a few minutes window before he'd officially be considered late, but that was just enough time for him to get there.

When he reached the employee entrance his leg felt like it was on fire. He bit his lip and pushed onward, through the door, past the other busy employees and to the time clock. He breathed a sigh of relief when he saw that he still had a minute left, and punched in as quickly as he could.

Not two minutes later Victor came storming across the floor heading toward Bowie and three others who were busy tearing apart pallets of stock to reorganize the freight by department.

When Bowie noticed him, he thought for sure Victor was going to ask Bowie back to his office again. He was surprised when Victor immediately broke into heated conversation in front of everyone.

"Swift!" Victor growled. "Why didn't you pick up your phone earlier? I needed you here."

Bowie didn't miss a beat. "I was taking care of some personal business. I must have missed your call." He said casually as he continued working while he talked.

"You need to answer your phone when it's work related." Victor said grumpily. "I needed you here earlier. We're nearly a truck behind and we've got more on the way."

"Did you call Bob or Matthew?" Bowie asked.

"Bob called in sick and Matt quit."

"Ah. That sucks. Sorry man." He said only half meaning it.

"So, next time I call you, you're going to pick up, right?"

Bowie stopped what he was doing, raised an eyebrow and slowly turned to Victor, not sure he'd heard him right.

The other three guys on the floor continued working but their attention was on Victor.

"What?" Bowie asked simply in disbelief.

"I said the next time I call you, you're going to pick up." It was a statement this time, not a question.

Bowie raised his other eyebrow. "If I'm in the middle of a personal matter, I'm not going to pick up the phone. I told you, I was taking care of something."

"You can always pick up the phone."

Two of the guys stopped what they were doing to watch.

"I can't pick up the phone if I'm in the shower. I can't pick it up if I'm at a funeral. I'm not going to pick up the phone if I'm doing something that prevents me from doing so."

"So why didn't you pick up then?" Victor asked. "What was so important it kept you from answering?"

Bowie shook his head and set down the box he still had in his hands. "That's not any of your business." He said quietly.

"It is my business." Victor objected. "I have a business to run. I need people here to do their job. Without people here, this warehouse will be so backed up it would take months to recover. I need you to pick up your phone so we don't have a catastrophe on our hands."

"That's what a schedule is for," Bowie pointed out. "I wasn't scheduled, so I was doing other stuff. I have a life outside of work, Vic."

The use of his hated nickname set Victor even more on edge. "I expect you to do your job!" He barked.

Bowie'd had it. "My *job*," he shot back loudly, "is managing ordering and inventory, not hucking freight. I came in to help you cover a few shifts in spite of the fact that I'm *supposed* to be on light duty due to my injury, but nowhere does my job description say that I am to come in to work beyond what I am scheduled for. It's called volunteering. And if I don't have the time to cover a shift, I don't have the time. If I want to not answer my phone, that's my own business. Hell, I'm here right now, *volunteering* to cover Joey's shift like you asked me to a couple of weeks ago. If I'm not on the schedule for a shift then there is no obligation for me to be here. Okay?"

Bowie noticed a couple of the guys nodding quietly in agreement.

Victor gave him a death glare. "You pick up your *goddamned* phone next time or else! Understand?" He yelled. There was a brief moment when the floor was dead silent. Everyone had heard the shout and stopped what they were doing. All eyes were on Bowie.

Bowie stood up straight and tried to compose himself, his lips tight in thought. He smacked his lips a little. "Well. Uh... Victor..." He began. He paused for just a moment, looked Victor in the eye and said very simply. "No. If that's the way you're gonna be you can go screw yourself."

"Excuse me?" Victor was beside himself.

"I said no. You wanna be a jerk, fine. You can do what you want, but I have no obligation to pick up my phone. It's my right to answer or not answer my phone as I so choose. So... sorry, but no."

Everyone present held their breath. The warehouse was so quiet Bowie could have heard a pin drop. If there was any question as to how angry Victor could get it had just been realized. The plump manager's hands balled up into fists, his face was tight and trembling and his breathing stopped, choked up with absolute anger.

Yet, before he could stop himself Bowie dared utter two words in defiance.

"Got it?"

"GET THE HELL OUT OF HERE!" Victor screamed at the top of his lungs, thrusting an outstretched finger to the door and sending a spray of spittle showering in front of him.

Bowie held his ground and calmly walked up to Victor, his head held high, looking down his nose at the enraged man before brushing past him without a care and left. Bowie knew if Victor were to strike at him or do anything violent, he would be in serious legal trouble, and he was somehow very comfortable tempting Victor to that end. It was his life. And nobody was going to tell him what do to or how to live it, no matter what.

As he walked through the silent warehouse, he knew he had just shattered the glass that had kept everything contained until now. He had crossed a line that separated him and his co-workers from Victor's wrath and he didn't care. He chuckled to himself as he neared the time clock. He was done here, one way or another and now that there was blood in the water, he doubted many people would stay and continue to work for him. That kind of attention would put Victor in the spotlight with the company and then a real investigation would begin. There was a good chance he'd get fired and Bowie was glad of it. He'd get a job somewhere else, and even if he didn't find something amazing, it was better than being where he was.

Bowie felt an odd sense of emptiness as he punched out. It was almost like the ground had left him behind and he was free falling.

He smiled and headed for the door, glancing over his shoulder as he passed friends and co-workers he'd known as long as he'd worked there. Many of them he never really knew, but they were his people just the same. He didn't notice their looks of pity and concern for his well-being. He had done something no one else had dared, and that was a place they could not follow him.

Outside it seemed even colder than it had before. Chilled with fog, the air bit at his skin but he didn't feel it. His nerves were on fire, his body hot with adrenaline. He let out a cry of victory into the night.

The shout fell and faded, echoing dimly off the asphalt and concrete. After a time, it became a lonely night once more as he headed back to his apartment.

XI

The next day was spent delivering applications and asking to speak with managers. No matter where he went it seemed as though the manager was either too busy to see him or was otherwise unavailable.

It was foggy and quiet on the bus ride through town. Echo City Rail was his last stop. He almost expected to see the creepy stranger on the way but it didn't happen. In fact, he hardly saw a soul. The fog had grown so thick he almost couldn't see across the street. Even so, he couldn't shake the ill feeling in his gut.

The lobby of Echo City Rail again was vacant when he entered. He felt completely out of place, as if he was trespassing somewhere he shouldn't. With the wall of fog outside, he felt extremely isolated, as if he'd just entered into some strange private sanctum.

"Hello?" He called out as he neared the desk. His voice echoed throughout the lobby. "Excuse me? I'm here to turn in an application." He waited for a few moments before trying the bell at the desk. It rang loud and clear and startled Bowie just a little. He wondered if it was the quiet or the fog that made him so jumpy. After three bell rings and five minutes of waiting, Bowie decided to take a look around the corner where the man with glasses had disappeared to the last time he'd been there.

It was a narrow, white painted hallway with blue-gray commercial carpet. It carried on a good twenty feet before it veered left. There was a solid gray security door at the turn and when Bowie knocked on it, no one answered. He really wanted to get his application turned in, but he felt silly knocking on closed doors inside the building. Looking to his left he could see the hallway didn't have far to go before it ended at yet another gray security door. He shook his head and went over to knock on that door as well.

Before his hand could knock a second time the door flew open and a different man in a pinstripe collared shirt came through, jumping a little when he saw Bowie.

"Oh. Geez. You scared me. Excuse me." He said as he brushed past and continued on his way.

"Pardon me." Bowie said. The man was walking so fast Bowie had to almost jog to keep up. He called out, "excuse me. Can you help me?"

The tall man turned around once he'd reached the front desk and had his hands in a drawer. "Yes? What?"

"I needed to turn in this application." Bowie said holding out his application.

"We're not hiring right now." The man said in an irritated tone.

"Oh." Bowie's heart sank into his stomach. "Well, could you at least give it to your manager in case something opens up?"

The man snatched it out of Bowie's hands. "Sure." Then he pulled a stack of papers out of the drawer and hurried back through the hallway and out of sight.

"Thanks." Bowie muttered to himself. He stood there dumbly in the lobby for a minute or two trying to figure out what just happened.

The chances that he'd get employed any time soon were dwindling, and the one place he had really hoped for didn't seem like it would pan out. He didn't know what to do. He had tried. He'd gone out on the street, kept his eyes open for employment. Anything to get him away from Fleischer Home and Garden.

He turned and left, venturing out into the thick mist.

He waited at the bus station for what seemed an eternity, running things over in his mind. He had promised himself to keep fighting to live an engaged life but what if there was nowhere else for him to go? This wasn't what he had envisioned for himself. For him it almost felt as if the world was telling him to just give up and go home.

In a way, he wanted to. He wanted to forget work and Victor and looking for work and making money so that he could live on his own without all of the stress and uneasiness. Why should he continue to tolerate his station in life and prolong his own suffering?

He could smell the diesel fumes from the bus as it came to a hissing stop in front of him. He didn't even remember walking to the bus station. His legs had moved on their own, propelling him forward. He got on and found a secluded seat in the back.

That's what Arsen had been talking about. His duplicate self had warned him not to lie down and die the slow death. Otherside was supposedly a reflection of the real world, but within such a distorted reality it was impossible to say just how far things had to progress here in the real world for it to really matter.

He was stuck and no matter how hard he tried he wasn't getting anywhere. It just felt like he was spinning his wheels.

He took a deep breath and tried to push those thoughts from him mind. He had to be stronger. Though he continued trying to convince himself that Otherside was just a bad dream he couldn't help but think of what had happened there. He wasn't certain if Arsen was even alive. The creatures in that dark twisted world were insatiable. It would be a miracle for his other self to survive long enough in Hellion territory to make it back.

Bowie thrust his elbow behind him into the wall of the bus. He didn't notice the bus driver looking back to see what the noise was.

Damnit! He thought. *What the hell was the point of all this? Did any of it even really happen?* He had spent so much time telling himself Otherside wasn't real. He had been attacked by a dog on the way home and it had torn up his leg. Then he passed out and had a bad dream. That was all. It had to be. He shook his head. It hadn't happened and that was the end of it.

The bus came to a halt and he got off a few blocks from his apartment.

He had only just started for home when he heard a strange whirring sound coming from down the sidewalk. He watched but couldn't see it through the mist. It was low, almost like a perpetual zipper with a slight, rhythmic undulation to it. Suddenly it stopped, and Bowie could hear something metal clattering around for a few seconds. Then the whirring picked up again. The sound made the hairs on the back of his neck stand on end. He waited where he stood, not sure of what to expect, when out of the mist a bizarre figure emerged.

Along the sidewalk of the quiet suburb an old man emerged from the fog pushing a bicycle piled with massive garbage bags. The black and white bags were full of empty plastic bottles, soda cans and other recyclables and were fastened to the frame of the bike, hanging on its sides like massive bulging tumors. The protuberant bags hid so much of the bicycle so that the only distinguishing features were the handlebars and the front tire, which whirred lazily as the mountain bike treads rubbed against the plastic bags.

Like a beast of burden, the old man trundled onward, walking beside the bicycle with his hands on the handlebars. A woolen cap did it's best to hide a balding head of mangled white hair which peaked out around the man's ears. His features were worn and graying with patches of stubble and a tattered white beard enclosing a wrinkled face. His clothes were tattered; A hand-me-down navy-blue jacket on top of a too well used shirt, faded khaki pants that had started to fray around the edges, and a pair of thick soled brown boots. His posture seemed tired and unhurried as he slowly walked along, scanning the curb for garbage cans.

Bowie was about to cross the street to give the man a wide berth when he realized that the man looked just like Hal.

He froze. Everyone had a duplicate in Otherside. Or, at least most people seemed to. Hal had even told Bowie about his own duplicate, but now Bowie couldn't remember the name Hal had given him. Of course, he couldn't be certain it was Hal's duplicate. They looked similar, certainly, but Arsen and Bowie hadn't been identical by any means and he doubted Hal's real self would look much like the strange organ grinder. Even if he was, there was no way he would know anything about Otherside or the war between the Effigies and the Hellion.

Bowie had nearly given up on ever trying to remember his name and was about to cross the street when the vagrant spoke.

"Hey. You got a sec?" The man said in a pleasant tone. When the man had spoken it sent chills up Bowie's spine. His voice was the same as Halloran's.

Damnit... Thought Bowie. He remained where he was. The old man whirred a little closer.

"I found this on the sidewalk and I want to return it, but I don't think the owner will be pleased to see someone like me with it." The old man said, holding out a thick wallet.

Bowie cautiously held out a hand. "Yeah. Yeah, that's fine."

Once he had it, he took a quick peak inside.

"Holy –."

"I know. I couldn't believe it either. Someone would be pretty sad if they found out they lost that much money."

The wallet probably had close to a thousand dollars in it, and at least a few credit cards, not to mention a driver's license for someone by the name of Bonds.

"You trust me to return it? I mean, how do you know I won't just run off and take it for myself?" Bowie asked.

The old man shrugged. "I suppose you could. And I wouldn't stop you. But you don't look like the kind of guy who would do that." He paused and jerked his thumb over his shoulder at the duplex they were standing in front of. "Besides, the address on the license is right here."

Bowie chuckled a little bit. "Alright, old man."

He walked up to the house and rang the bell. The man pictured on the license opened the door. Bowie didn't say anything, just held out the wallet for the man to take. The man's eyes went wide and he took it gratefully.

"Thank you!" He said. "Oh my God. Thank you so much. I didn't even know I'd lost it!" He withdrew into the house, leaving the door open.

"Yeah no problem." Bowie said and then turned to walk back to the sidewalk.

The old man had already started down the street. Bowie hurried to chase after him. "Wait. Where are you going?" Bowie asked as he caught up.

"Nowhere in particular. Why?"

"Well, dude. What was all that about?"

The old man turned to look over his shoulder as the owner of the house came back outside and looked in their direction as they walked away.

"You found all that money, and what? You just give it back? I mean..." Bowie considered his words for a moment. "You look like a homeless person, right?"

The old man nodded and smiled a little as they continued down the sidewalk. "I am homeless, yes."

"Couldn't you use the money and just give back the wallet?"

The old man shrugged.

"Or even given it to him yourself. He came out of his house just a moment ago. He might have given you a reward for returning it or something."

Again, the old man shrugged.

"So why did you give it back?"

The old man looked Bowie over for a moment. "Who are you kid?"

"I'm Bowie." He said with a little hesitation, offering his hand.

The old man looked down at Bowie's hand, at again at his own hand which was grimy, smiled a big grin and shook his hand. "Geoff." He said. "You know, you're the first person to offer me a handshake in a long time."

"Really?" Bowie said as they both let go.

Geoff looked down and gestured at his own clothes. "Not a whole lot of folks lining up to shake my hand, if you know what I mean."

Bowie laughed a little, feeling a little uncomfortable. "So, why didn't you keep the money? You just said you were homeless."

Halloran shook his head. "Honestly, I'm not sure a young fellow like you would understand. You see, there's a lot more to life than just money and things. Like doing the right thing." He pointed back down to the house they had just visited.

"What about a place to live?"

Geoff shrugged. "I don't need much but a warm coat and a place to get out of the rain. There are shelters, and places to stay warm and dry during the winter. Money's not much good for me, you know?"

"What do you mean?"

Geoff made a gesture to indicate drinking.

"Ah." Bowie understood.

"Besides, what matters most to a man like me isn't what I have, it's what I give. You understand?"

Bowie paused. It was no wonder Hal had such a command over the other Effigies when his real self seemed to be living a completely selfless life, even if he was homeless.

"What do you do about food?"

Geoff let out a hearty laugh. "Well, I buy it when I need it. I do have a little money. And I take charity from those who want to give it. The way I see it, it makes them happy to give it, and it keeps me fed."

Bowie was somewhat dumbfounded. "You just... live. That's it. You don't work or anything, you just wander around living off of handouts?"

"Well, I wouldn't say I don't work or anything. I help out where I'm needed. Like the wallet. That's all I can really offer the world anymore. There's not much place for retired war veterans in the civilian world, you know? Listen, it's been nice talking to you, but I should probably go," Geoff said, gesturing over to some people coming down the sidewalk and giving them both looks. "It would be better for you if you weren't seen with me, if you know what I mean."

Bowie stopped and watched as the old man continued walking for a few paces. Suddenly, the old man shivered and turned, clutching his arms. He looked around frantically for something but didn't see anything. He turned back to Bowie and said with a slight rasp in his voice. "Something's coming. I can feel it. Be on your toes, Bowie. Whatever it is, it's bad."

The old man hurried off with his whirring, garbage laden bicycle, leaving Bowie alone on the sidewalk. He stood there for a few minutes, thinking about what Geoff had said. It was strange to have met the man's Effigy before meeting the man. Had things happened the other way around, Bowie probably would have stayed as far away from Geoff as possible, not knowing what kind of man he really was. Muggings and other crimes were common in Echo City. He had learned from a young age not to talk to strangers, and to be wary of people like Geoff.

Bowie chuckled to himself a little when he thought of how ironic it was that the very type of person he had been told to avoid was one of his greatest allies in Otherside. Maybe that was the problem. Perhaps one of the reasons so few Effigies existed in Otherside was due to subconscious prejudice in the real world. His world was filled with people mostly interested in buying and consuming things in their own self-absorbed lives. The more he considered it, the more it seemed to make sense.

As he was thinking about it on the way home, he remembered he had wanted to stop by the Tri-Feed hardware store to see if there was anything he could get to help spruce up his apartment a little. He'd wanted to make a change in his life, and when he'd returned home from the hospital, he'd seen just how dull and lifeless his apartment had become. He only had about twenty bucks to spend, but he figured that would be enough to add at least a little color to his living arrangement.

He took a side street past some small houses on a gently sloping hill. The neighborhood was another quiet one. At that time of day most people were at work.

He had just passed a boxy beige house, its lawn creeping up to meet the asphalt for lack of a sidewalk, when Bowie lost his footing. He managed to tumble to his side instead of forward, narrowly missing a pitfall as a gaping hole opened up in front of him.

The cold asphalt scraped against his hands as he pulled himself up. Looking down he expected to see a small pothole, maybe the size of a basketball but what he found was nothing of the sort.

The hole had collapsed just like any sinkhole, only this one seemed to stretch impossibly downward into darkness. It was as wide as Bowie, and about three feet long.

His heart raced as he realized how close he'd come to falling in.

He gave the hole a wide birth and picked up his pace. He was only a block away from Tri-Feed when suddenly another hole sucked down the asphalt, collapsing beneath an old red Volvo just a few feet from where Bowie stood. The car was too big and got wedged for a few seconds before the ground gave way and took the Volvo down.

Bowie began jogging. He wanted to tell himself that it was just a coincidence but in his gut he knew better. Something was after him. When he'd hit the Eidolon with steel in the suburb it had turned into black sludge and slithered away until it found a hole just like the one that had just nearly taken him.

As another hole nearly swallowed him, sinking behind him by mere inches, Bowie broke into a dead run. He ran through the parking lot, leaping over small pits as they appeared, and burst through the double glass doors of Tri-Feed.

Inside an eerie quiet had settled. Bowie stood at the glass door panting, looking out to see if any more sinkholes were tearing away at the parking lot. He had only been there for a few seconds before he became acutely aware of just how quiet the usually busy Tri-Feed store had become.

It was your typical hardware store mixed with sporting goods and a few housewares. He had come in through the housewares section, where an assortment of colored glass bowls and cups topped off small square display stands for a wide array of cheap products. Further on, the store was cramped aisles filled with small appliances, chain by the foot and the beginnings of the screws and nails. He could only see a little way down the main center aisle as he crept forward, hoping to find an associate wandering around. The main aisle veered to the right, leaving a swath of products and a few aisle-ways blocking his view in a strange attempt at a more "contemporary" retail design.

Bowie remembered the incident at the gas station near his home. Cautiously, Bowie stepped over toward the register and leaned over to peak behind the counter.

"Can I help you?

Bowie jumped. He whipped around to find a pleasant looking young man with a pair of silver rimmed glasses and a round face smiling at him.

"No. I'm good. Hi. Sorry. Just a little jumpy today." He explained.

"Do you need help finding anything?"

"Uh... Yeah. Where is your spray paint?" He asked, trying to remember what he'd come for.

"Aisle six."

"And do you guys sell picture frames, or mirrors?"

The associate nodded and pointed down toward the back of the store. "Frames, no. Mirrors are going to be back there next to bath hardware."

"Okay. Thanks." Bowie smiled and let out a sigh as he headed down the main aisle toward paint.

It was relief to see someone else. The store had been so quiet. He wasn't certain he'd want to leave any time soon. He felt a little safer knowing someone else was there. Another encounter with the silent Eidolon was something he preferred to avoid.

While he perused the wide selection of spray paint, Bowie considered stopping by the guns and knives at the counter in the back. He'd neglected to bring his knife with him and he was starting to feel naked without it.

He was pulling a can of burgundy spray paint off the shelf, when a massive crash shattered the silence. The can fell from his hand and clattered uselessly on the floor.

Bowie walked down to the end of the aisle to see what happened, but the store was quiet once more.

"You okay?" Bowie shouted, hoping someone would answer. Anxiously, he peered around the corner.

No one answered. The aisles were vacant and everything was still.

"Hello?" Bowie called out again. "Is everything okay?"

Under ordinary circumstances he might have felt a little awkward saying those things, but given the eerie silence, Bowie would have been grateful to hear the sound of another person's voice. He left the spray paint aisle and began walking in the direction he thought the sound had come from.

You're an idiot. He told himself. *You need to get out of here.* The sinkholes erupting, the strange staring man who kept following him. All these things were screaming to him in his mind that he was not safe. Four aisles away, he found the source of the racket. Several ladders had fallen down haphazardly around the guy who had helped him only moments ago. His body was sprawled unconscious against the racking.

Bowie checked both ways down the main aisle before he turned and crept over to the poor associate who was laying at a funny angle. When he got closer, he saw that it had been no accident. A sticky crimson splotch had matted the man's hair on one side, disguising a serious wound where the man's head had been bashed in.

At first, he thought maybe the employee had hit his head on the ladder, but there was no blood anywhere else, and none of the ladders had fallen even close to his head.

Bowie immediately pulled out his cell phone to dial 911. He wasn't in the least surprised to see that the screen read "no signal" at the top. He shook his head and pocketed the device before he decided it might be best to leave the store as quickly as possible. He may have to brave collapsing streets but at least he wouldn't be trapped indoors, anxiously waiting for something to happen.

When he rounded the corner of the aisle to make a dash for the exit opposite from where he'd entered, he came skidding to a stop. Four big guys in t-shirts and jeans stood there, watching him with blank expressions.

Bowie waited for a moment to see what they would do, but they remained where they were. He turned to try the other direction instead, but as he turned around his heart leaped up into his throat.

Standing no more than twenty yards behind him was the stranger. He wore the same clothes as before, the same intense stare, only this time he was smiling. His lips seemed to curl up to his ears in a big sinister grin. In his hands he carried two things. The first was a signal flare, burning fierce scarlet in his hand, hissing quietly. The second was a long, plastic handled gun made for driving nails through concrete with a powdered charge. Its muzzle rested gently against a white propane tank that sat neatly on the ground in the middle of the aisle.

In less than a second, Bowie realized two simple, terrifying truths. First, the stranger was pulling the trigger which, with the help of the flare, would cause a big explosion; Second, the stranger didn't care in the slightest.

Click.

Bowie dove for cover behind an aisle as the shockwave blasted debris in all directions. The aisle itself warped and threatened to come crashing down where Bowie had landed. His ears rang with the enormous boom that shook the store as he lay coughing in a cloud of dust on the floor.

He forced himself up slowly and started half-walking, half-crawling down the aisle to get away as fast as he could. He didn't need to turn around to know what was behind him. The stranger was from Otherside which meant only one thing could even hurt him; Iron. Bowie knew propane tanks were made with brass. The explosion had probably done nothing to the Eidolon.

He darted around the corner and only barely caught a glimpse of the stranger following.

Iron or steel, thought Bowie. He needed to find something to protect himself with. He turned down an aisle of nails and screws and tore product from the shelves, scattering it behind him as he ran. With any luck it might at least slow the creatures down. He knew he was making a racket but it didn't matter. They would find him eventually. He had to run.

When he reached the back of the store, he had a choice. He could try to make a break for the exit and brave the swallowing pits outside, or he could try his best to get to the gun counter and find a proper weapon.

He opted for the guns and began sprinting through the store. Along the way one of the four Eidolon burst out in front of him. He yelped and back peddled hard, managing to gain only a small distance as the Eidolon swiped at him, missing by mere inches.

Bowie looked around frantically for a weapon. He had managed to stop right in front of the sledge hammers and axes. He didn't have time to think. He grabbed and handle and started swinging.

The hammer head from the sledge struck home easily and knocked the Eidolon to the ground.

Bowie didn't bother waiting around to see if it would get back up or not. He dropped the unwieldy sledge and leaped over the fallen enemy.

He thought he could see the counter up ahead, but two Eidolon blocked his path. He whipped down another aisle in an attempt to get around them but by the time he reached the end of the aisle, they had already moved to counter him. They were coming at him from both sides, and a third one was coming behind him down the aisle. As they closed in, he bolted across the center aisle and veered to his right. The one on his right was quickly closing in. He faked going straight toward it and darted to his right, causing the Eidolon to crash into a rack of clothing. It hadn't bought him much time, but at least his assailants were all on one side of him now as he ran once again toward the back of the store.

He quickly cleared the aisles and reached the gun counter.

... Where the smiling Eidolon waited.

Bowie cursed, ran past the counter and burst through an "Employees Only" door into the back rooms.

A narrow plywood hallway to the left led to a dead end with locked doors and to the right it opened up into a large receiving area littered with wrapped pallets. Bowie chose the receiving area and made a dash for the exit door on the far side. When he rammed against it, it wouldn't budge. The push-bar on the door was working fine, but something had wedged the door shut from the outside. He tried again but still it wouldn't open. When he heard the door from the hallway open, he hid behind a tall pallet of boxes in the corner. His hiding spot wouldn't last forever, but at least they'd have to spend some time trying to find him. In the meantime, he had a few moments to try and think of a way out.

He sorely wished the big roll-up doors had been left open and a part of him wondered what the hell had jammed the door shut. Emergency exits were always locked from the outside, but never from the inside so people could escape in case of a fire.

He could try to make a dash for the hallway once the Eidolon entered the receiving floor, but he'd have to be quick. If they caught him, he'd have a hopeless fight on his hands and if he got caught between them on the way out it was over. What he really needed was something to defend himself with.

He searched the area near the roll-up doors for anything that might be of use. There was a massive iron pry bar leaning up by one of the doors, but it was way too unwieldy to use as an effective weapon. The two by four next to it would be even more useless. Other than scattered remnants of garbage, the only other thing close by was a cardboard box with a pile of tools tossed carelessly inside.

Bowie noticed a plastic grip handle protruding from the box that he recognized immediately. It belonged to an outdated, battery powered nailgun and the battery was still attached at the base of the handle. He quickly crept forward, keeping his body low and snatched the handle from the box before hopping back behind the pallet. He gritted his teeth as the pain in his leg caught up with him. He'd been running on it pretty hard and now that he had stopped it felt like it was on fire. He did his best to ignore the pain and focused.

The battery was attached to the handle of the nailgun but he couldn't tell if it had a charge or not. Turning it over he saw nails in the clip. There was a chance it might work. There was only one problem. The nailgun required the tip to be pressed down in order for the gun to fire. He couldn't hold it in with his finger or he'd blow a nail through it. He needed something to hold it down or else he had to get in close and push it in to his opponent.

He heard someone knocking over boxes just a few yards away. They were looking for him.

Bowie pressed his back against one of the pallets, and cautiously peered around the corner.

The Eidolon was tearing boxes off a pallet stupidly. The creature moved on to the next pallet and started tearing at the plastic wrap. As the creature disturbed the freight a heavy box tumbled down and the corner struck the Eidolon sharply on the head. The Eidolon didn't flinch. In fact, the box didn't cause the Eidolon to move at all.

Bowie thought it strange that the reflections of real people seemed to be unaffected by the real world. It was as though certain laws of physics just didn't apply to them. Gravity still had its way, and they couldn't pass through solid objects, but it was like they were so incredibly dense and heavy that normal materials didn't affect them at all. Except for steel.

Bowie checked the nailgun one last time. It sickened him to have to fight like this but it was either them or him.

Just as the Eidolon turned its back, Bowie took a deep breath and made a rush for it. He pressed the nailgun against the small of the creature's back and pulled the trigger.

Gat.

The steel sliver spat right out the other side, leaving a small hole in the Eidolon. The creature arched its back in agony before spinning around to grab Bowie by the throat.

Surprised that his adversary hadn't gone down, Bowie angled it up and tried to take a shot at the creature's heart. However, the angle was too steep and awkward and the tip didn't depress like it was supposed to. He squeezed the trigger but nothing happened. Before he could adjust the angle, the Eidolon gripped Bowie's throat hard. Despite it's impossible immovability, the Eidolon's strength was no more than that of a human, which was more than enough to choke him to death.

Bowie's eyes went wide and he brought his free hand up out of instinct to pry the creature's grip from his throat but his efforts were useless. Every second that ticked by drained more and more life from his lungs as he struggled to breathe. He slapped his arm around to break the hold, clawing at the Eidolon's face, trying to tear loose the creature's grasp. His vision started to blur as he gasped for air, his face turning red as the Eidolon continued to strangle him. It would all be over in a few seconds. He was rapidly losing his grip on the heavy nailgun as his strength left him. He just barely managed to fumble the gun against the Eidolon's sternum. The tip depressed.

Gat.

A blot of black sludge spattered over Bowie's front as the nail struck home. If Eidolon had a heart, he'd just hit it.

The grip on his throat loosened and he stumbled back, gasping for air. The Eidolon was stunned and Bowie had a brief moment to collect himself before he moved forward and pulled the trigger again and again, shooting steel nails through the Eidolon's flesh like a soft fruit.

Its body collapsed and the Eidolon fell noiselessly to the ground, dissolving into a thick rancid puddle of black.

Bowie took a moment to catch his breath, still coughing as he massaged his throat.

There were still more of them. A quick mental count reminded him that there were at least three more in the store plus the smiling one.

Bowie heard more footsteps, this time rapidly approaching. They must have heard the nail gun. They knew exactly where he was.

He needed to defend himself. The nail gun was effective, but at close range, he wasn't going to last against three more. He needed something to hold the damned tip of the gun down if he was going to continue to use it. He looked around again for anything that might help him but all he saw were boxes and shrink wrap.

An idea struck him. He saw a box that had torn when the Eidolon had disturbed one of the pallets. One of the cardboard flaps was sticking out at an odd angle. He grabbed hold and ripped at it until it came free. The cardboard was just thick enough that Bowie could hold it in one hand and apply enough pressure to depress the tip.

And just in time.

Two more Eidolon had found him and were making a bee line for him.

He spun to face them, pressed the cardboard against the gun and rattled off the trigger as fast as he could.

The first nail shot through the cardboard and veered off, striking a steel pipe that ran up the wall, sparking as it rang against steel.

The second nail struck the forward most Eidolon in the leg, sending the creature crashing into a pile of boxes.

Bowie screamed as he spat off nails in a spray at each Eidolon, pumping the angry shards into one, then the other. He switched back and forth every three or four shots, peppering the receiving dock with speckles of black ichor.

The Eidolon didn't stand a chance. Several nails went into the skull of the first, and it was already dissolving by the time Bowie sent a second volley into the creature's torso. The second clutched at its stomach in agony before its torso became little more than a sticky mass of sloughing black sludge.

Bowie kept firing until the clip ran dry. It took several lifeless clicks of the trigger before he realized it was empty. He dropped his hands and breathed heavily for a while. He looked down at the gun with a nod of satisfaction. Bowie couldn't believe it. It had worked!

After a few moments, the loading dock felt silent. Wondering what had happened to the last Eidolon, the smiling one, he listened. All he could hear was the sound of his own breathing. He watched the black puddles of sludge that were already coursing their way across the concrete floor and down the hallway.

He was out of ammunition.

Cautiously, he went back to the box he'd found the gun in to see if there was a spare clip of nails he could use.

As he searched, he thought he heard a noise from the hallway.

Bowie remained still and listened again. A loud air compressor blared to life and he jumped. It was an automatic compressor hooked up to the building and had to recharge its lost pressure, grinding and pumping air noisily into its chambers.

"*Shit!*" He cursed. His heart was racing. He knew the larger retail stores used compressors to charge their water lines when the pressure dropped too low but it had scared the hell out of him all the same. He took a deep breath and continued rifling through the box. To his relief there was a spare clip of nails tossed carelessly in the bottom. He loaded the gun and began slowly limping back toward the entrance with the nailgun at the ready.

The store was very still, the silence only broken by Bowie's feet as they crunched over debris left by the explosion. He wondered where the last Eidolon was hiding. They had come for him in force. They meant to kill him. They wouldn't just leave. None of it made any sense. How could they be so well coordinated?

As he crept closer to the glass front doors, Bowie got a sick feeling in his gut. He could see the grey skies opening up over the pitted parking lot that had nearly swallowed him.

Out in the parking lot the smiling stranger stood facing the building. He was halfway across the asphalt near a white minivan that had been lodged in a sinkhole. He waved at Bowie with that same wicked grin on his face.

Bowie stared, confused. He turned around to check if any more of them were behind him, but he was alone. He was a little confused. Was he being taunted? He could try to wait it out but he had no idea how long the Eidolon could remain in his world. Or if the Eidolon needed to eat. Or sleep. He took in a deep breath. He had to leave at some point. He pushed on the front door.

It was locked.

He grabbed it with a hand and rattled it back and forth but it didn't budge.

Across the parking lot, the stranger turned and hopped down into one of the holes and out of sight.

"What the hell?" Bowie dropped the nail gun and grabbed the door handle with both hands and shook it but to no avail. Bowie searched to find the deadbolt, but the latch required a key. *How the hell did he lock it?* Bowie thought. It wasn't like the Eidolon had a key. Or maybe he took one from the dead employee. Not that it mattered now. He was trapped. He had to find another way out.

He had just turned to head to the other entrance when he shook for a brief moment. Or rather, the floor shook.

Then suddenly the floor dropped several inches, settling at a slight angle. Bowie could hear a deep rumbling sound echoing through the building.

He started to panic and began desperately shoving at the door. It still wouldn't move, so he took several steps back and rushed the door to burst it open with his shoulder.

He bounced back in agony, clutching where he had struck the door.

"Crap." He snatched up the nail gun and pressed it against the door, just as the floor sank another six inches. He pressed the trigger but nothing happened. The battery had come loose. He smacked it back in with his hand and pressed it against the window once more.

Crack!

A seam split the glass in two but it did not shatter.

Bowie pulled the trigger again and again, and the crack grew wider and wider.

The floor began a constant, resounding rumble.

He didn't have much time. Bowie took another running start and threw his weight against the door with all of his might.

The glass gave way and showered out onto the concrete walk, Bowie tumbling with it to the ground. He scrambled to get as far away from the building as he could. He made it about halfway across the parking lot before an enormous rumble filled the air and he turned just in time to see the groaning earth swallow the entire building.

All that remained was a massive hole stretching down into oblivion.

XII

Bowie rushed home as fast as he could. There was no telling if the smiling Eidolon would return. He had thought the whole business with Otherside was over, that it had been a fabrication of his mind. He'd been under enough stress lately that he'd been convinced none of it had happened. Now he knew he'd been mistaken. It was happening all over again, only this time Halloran wasn't around to help him. He was on his own.

As he turned the corner of his street he was met by a marching mob of neighbors. People he'd lived next door to; men, women and children, were walking down the street heading straight for him.

He recognized their blank expressions and uniform step immediately. They were all Eidolon.

He had held on to the nail gun but he only had a few shots left and there was no way he'd survive an entire mob before he ran out. He sorely wished he had his grandfather's knife but he'd left it in his apartment. He considered making a break for it but there were just too many people. They'd overtake him in a matter of seconds.

He darted across the street and behind a fence. If he could lead them closer, and further away from his apartment building, he might be able to circle around and reach it.

As he waited and the first of them came into view around the fence, something wasn't right. They weren't running. In fact, none of them seemed the least bit interested in his presence. They stared right on down the street as if they were heading somewhere else.

Bowie watched curiously. He was certain they were coming after him, but they had some other objective in mind as they continued past. He decided to count his blessings and made his way around to the back of his apartment complex.

He reached his front door without any trouble, went inside and got what he needed. Once his grandfather's knife was in his hand, Bowie felt a little more secure. However, he was still uneasy about what had just happened.

He looked himself over in his bathroom mirror.

"Alright, get a hold of yourself," He said. "They weren't after you. They're just passing by. Maybe they're going back to wherever they came from."

Bowie said the words but he didn't believe them. Those Eidolon had a purpose. They weren't just there by happenstance. They were up to something.

"If you follow them, you'll just get yourself killed," He tried to convince himself. "Your leg still hurts. You wouldn't stand a chance out there. Besides, maybe they weren't after you. Maybe they're after someone else."

No sooner had the words left his lips than he realized he was probably right. They *were* after someone else. There could be another person out there just like him being pursued by the same demons. He winced at the thought.

He understood what Geoff was talking about. If he couldn't help someone else, even if they didn't ask for it, what good was Bowie to anyone?

You have to follow them, he decided before he turned and quickly left his apartment. *Even if it kills you...*

It wasn't long before Bowie had caught up with the several dozen Eidolon that marched ever onward into town. For a moment he considered sneaking up on them and taking them out one by one with his knife, but if they realized what he was doing and turned on him he'd be in trouble. He didn't have enough nails left to take them all on and against such numbers the knife would only last him so long before they completely overwhelmed him. He had to play things smart. If he could just observe them from a distance first, figure out what they were up to, maybe he could stop them.

After about ten minutes of walking, Bowie was starting to wonder if they'd ever reach their destination. However, as they got closer to one of the street corners, they veered left and headed straight down Keene road.

They marched single file now, careful to stay away from the chain link fence, sometimes walking on the gravel beside the sidewalk, sometimes swerving around the light posts. It seemed so strange to watch them, almost like ants diligently traveling their own twisted path to forbidden food. It wasn't until they started to fan out at one of the intersections that Bowie realized exactly where they were heading: Fleischer Home and Garden.

They went right past the warehouse and headed on further toward the store itself which sat about a hundred yards away bordering Duportail Avenue. The street was busy and it was a wonder nobody stopped to pay attention to the wave of people marching in unison toward the large home improvement store.

Bowie smirked as he wished the Eidolon were there to swallow up another building, but he doubted that was going to happen.

As they walked by, one of the workers driving a forklift down the runway from the warehouse to the store stopped as he saw the oncoming mass of people. They got right in his path. He unbuckled and stood up, saw Bowie and shouted "What the hell is this?"

Bowie recognized the voice instantly. It was Eduardo. *Shit.* Thought Bowie. "Run!" Bowie shouted as hard as he could. "Get out of there!"

Ed started laughing loudly. "Oh no!" He pretended to be frightened.

"I mean it! RUN!" Bowie cried.

When Eduardo saw their vacant expressions and realized that Bowie wasn't kidding, he set the break, jumped off the machine and ran for the main store.

The Eidolon still paid no attention to Bowie or Eduardo. Bowie knew they could see, but in truth he wasn't sure exactly what Eidolon were capable of. It seemed as though they were following some sort of command, as if someone were controlling them.

The filing mass of Eidolon entered through the large sliding glass door at the rear of the building. It had been left open for Ed to transport pallets from the warehouse and he hadn't closed it behind him when he ran through.

There was nothing Bowie could do to warn anyone. The store wasn't busy by any stretch of the imagination but even so evacuating everyone before the Eidolon got to them wasn't a possibility. Everyone would think he was crazy. Eidolon looked just like humans. Boring lifeless humans. Besides, even as they continued over the concrete floors, they were disinterested in everyone they passed.

A few associates gave puzzled looks as the mass of Eidolon walked by. One tried to offer his assistance only to be completely ignored.

They split up into multiple groups and worked their way to the front registers. There were too many to see over, and Bowie couldn't tell what was going on until he heard a piercing scream.

He skirted around the registers to come around from the front of the store.

He heard a desperate cry, "Let me go!" followed by another scream. Bowie leaped up onto one of the registers to get a better look.

To his horror, four of them had Amy stretched out, each holding a different limb. She was struggling with everything she had and screaming in terror as they lifted her up and began moving her away.

Bowie's eyes went wide.

Left with little choice, Bowie did the only thing he could think of. He jumped from the register and tried to reach her before it was too late. He pushed wildly through the crowd of Eidolon, slashing furiously with his knife when the Eidolon tried to block his way.

He had nearly reached her when they all turned on him.

As patrons at the store panicked and fled, the Eidolon completely surrounded him and rushed in savagely. He rattled off what was left of the nail clip and sent several sprawling before he had to drop the gun and grab hold of his knife. He swung it left and right but it was all he could do to stay vertical as fists and fingernails tore at him beating him down to the ground. He plunged the knife into an Eidolon, but when it twisted to the side it nearly wrenched the knife free from his grasp. He fought for dear life and managed to keep standing, but a pair of arms came slamming down over his shoulders, driving him to his knees. He spun on his knee and clumsily made a wide arc with the blade, causing several Eidolon to back off, giving him time to get off the ground.

Seizing the opportunity, Bowie made a mad dash into the crowd using his shoulder as a battering ram with the knife firmly pointed at his target. As he rammed into the Eidolon and the knife pierced it at the same moment, the body crumbled and moved with him, giving him enough momentum to make it those last few feet. He stumbled and yelled wildly before he leaped into the air and brought the knife down through the last Eidolon standing between him and Amy.

The creatures holding her stood there staring and Bowie didn't give them time to react. He slashed at their limbs to free the her and they recoiled, letting their grasp slip until Amy was free.

The fight wasn't over, however. They quickly formed a circle around Bowie and Amy, each one leaning in, ready to attack at any moment.

Bowie kept his knife up, waving it and pointing it at the Eidolon, trying to create a perimeter.

"Are you okay?" He asked.

Amy massaged her bruised wrist as she stared wide eyed at the Eidolon. "I'm okay. What the hell is going on?" She looked down at the black sludge splattered over the concrete floor and staining her shirt.

"Uh," was the best Bowie could manage. He had no idea where to even begin. As he moved the knife around, walking a small circle around Amy to keep the assailants at bay he tried hard to come up with an answer. "It's kind of hard to explain, but these aren't people."

"What do you mean they're not people?" She looked into their vacant expressions, but some of them she swore she'd seen around town.

"You just have to trust me. We need to get out of here."

"Okay." She said, scared. "What's your plan?"

"Uh," he began, "I'll tell you as soon as I come up with one."

Bowie looked for a gap in the crowd but they had clustered in so close that it was difficult to see past them. The thinnest spot was near a tall locker of propane tanks against the front wall of the store.

"Okay." He began. "First part of my plan. We make for the wall. Take my lead and stay close. Don't let any of them get near you."

"Okay."

They moved slowly in unison. Bowie kept the knife darting around just enough, warding off the threatening creatures who didn't dare come close to the knife. It wasn't quick but they made progress.

As they moved, Bowie wasn't sure what was keeping them from charging in and simply overwhelming them by sheer numbers.

At last the Eidolon parted and they had the propane lockers at their backs.

"Why are they moving away instead of attacking?" Amy whispered, holding close to Bowie's back.

"It's the knife. They can't touch iron." He explained.

She paused briefly. "That didn't stop them earlier."

"I don't know. I'm counting my blessings, okay?" He whispered back.

"Sorry."

"Okay. Now we're going to make our way to the front door. If we can get outside, we might have a chance."

"And just what chance do you think you have?" Came an unfamiliar voice from amidst the crowd.

Bowie froze.

The crowd of Eidolon slowly parted, making way for a figure walking casually toward them.

It was the smiling Eidolon.

He was completely undamaged by the earlier explosion. Even his clothing remained unblemished. He walked with a sort of swagger, one hand swinging loosely back and forth as the other lay tucked inside a pocket. His grin seemed even more twisted as he moved closer, stopping just a few yards away.

Amy whispered to Bowie. "Who is he?"

Bowie shook his head and replied quietly. "I have no idea."

"I'll make you a deal." The smiling Eidolon chuckled. "You can walk right down this path and out of here to safety. I promise they won't stop you." He gestured to the Eidolon. "All you have to do is get past me. How does that sound?"

Bowie hesitated before eyeing him warily. "Who are you?"

"Who? Me? Please." The stranger snorted. "I'm known as Scratcher." He bowed. "At your service," he said almost politely.

Bowie swallowed and tightened the grip on his knife. Eidolon didn't talk. They didn't smile. They certainly didn't play games. This one was different. Bowie didn't have a choice but to ready himself.

Scratcher saw that his prey was ready to fight. He cracked his neck and shrugged his shoulders, hunched over and dug his toes into the ground, ready to pounce.

A palpable tension hung in the air as Scratcher and Bowie traded stares. Suddenly, his weight shifted and he sprang.

Just then a shrieking cacophony shrilled through the air. The glass front of the store burst. Amy and Bowie bent over, clutching their ears as the sound mercilessly ripped the very air to shreds. All around them, Eidolon started rippling and roiling beneath their skin, shaking at the very seams and at last bursting apart into ichorous splatters across the floor.

The sound stopped as suddenly as it had begun.

Bowie looked up to see what had happened. He was half covered in inky remains and his footing slipped on black sludge as he stood up straight.

For a moment, he was back in Otherside, staring over a sea of carnage. He imagined the Effigies, the bodies of the fallen Eidolon and the retreating Hellion in the distance.

He snapped out of it. The floor surrounding the registers was awash in black sludge. The Eidolon had all exploded.

Before them stood the old man, hunched and powerful: Halloran.

He wore the same outfit he'd worn the first time Bowie had seen him. The grey hoodie, the jeans. In the full light of the store he looked like some kind of homeless person. His expression was wearied, but he was smiling. In his hands he held the grinding organ, much the same as in Otherside.

"Hal!" Bowie cried out, glad to see his friend.

Hal held up a hand of warning to stop Bowie from coming any closer. He opened his mouth to speak but his voice was haggard and difficult for Bowie to hear. "I cannot stay much longer. I will return. Meet me at the sewage plant. Bring her. Stay armed and be careful."

With that, Halloran evaporated into a cloud of black, acrid smoke, leaving Bowie and Amy alone in the quiet store.

Amy looked down at her clothing as the black stains began leeching themselves out of the fabric to drip and drop to the floor before trailing away. She remained tense, still afraid something worse might suddenly happen.

"What the hell was that?" She demanded, turning on Bowie. "What is going on? Are they coming back to life or something?"

"Huh?" It took Bowie a moment to realize she was talking about the black puddles that were flowing toward the rear of the store. "No. They're gone. I think we're safe for the moment. Those creatures will be back, but it takes a lot of energy for them to manifest here. We need to arm ourselves and head to the sewage plant like he said."

She raised her voice in protest. "Now hold on! You need to tell me what the hell is going on. Now! What the hell were those things?"

Bowie sighed and motioned for her to follow. "Those were Eidolon. In this world they look just like people. They're like reflections of people in this world who have gone dead inside."

"What? Why did they explode?" She said, carefully stepping around a stream of Eidolon remains as she followed him.

He laughed a little. "I'm not sure. Hal has some kind of power with that grinding organ. I have no idea how he does it, but I think he used it to destroy them."

"Who's Hal?"

"Hal. The old man you just saw."

"Is he an Eidathing too?"

"No. He's an Effigy. He's a friend of mine. He saved my life. Look, if he's here then we need to listen to what he says. Otherwise, we'll probably get killed."

Amy remained quiet for a moment, not sure if she should believe any of it. To her, Bowie seemed way too calm considering what had just happened. None of his answers made any sense to her.

"Okay. Let's start there. What the hell is an Effigy?" she asked.

"Eidolon are reflections of lifeless people. People who just go through the motions instead of truly living. Effigies are reflections of people like you or me.

They're powerful, alive, and they try to do right by those around them."

"What do you mean by reflection anyway? Are you saying there's another one of me? An Eidathingy?"

"Eidolon. And no, your reflection is an Effigy." Bowie said casually. He was busy checking down the aisles to find what he was looking for.

She looked at him incredulously. "How do you know that?"

"Look, I'll tell you more about that later. Right now, we need to arm ourselves. Help me get one of these nail guns loaded."

Amy gave him a strange look of excitement as they entered into the power-tools aisle.

"Okay, seriously. I mean, thank you for saving me and all, but I don't understand why you're grabbing a nail gun. Why don't we go get some real guns or a bat or something?"

Bowie turned to face her directly, put a hand on her shoulder, took a deep breath and said with honest sympathy. "I'm sorry. This is all pretty complicated and honestly even I'm not sure I believe half of it, but you're going to have to trust me on all this. Those things can only be hurt by iron or steel. I'd be happy to get a gun and blow them away, but most ammunition isn't steel jacketed. Most of it's lead. Also, we're going to need a lot more ammunition than a standard clip can hold. Nail guns also happen to be readily available and if we get attacked again before we get a real gun, we'd be screwed." He pulled a white nailer from its box and looked over the data plate on the gun. "Grab a box of twenty-one-degree nails in a coil."

She looked at him in wonder.

He shot her a devious smile. "It's drum fed. I'd rather not have to lug around clips and reload after I've gone through a bunch. That'll give us about a hundred shots before I'm out. Grab two, one for you."

"You're nuts." She said with a half-smile.

"Alright, suit yourself, but you need to get something to defend yourself." He started loading the drum. "I'm really sorry about all this, by the way."

She gave him an odd look. "Why are you sorry?"

"I'm the one who got you mixed up in all this?"

"What do you mean?"

"If I hadn't met you none of this would be happening to you right now."

"If you hadn't met me you would have bled out on the sidewalk," she reminded him dryly.

Bowie stopped what he was doing and looked at her. He hadn't considered that. She looked back at him and for a moment they seemed to understand one another. Bowie owed her his life and she owed him hers. Even if she didn't understand what was truly going on.

"So why are they hunting us?" She asked as she held the battery out for him.

He grabbed it and locked it into the gun. "I'm not sure. I think it's me they're after. I don't know. Remember when you found me on the street?"

She nodded.

"I was there that night because of them. My other self was trying to kill me."

She raised her eyebrows. "Okay. Seriously. What the F."

"Sorry." He interrupted. He shrugged and shook his head. "Sorry. It's complicated. Last time the Eidolon showed up because of me. Now, I'm not so sure. My other self..." He paused for a moment. "I'm not sure if he's even alive right now."

"Why did they want to kill you?"

"I..." His voice trailed off. "Let's save that conversation for another time. I need some heavy-duty tape."

She led him back over to one of the registers and handed him a roll of duct tape. "Will this work."

He nodded and tore off a piece, placing it over the tip of the gun and pulling it back tight. He raised it up, aimed down the aisle and pulled the trigger, popping the gun and sending a nail clinking down the aisle way. "It's probably only good at close range, but at least it's something. I have my knife if they get any closer. Now we need to get you one."

She frowned at him. "I still think you're nuts."

"Tell that to the puddle of goo flowing past your feet."

She looked down and let out a slight squeal before hopping to the left. "I am not carrying a nailgun around town. Those things are heavy and awkward. Besides people are going to notice someone carrying a nailgun that big around town."

"You think I should have grabbed a smaller one?"

"I think this is all really messed up and that I don't want anything to do with it, but hey, what do I know?"

"I'm just saying..." He shrugged. "You know, you're remarkably calm about all this."

"I just watched a dozen people explode into black sludge because of a creepy hobo with a grinding organ. It doesn't get much weirder than that. Besides, I nearly got killed back there. I owe you."

"Nah. You don't owe me. You helped me out and I returned the-"

She held up a finger. "I have an idea." She left him at the register and jogged down a nearby aisle. When she returned, she had a wide plastic package that she started tearing open with a pair of scissors she found beneath one of the registers.

"What's that?" He asked just moments before she brandished a machete.

"It's a Gerber, and I love it." She said, grinning from ear to ear.

"I didn't think their machetes were that good?"

She shrugged. "They re-released it last year. I'm guessing it's better than the first one. I mean they make military issue multi-tools. How could they screw up a machete twice, right?"

Bowie bowed. "Please, teach me your ways." He joked.

She let out a giggle. "Besides, if we're stealing stuff from the store..."

"Yeah, let's not call it stealing. We're just... borrowing a few things for the sake of our survival." Bowie corrected her.

"I think I might understand people who steal from here." She said drooling over the machete. "So awesome."

"And you thought a nailgun would be conspicuous. How are you going to pass off a machete?"

"By putting it in my backpack, duh." She said, heading toward the offices at one end of the building.

Bowie kept close by as she retrieved her backpack. By the time they reached the front door she had managed to get it zipped up so the only thing showing was the machete's handle.

"You seriously take a backpack to work?"

"I'm taking a couple of courses at ECC. Sometimes I do my homework here. It's better than lugging around a couple of books and pens and paper. by hand."

Bowie held his hands up in a defensive posture. "Whatever you say." He smiled. As he turned to the front doors of the store, looking out across the parking lot his smile faded. "It's a long way to the sewage plant." He said, dreading the long journey. Last time it had taken him quite a while and that was on a bicycle. He didn't look forward to making the trek on foot.

"I'm driving." She called out as she went through the double doors ahead of him.

"Oh." Bowie felt kind of foolish. He'd forgotten that she had a car. He was a little leery about getting into a vehicle after the sinkholes he'd dodged earlier. Being trapped in a steel cage if one suddenly opened up under the car did not appeal to him. He decided not to think about it and got in her car, keeping his eyes open for any signs of trouble. Amy didn't wait around. She hopped into the driver's seat of the sedan, pulled into the empty street and gunned it in the direction of the sewage plant.

Bowie thought it was strange how empty the roads were. With the heavy fog, it was impossible to see traffic on any of the side roads but even on their route they passed no one. The fog was growing thicker by the minute and Amy had to drive slowly. He checked his nail gun over, testing it in his hands.

"This is so cool." She smiled as she glanced over at him in the car.

"Cool?" He raised an eyebrow.

"Haven't you ever seen *The Ravenous*? This is so like that." She said with excitement. He clearly had no idea what she was talking about. "The movie?" She hinted. He shrugged and started inspecting his nail gun. "If you shoot that thing in here, I'm making you walk."

"Sorry. I'm just a little uneasy, that's all."

"Man, this fog is thick. Have you ever seen anything like this?"

"It was foggy the last time this happened too." Bowie noted.

"Really? Why is that? Do you think it's related?"

"I have no idea. I mean, it is winter, so it's not like we don't have fog sometimes."

"So where is the sewage plant?"

Bowie blinked in disbelief. "You don't know where you're going?"

"Well, I kind of knew it was this way. I have a vague idea but I've never actually been there. My mother used to go on hikes out in that area to look for wildlife."

"Okay. Do you know what street we're on?"

She smiled sheepishly in response.

"Great... Okay." he leaned forward to get a closer look at a passing street sign as they went through an intersection. "Take a left up here. That should get us to Goethals. From there I know where to go."

They drove in silence for a while before Amy spoke up. "So, that night I found you on the side of the road. That wasn't a dog attack was it?"

He shook his head. "No. No, that was... this." He gestured all around. "Only I didn't have someone else caught up in it with me."

"What happened that night?"

He bit his lip uneasily. "That night a lot of people died. I was lucky to come out of it alive. Well, not people really. A lot of Effigies were killed by a bunch of Hellion.

"Hellion? Dude, seriously? Where did you come up with these names? They're really weird."

"That's what the Effigies call them. Hellion."

"Okay, what are Hellion?"

Bowie turned his head to look out the window. It took a few moments before he could find the right word. "They're basically monsters."

"Like, creatures from another world, or what?"

"Like the worst humanity has to offer. They're reflections, just like the Eidolon and the Effigies."

"But they belong to bad people."

"Yeah. Something like that."

"And how do they fit into all of this?"

"They're bad business. That's all I know. They're only in Otherside though, so we shouldn't have to worry."

It took them about fifteen minutes to get onto the old gravel road that led to the sewage plant. Amy parked the car just outside the front gate which stood wide open.

As she and Bowie got out of the car she asked "is this place always unlocked like this?"

Bowie shrugged. "It was last time I was here too. I guess they figure people looking for trouble aren't going to mess with a sewage plant."

"So, where is he? That guy from earlier."

Bowie looked around but the fog was still thick and it was difficult to see very far. "His name is Halloran."

"Halloran? Dude, I'm telling you..." She gave him a look as she put on her backpack.

Bowie shrugged. "I call him Hal."

"How do you know we can trust him?"

"Because he saved my life. Several times. He's one of the good guys."

"I'm still having a hard time believing all of this." She said as she took a few steps away from the car in the direction of the plant.

"How do you explain the black puddles of goo then? You know, the ones that were moving around after a mob of zombie-like people attacked and then exploded."

She shook her head. "Yeah, that was just freaking weird. I don't ever want to see that again, okay?"

"Well, hopefully Hal will show up, we'll get this all fixed and you won't have to. Here, follow me." He said as he started toward the open gate.

"Where are we going?" She said as she followed suit.

"Last time I was here, Hal took me to a specific spot for a weird ritual thing. He said something about the energies of this place. I think maybe that's where the energy was the strongest. He might need us to go there. Maybe that's the only place he can appear."

Amy didn't argue as they crossed the gravel lot. When they reached the narrow path that ran between both of the pools used by the sewage plant, she hesitated. "Is that all sewage?" She asked, pointing to the water.

"Uh... You know, I'm not sure. Maybe. Probably don't want to drink it if that's what you're asking."

She shot him a look. "Yeah, no thanks."

When Bowie reached the middle of the path, he let out a sigh of disappointment. "He's not here. I thought he'd be here already."

"Do you think something happened to him?"

Bowie hadn't considered that. He had no idea what was going on in Otherside while the two of them were driving. "I don't know. Let's just hope he shows up before more Eidolon get here."

They waited there for ten minutes before Amy sat down on the gravel and huddled up.

"Aren't you cold?" He asked.

"Yeah. I'm also really tired. I didn't get much sleep last night."

"Ah." Bowie said simply. He decided to remain standing. After a few moments he started heading back to the car.

"Where are you going?" She asked, anxious about being left alone.

"I'm going to see if he's waiting for us over by the gate."

"Oh. Okay." She said. It wasn't a far walk, so Amy stayed where she was.

A quick look around by the gate told Bowie that Hal hadn't shown up yet. He was getting a little impatient, so he kicked at the gravel and turned to head back to Amy.

"Strange place to run to." Came a voice.

Bowie jumped a little, and leveled his nailgun at the intruder. To his surprise it wasn't Scratcher. In fact, he didn't recognize the person at all. It was a squinty eyed man with a cherubic face and delightful grin perched on the top of the gate much like a cat. Bowie watched him warily, taking slow cautious steps back in Amy's direction.

"You look surprised." The stranger on the fence laughed. "You were expecting someone else, perhaps?"

Bowie didn't answer. He wasn't sure if the man on the fence was friend or foe. It could be another smiling Eidolon, or an Effigy. He might have been just some strange guy but Bowie doubted that.

"Not much of a talker? Well, that's alright. Lovely day for a stroll wouldn't you say? Especially in a place like this." The man hopped gracefully from the fence in Bowie's direction.

"Who are you? What are you doing here?" Bowie demanded.

"Oh, come now." Said the stranger. "I asked you if you thought it was a lovely day." He took a few steps in Bowie's direction.

Bowie took a few steps back of his own. "You can either answer me or I can put a nail through you."

"Ooh." The stranger feigned terror. "Playing hardball. You're not as much of a pushover as everyone says."

Bowie trained his gun on the man's head. "You haven't answered my question. Who are you, and what are you doing here?"

"They call me Mouth." The man bowed deeply with an overly dramatic flourish.

Bowie waited, expecting Mouth to continue his introduction but he simply stood up straight and watched with great interest.

"What are you doing here?" Bowie demanded.

"Why, I came to find you!" Mouth smiled pleasantly.

"Why? What do you want with me?"

"Why, I wanted to keep you distracted of course."

Bowie raised an eyebrow. He was about to ask what Mouth meant when a piercing scream filled the air. It was Amy.

Bowie kept an eye trained on Mouth for a brief second before risking a glance over his shoulder. He couldn't see anything through the mist. When he looked back, Mouth had started moving closer at a casual pace.

Bowie turned and ran as fast as he could. In a few short seconds he could just make out the spot where he'd left her, but Amy was gone. He skidded to a stop and looked around in a panic. Her machete lay on the ground just a few yards away.

He spun to face Mouth, who had just come into view from the mist. "Where is she?" Bowie shouted as he aimed the nailgun at him.

A familiar voice rang out over the sewage plant. "Looking for someone?"

The voice belonged to Scratcher. He was standing on the thin path between the two pools, barely visible within the mist. In his arms he clutched Amy from behind, his fingers clamped around her lower face. Her expression was one of sheer terror, and a trail of blood ran down her left arm which hung limply to her side.

Bowie trained his gun on Scratcher, who grinned menacingly. "Put the gun down," He ordered.

Bowie hesitated.

"Put the gun down and toss it over there," Scratcher nodded to where the machete lay, "or I'll snap her neck."

It took a few seconds for Bowie to realize the severity of the threat before he submitted and lowered his weapon. Amy was defenseless. Scratcher had the upper hand. He'd won. If Bowie got rid of the gun, all he'd have to defend himself was his knife and even then, nothing would prevent Scratcher from killing Amy. But what choice did he have? He swallowed and tossed the nailgun to the ground.

"There. That's better." Scratcher smirked. "Not so tough without your precious iron, are you?"

Bowie didn't answer. He was still trying to think of some way to get Amy out of Scratcher's grasp. If he could buy some time and move in close enough, he might be able to strike but if he tried anything, all it would take is one snap and the Hellion would break her neck. Bowie needed to keep him occupied until he could think of something.

"Why are you doing all of this?" He asked, trying to keep Scratcher talking.

"Oh, come now. Do you really think we'd tell you anything?" Mouth said as he circled around Bowie, heading for the weapons lying on the ground.

"Why not? You've won. I'm defenseless and you'll just kill us both anyway."

"He's got a point," Scratcher said with an air of sarcasm. "Go ahead, reveal our dastardly evil plan."

Mouth stopped and slouched just a little, giving Bowie a mocking look. "He's just no fun, you know. We're here for you, of course. As if it wasn't the most obvious thing. So simple, yet so delightful, wouldn't you say? Watching you run for your tiny little lives like you might actually escape. Quite amusing, really."

It occurred to Bowie just then how easy it had been for Scratcher to find him. They were out in a very remote area away from the bustle of the city. "How did you know where to find me?"

Mouth snorted. "It was easy. You practically reek. All we had to do was follow your wonderful stench and we were led right to you. It'd be difficult *not* to find you. Like not seeing fire in the dark. Now the girl on the other hand. That was a trick. Had to find her the old-fashioned way."

"Because she's never been to your world." Bowie theorized. "That's why you didn't attack me. You wanted her too."

"No. That's not..." Mouth started but never got a chance to finish.

A piercing shriek rang out over the sewage plant and Bowie clutched at his head in pain. He knew the sound. It was Hal.

Mouth and Scratcher did likewise and Bowie seized the opportunity to make a break for Mouth. He drew his knife and charged, taking a long sweep with the blade. Mouth dodged backward and to the side, just as Bowie had hoped, leaving a clear path to their weapons.

Mouth realized his mistake faster than Bowie had anticipated and pounced, driving him down to the ground.

Bowie landed on his side and was pinned there. Mouth had his knife hand in an iron grasp and was twisting it with glee. Bowie couldn't hold on; the pain was too great. He could feel the tension in his bones threatening to snap. The blade rolled from his grasp as he tried as hard as he could to push out from underneath his adversary.

However, Mouth didn't budge at all. He was just like the Eidolon: Unmovable.

Bowie's other hand was still free. Just outside his reach lay the nail gun, ready to fire. He reached hard, stretching his fingers further than he thought they could go. Meanwhile he struggled against Mouth, his wrist twisting even further as Mouth looked on with an expression of sheer ecstasy as Bowie cried out in pain.

Bowie 's fingertips brushed against the gun handle. He reached just a little further, the muscles in his arm stretched to their limits.

He grabbed the gun.

He angled it up at Mouth but it was too late. Mouth had already seen what Bowie was reaching for. He swatted out with his hand, knocking the gun from Bowie's grasp. It tumbled clumsily from his hand, landing on the blade of the machete with a dull *tang*.

Mouth's gleeful expression was suddenly one of fierce anger. He leaned down over Bowie and opened his mouth wide. Only it didn't just open. It split in two, confirming what Bowie had feared in the back of his mind ever since he'd seen the smiling stranger. They weren't Eidolon. They were Hellion.

His jaws grew wider and wider, beckoning towards the now vast gullet beneath. As it did, Mouth's skin peeled and tarnished, revealing mottled brown Hellion flesh.

"Bowie!" Amy cried out.

There was nothing he could do. The gun was out of reach.

"The Blade!" Came Hal's voice. "Grab it!"

I dropped it. Bowie told himself. Then he remembered the machete. He looked over at it as the strings of drool from the Hellion's mouth reached his face.

When Mouth had knocked the gun out of Bowie's hand, it had fallen on the end of the machete. The gun was just heavy enough that the handle had bounced up and was just within reach.

Bowie snatched it and swung it as fast as he could.

Mouth reacted instantly, half pushing, half leaping off of Bowie and skirting back several paces, snarling. The blade missed by less than an inch.

Now free, Bowie scrambled to get to a standing position. He swiped several times with the machete, warning Mouth not to come closer as he stepped over to the gun. In the corner of his eye he saw Halloran squaring off against Scratcher but he didn't have time to watch. Mouth made a dash at him. He did his best to sidestep but Mouth swiped at him with a hand and Bowie felt a searing pain in his side. He swung wide with the machete, forcing Mouth back. Clutching at his side his fingers felt wet. He looked down where crimson painted his hand.

Bowie looked back at Mouth. The Hellion was sneering, holding his hands wide apart, inviting him to try his luck. His fingers had now split open and fierce, bone-like claws protruded from their tips.

On the other side of the clearing, Halloran squared off with Scratcher, who kept himself between the old man and the girl. Scratcher didn't consider Amy a threat so his attention was almost completely on Hal.

The Effigy was analyzing his opponent, reading the situation and trying to come up with a plan. He knew the Hellion was eager to kill the girl, but doing so would leave him vulnerable to an attack, if only momentarily.

"Shouldn't you be worried about the boy?"

Scratcher sneered, "he's about to be torn to shreds over there."

"I wouldn't be so sure." Hal said confidently. Scratcher was stalling for time. He needed to act before things got out of hand. Hal's fingers gripped the handle of the organ and he started to rotate the handle.

Scratcher didn't wait to find out what would happen. He snarled and charged. Hal was ready for the attack and ducked beneath a vicious swipe at his head. Scratcher's claws missed but he immediately followed up with another attack. The onslaught made it difficult for Hal to concentrate on the organ. His hand turned the crank but it was all he could do to maintain focus while Scratcher swung at him over and over again. He couldn't keep dodging for long. Eventually a blow would strike home and he'd be in a world of hurt.

"Bowie!" Hal shouted. "Keep him busy!"

The fight between Hal and Scratcher was slowly moving closer to Mouth and Bowie. If Hal wasn't careful the fights would bleed together. He tried to maneuver himself to one side, to get himself between Scratcher and Amy.

Amy, who had been too terrified to move at first, had managed to get herself back on her feet. Hal had moved Scratcher enough to give her an opportunity to get away. She turned and ran. She had only gone a few steps before she looked back and saw Bowie staggering, clutching at his side.

She skidded to a halt. She couldn't leave him there to die.

Quickly surveying the scene, she saw it: the nail gun laying in the gravel. She made a break for it.

Scratcher was busy chasing after Hal and Mouth was making passes at Bowie, ducking under the machete to tear at Bowie's sides.

Amy saw Bowie take another slash to his leg and he cried out, nearly falling to his knees. She had precious few seconds to spare.

Scratcher heard her footsteps and spun around. At the same time, Hal saw the girl and Scratcher turning to go after her. There was no way she would make it to the gun. Hellion were too fast. He moved as quickly as he could to get to Scratcher before Scratcher could get to the girl. He was just behind the Hellion who was inches away from grabbing the girl when Scratcher heard him.

The Hellion immediately turned on his forward foot and dug in, bringing all of his momentum into an upward swing with his clawed hand.

Hal tried to stop but it was too late. The Hellion's blow struck the grinding organ, blasting it to pieces and sending splinters flying in all directions. The shockwave, as the device's power was released, sent Hal hurling backward until he landed sprawling on the gravel.

Scratcher was upon him before he could even breathe. The Hellion pounced and raked his claws across Hal's body in vicious strikes, ripping his body to shreds.

Amy was too terrified to scream. She had reached the nail gun but it was too late to save Hal. It didn't matter. She raised the gun and took aim. Scratcher turned to face her as Hal's body burst into smoke and dissipated in the mist.

"No!" She screamed at him as she started pulling the trigger over and over again, sending a spray of nails popping over the gravel.

Scratcher was too quick and had anticipated the shots. He dove to the side and, as she focused the stream of nails in his direction, he kept ahead of them, swatting them aside when they got too close.

When she saw that her shots weren't working, she backed up until she was just behind Bowie. He was nearly out of breath as he tried to fend off Mouth.

"It's not working." She said, starting to panic.

"He's too fast," Bowie panted.

Scratcher and Mouth moved into position so that the pair were flanked on either side.

"What's the matter?" Mouth said, his speech echoing strangely across the gravel from his split mouth. "Having troubles?"

"Why do assholes always smile?" Bowie grumbled to Amy.

She was far too afraid. She had thought the gun would at least even the odds but it hadn't. She had only wasted precious ammunition.

"I can't get a clear shot." She said whispered to Bowie as Mouth and Scratcher circled them, forcing Bowie and Amy to turn slowly around each other. "What do we do?"

Bowie shook his head. "No idea."

"Great..."

"Sorry. I'm all out of ideas." Bowie said.

Amy wasn't. "Do you trust me?" She asked hesitantly.

"What?"

"I need you to trust me."

He had no idea what she meant but she was fighting on his side, and for the time being that was enough for Bowie. "Okay."

"I need you to look over your right shoulder at Scratcher."

"What?"

"Just do it."

He turned. Scratcher was smiling and ready to pounce as he watched intently.

Mouth saw the brief opening as Bowie looked away and sprang, claws extended, ready to disembowel his victim.

He was lightning fast, but Amy was ready. She turned right into a kneel to get the gun around Bowie's waist, just as Mouth leaped. Amy screamed and didn't stop squeezing the trigger as the nails punctured him again and again. The Hellion was unable to react fast enough to avoid the nails as they tore through his body. He convulsed with each shot, twitching and writhing in agony as he fell to the ground, helpless against the onslaught. She had fired almost twenty nails before he stopped moving and lay pooling on the gravel.

While Amy was had her back turned, Scratcher made his move. He forced Bowie to take a swipe at him by moving in close, but kept just out of arm's reach. When Bowie took a step forward and swung hard with the machete, Scratcher clapped the blade between the flat of his hands. The machete sizzled against Scratcher's flesh, but he grit his teeth and held on. Bowie couldn't wrench the blade from the creature's grasp and with a quick twist and pull, Scratcher ripped the weapon from Bowie's hands. Bowie stumbled forward, completely exposed.

Scratcher did not waste any time. He sank his claws down into Bowie's shoulders.

Bowie screamed in pain and fell to his knees. When the creature ripped its claws from his shoulders, he closed his eyes, expecting to be torn to pieces. However, when he looked up, Scratcher had moved back.

Amy had finished dealing with Mouth and was standing right behind him, the nail gun aimed over his shoulder at Scratcher.

"Back off!" She roared fiercely, adrenaline pumping through her veins.

Scratcher opened his arms wide, leaned forward and let out a bellowing roar in anger. The deafening sound filled the sewage plant and before the echoes had died down, Scratcher's body disintegrated into the mist, leaving Bowie bleeding on the gravel with Amy beside him.

As quickly as he left the air fell silent.

The adrenaline rush faded and Amy turned her attention to Bowie. His shoulders looked gruesome and his clothes had been shredded.

"We need to get you to a hospital." She said, examining the wound. "Can you walk?"

Bowie felt dizzy from the pain. "I'm not sure, but we should wait for Hal to come back. He had us come here for a reason, and if we head back into town we might run into more trouble."

"He's dead." She pointed out. "I watched him die. We can't just wait here like this. Those things might come back!"

Bowie shook his head. "No. I don't think he's dead. That wasn't the real Hal."

"Huh?"

"He's... That was like a projection or something. I remember him saying once that it took a lot of energy to create an image in this world. I think that was like a double or something. I don't think it was real."

"It sure looked real to me. I mean, he fought those..." Amy stopped short. She remembered the horrific sight of the creature's jaws splitting and opening to reveal the large gullet.

"Hellion." Bowie finished for her. "Those were Hellion..." His voice trailed off at the end.

He had seen the Eidolon before, and Hal's projection, but he had never considered the possibility that the Hellion could do the same. Halloran had told him they didn't even know about Bowie's world.

With Amy's help he got up. The pain in his shoulders was still immense, and he nearly passed out, barely managing to keep himself upright.

"There's no guarantee that he'll be back any time soon. You could bleed out before then. We need to get you medical attention quickly."

Bowie nodded in agreement and started staggering toward the car with Amy close by to help him keep his balance.

"Wait." He stopped. "My knife."

She understood and quickly went to retrieve it. She grabbed up the machete too and stuffed it in her backpack before returning to his side and helping him back to the car.

They had reached the gate of the Sewage plant when a figure emerged from the mist. Amy immediately raised the gun, her finger on the trigger. However, she froze in complete shock.

The woman standing before her was a mirror image of Amy. Literally. She bled from the opposite arm and her hair was messed up on the opposite side. Her clothing was the same right down to the wrinkles, but everything was reversed. Had they been standing on opposite sides of a pane of glass, she'd swear it was her reflection.

Bowie was surprised. When he'd seen his own other self in Otherside, there was little resemblance. Amy's duplicate had also been distinctly different. The only similar feature was the scar through her eyebrow. Here though, the Effigy looked just like Amy, through and through.

Snapping out of it, Amy retrained the nail gun on her duplicate self.

"Whoa." Bowie cautioned her. "Easy. She's not here to hurt us."

"How do you know that?" Amy said bitterly.

Bowie let out a sigh and took a few steps, placing himself between Amy and her other self. "Do you really think you're a monster?" Bowie asked simply.

The question gave Amy pause. "I... Uh... what?" She let her arms fall to her sides.

Bowie turned and limped a few paces to give Amy a clear view.

"I'm glad you're okay, Varela. I didn't know if you made it back after the fight."

Amy's duplicate nodded respectfully. "We got back just fine, but it looks like you brought all the trouble back with you."

Her comment gave Bowie pause. "Did Arsen make it back?"

"He's fine. Listen, Hal sent me. I'm here to warn you."

Bowie chuckled a little. "It's a little late for that."

The glare Varela gave him froze his blood. "No. It's not." She paused, "They are going to keep coming for you, now that they know about this place."

"What do you mean?" Bowie asked.

She began circling around Amy, sizing up her original self, unsure if she could really believe they were the same. "They knew. Of course, they knew. They just didn't know how to get here. It takes a great deal of time and patience to send a working image here, and even then, one gets lost without some way to hone in on a specific location." She stopped just behind Amy, looking at Bowie over the girl's shoulder. "The Hellion are too impatient. Without sufficient reason to come here, there was no point. They were better off slaughtering Effigies and hunting down newborns."

"So why are they here?" Bowie interrupted.

"For you, of course."

"What do they want with me? And how did they even find me? I can understand Arsen finding me. We have a connection to one another. But Hellion?"

"We think they're after you because you crossed over between worlds. They followed your scent." She said sharply.

"My scent? They can smell me from Otherside?"

"Yes. They can smell you. You practically reek."

Amy sniffed at Bowie but shook her head. "He doesn't smell like anything."

Varela gave Amy a warning look. "Every time you hurt someone, every time you think of yourself instead of others, they can smell your selfishness. It's like the smell of meat. The stench draws them in where they can feast. You're lucky we figured it out in time. They've never done something like this before."

"I don't understand. What did I do?"

Varela shook her head in disappointment. "I don't know but you better figure it out quick, or they'll be back and chances are we won't be able to intervene."

Amy took a step toward her other self. "Thank you for the help." She said earnestly.

Varela shrugged and was enveloped in a cloud of smoke. When the smoke cleared, she was gone.

Bowie didn't say anything. He didn't bother looking at Amy. He began quietly hobbling toward the car.

She followed behind him and asked "What was that all about?"

He didn't answer. Everything was so confusing. He had tried so hard and now he was apparently doing everything all wrong again. He didn't know what to do.

Amy waited until they had both gotten into the car before she said anything. It was pretty clear something was bothering him. "Are you okay?" She asked.

"Yeah, I'm fine." Bowie said dryly as he turned his head to look out the passenger side window. "Let's get to the hospital. I'm kind of light-headed."

"So, that was my duplicate? My other self?" She asked trying to change the subject as she started the car. It still had her pretty rattled, though she was still concerned about him. She pulled away from the sewage plant and drove back into the center of town.

"Yeah. That was Varela."

"You knew her. How did you know her?"

Bowie let in a deep breath. "Well... I've been to their world. Hell... I nearly died there."

"She doesn't seem anything like me."

Bowie laughed. She was right. "Nope. She definitely doesn't seem like you."

"But she's my other self?"

"Your Effigy." Bowie corrected her. "And yes. She is."

"I don't get any of this." She said, feeling well out of her depth. "What was your double like?"

"He looked totally different over there. In Otherside."

"Otherside?" She gave him a weird look.

"Look, I didn't name it, okay? But yeah. He and I look almost nothing alike over there. Same for yours. Varela seemed older over there."

"What was she like?"

"Like a total..." He caught himself. "Like a total badass, actually." He admitted. "She was fierce, completely ready for a fight at a moment's notice. Like a warrior. Kind of scary, actually. She was so focused on the fight. She and Hal butted heads a lot I think, but if you need someone to have your back, she's definitely my first choice."

Amy was a little surprised, but she nodded as she listened. In a way it struck a chord with her. "So, what's it like over there? In the other side?"

Bowie winced as his pain flared. "Otherside is hard to describe. It's like a shattered landscape. Everything isn't like here. It's like the parts of our world we connect with most take on other forms more suitable to our emotions rather than what they actually are. Or something like that, I think. Only some of it isn't like that. I don't know. It's all pretty confusing and distorted." He paused for a moment to catch his breath.

The drive seemed a little quiet, so Amy turned on the radio. The reception was lousy, and all she could manage were faint bits of classical rock underneath the static.

"Man. What's up with the radio?" She asked.

"I'm not sure. Your cell phone probably isn't working either."

"Huh? Why not?"

Bowie shrugged. "I'm not sure why, but whenever people from Otherside are around, the cell phone signal cuts out."

"You mean, like electromagnetic radiation maybe?"

Bowie looked over at her and raised an eyebrow.

"I'm just saying. The only way radio gets cut out is interference." She glanced over at him and saw that his eyelids were beginning to droop. "Hey." She shook him with her arm. "Hang in there. We're almost at Echo General Hospital. Just don't fall asleep, okay?"

He nodded. "Sorry. I'm just very tired."

When they pulled into the emergency entrance a couple of EMT's who were standing nearby rushed to help Bowie inside.

"What happened to him?" One of them, a tall man in his thirties, asked.

Amy had thought about what she was going to say to the doctors when she brought him in. There was no way they would believe the truth. "It was an animal attack. We were out by the old sewage plant when we got attacked by a..." she was about to say bear. However, bears didn't live anywhere close to echo city. There were coyotes and snakes and smaller animals. "A cougar." Was all she could think to say.

"Weird," said the other EMT, a somewhat younger, barrel chested man. "I didn't think we had cougars down here."

She gave them a weak smile. "Neither did we. Don't know what is was doing near Echo City."

"Are you alright?" The first EMT asked, looking down at her arm which had bled through her shirt at the shoulder.

"I'm fine. It's just a cut. I tripped and fell." She hated lying to these people, but she didn't have much choice.

"Do you mind?" The taller EMT asked as he moved to check under her sleeve.

She allowed him to do so, and he inspected it closely while he let his partner get Bowie the medical attention he needed. "Looks alright to me. You don't need stitches or anything. You might want to clean it up though." He said. Then he left her to follow his partner.

After she parked in the hospital parking lot, Amy found a chair in the emergency lobby and tried to relax. She found herself anxiously watching the faces of everyone who walked by. Any of them could be Hellion.

Or Eidolon or Effigies. She couldn't tell. They looked just like ordinary people to her She let out a sigh after about ten minutes had passed. If they were after her, they'd come straight for her, she decided. Chances were, they'd avoid such a public place. Although, they came en masse to Fleischer Home and Garden. It was during the slow part of the day, but still. It was in broad daylight. Anyone could have seen what had happened, so perhaps public visibility didn't matter to them. It was hard to say.

Her fears and anxiety made time slow to a crawl. When at last Bowie emerged from the hall and hour or so later, limping slightly, she leaped up to greet him. He was walking unusually fast when she caught up to him and she had to take a few jogging steps to stay beside him.

"Are you alright?" She asked.

Bowie nodded but didn't say anything. He just kept walking with her right out of the emergency room and into the parking lot. Once they were outside, he asked simply "Where's the car?"

She pointed.

He started immediately in that direction and Amy followed behind.

"Where are you going?" She asked him, almost afraid of what he might say. She wondered if he had met with more Hellion or Eidolon inside.

"We need to get out of here. I know what I have to do."

"What about your injuries?"

Bowie lifted his shirt and revealed the tight bandages beneath. "They patched me up and got me some fluids but I can't afford a medical bill right now," he said sheepishly, "and besides, there are more important things."

She reached out and grabbed his arm to stop him. "What things? Wait. So, you just ran out and left them to pick up the bill?!"

He stopped and laughed a little. "Medicine is the one industry that doesn't need the help. Everything is overpriced and the price has nothing to do with the cost of producing the goods. I think they'll manage to spare two rolls of bandaging. C'mon. We need to go."

She led him to her car and helped him inside. He was stiff and groaned when he leaned into the car to sit down. "Why are you in such a hurry?" She asked once she'd turned the key and started up the car. "And don't tell me it's the medical bill. Something is up."

He looked over at her as she pulled out of the parking space and gunned the engine to make a hasty retreat from the hospital premises. "The Hellion will be back. They can smell me remember? Because I'm an asshole. If I had waited in the hospital, even if I could afford the bill, I'd be a sitting duck. There's no telling when they'd show up. I wouldn't last the night in that place and it'd put everyone else in danger. That's not something I want on my conscience."

"They'll come for you anyway." She pointed out. "Maybe having others around might be safer."

"There's not enough time to convince them any of this is real. They'd think I was insane. Then I'd have to make them understand that the Eidolon and Hellion can only be harmed by Iron. There's no way I would be able to protect them enough to make that hospital safe. The only way for me to keep them out of harm's way is to leave. Which is what we're doing."

"Okay. I get it." She said with a little edge in her voice. "So, we can't stay there. Where do we go then?"

"Fleischer Home and Garden." He said confidently.

She stopped at the edge of the parking lot. "What?"

"Trust me. That's where we need to go."

"There's people there too!" She insisted. "C'mon. First you want to protect the people at the hospital and now you want to put everyone at work in danger?"

"We don't have time to argue. Just go." He urged.

She rolled her eyes and shook her head. With a short sigh she turned out of the parking lot and started heading in the direction of the home improvement store. She waited until she'd passed a few blocks before she spoke up. "I mean, there's some people at work I can't stand, but come on. You got to tell me what's going on. You owe me at least that much."

Bowie averted his gaze out the window. "Because I'm an asshole. Okay?" He said quietly. It pained him to say it.

"You're not an asshole." She said in a soft tone.

"Tell that to the freaking Hellion..." He muttered. "You heard Varela. They can smell me. I've been doing things all wrong and I hurt someone. That's what assholes do!"

She waited until he had calmed down a little. "What did you do?"

He debated back and forth whether or not he should tell her. Sure, she was cute, but that made it all the harder to admit his fault. On the other hand, he owed her his life. She deserved an explanation, even if he wasn't proud of it. He took in a deep breath and let it out. "You know Victor at the warehouse?"

Amy gave pause for a moment. "You mean *the* Victor?"

"*The* Victor?"

"The one everybody hates?"

Bowie chuckled a little, "yeah, that Victor."

"I've heard horror stories, but that's about it. I'm still pretty new and I don't interact with the guys from the warehouse very often. So, what about him?"

"Well. He's the guy."

"What guy?" She asked.

"The person I've been treating like crap."

"Wait? What?! They can smell you because you've been treating a total jerk wad poorly? Seriously?"

Bowie shrugged a shoulder. "It's the only thing that makes sense. When I was getting bandaged up, I was going over and over in my head everyone that I might have selfishly hurt, and he's the only person I could think of. I mean, I know he's a terrible person, but that doesn't mean I should have talked to him the way I did."

"What did you say to him?"

"I basically called him out on all his shit. I challenged his authority because I don't care about my job anymore. He deserves it, but that's what I did. I made him look like an angry jackass in front of the whole crew too, instead of discussing it in private. And I'll be honest. It felt pretty good."

"But he deserved it." She agreed.

"That doesn't make it right. I think that's what Varela and Hal were trying to warn me about. I can't just go crazy and treat assholes like the scum they are. I can't be that selfish and heartless, even if they deserve it."

"Sort of like it's not your place to give them what they deserve?"

Bowie gave a slight laugh. "Something like that. If I'm going to get this 'stink' off of me, the only way I can think to do it is to make amends. It's stupid, but I think it's the only option I have right now."

"This is nuts." She muttered. "But if you think it's worth a shot..."

XIII

It wasn't long before they pulled into the parking lot of Fleischer Home and Garden. Amy brought the car around back and parked next to the employee entrance of the warehouse.

It was getting late and Bowie knew Victor's shift would be ending soon. He considered waiting until everyone went home but there was no guarantee the Hellion wouldn't come back by then. He opened the passenger door and had some difficulty getting out. Amy went around and helped him get out of the car.

When Bowie started for the door to the warehouse Amy asked "You're going right now?"

"Yeah. Right now."

"It's the middle of the shift! Aren't you going to wait until everyone else is on their way home?"

"Nope." He said simply. He didn't like it either, but he had a pretty good reason.

"Are you just going to ask him into the office or something?"

"Nope." He said again. He'd been thinking about it on the drive over. It wasn't enough to say he was sorry.

"So, you're just going to go in there in front of God and everyone and apologize? Is that even okay? I thought the company had rules about how you should handle situations like this."

He paused when he reached the door, his hand on the handle. "They do. Victor doesn't play by those rules. Victor does whatever the hell he wants and so long as the job gets done and his numbers are in line, he doesn't care. I have to do this in front of everyone. The only way I'm going to give Victor his pride back is if I make it public. Everyone has to see it and he has to know that everyone sees me submitting to him. That's the kind of monster he is. If he doesn't feel like he's won, then there's no point in doing this. I'll have done the right thing by apologizing, but I damaged his image in front of everyone and there's only one way to fix that before the Hellion come back." He turned the handle and entered the building as Amy gave him a skeptical look.

Things were operating as usual. It was the end of the day so a few people were standing around trying to look busy. Victor was center stage, barking orders and watching everyone, waiting for them to screw up. He had his back to Bowie with his hands on his hips as the last stack of pallets was being dragged away on a jack.

Amy followed Bowie inside mostly because she didn't want to be alone if the Hellion manifested again. She wasn't too keen on watching what was about to happen but she couldn't stop herself. She stood at the corner of one of the aisles and peered around the racking to watch the scene.

Bowie took in a deep breath and thought for a brief moment what it would be like to just leave, to spend the rest of his short-lived life trying to survive the brutal onslaught of the freakish Hellion. There were still a few moments left for Bowie to back out. Victor hadn't seen him approach. He could just walk away. He wanted to. His heart was racing but he couldn't do it. Amy was involved now, not to mention that he'd have to stay away from the rest of society just to keep them out of harm's way. This was the one thing he desperately did not want to do but he had no choice. It was either this or get mauled to death. This was the man he had to be whether he liked it or not.

He stood up as straight as he could and walked up to Victor. "Hey, Victor. You got a moment?" It sounded so casual when he said it, but he knew better.

Victor turned and was somewhat surprised to see him. He eyed Bowie for a few seconds before he answered. "What is it, Swift?"

For a moment Bowie considered correcting Victor about calling him by his last name but he decided against it. He wasn't here to argue.

"I wanted to apologize for my behavior lately." He said just a bit louder than he needed to. He wanted to make sure everyone could hear him. "I've been really out of line and I've said some things to you that I shouldn't have."

Victor did his best to hide his shock but it was clear to Bowie that the man's jaw would have dropped down to the floor if it could.

"I was way out of line as your employee and as a member this company. I set a bad example for my associates and co-workers. The way I acted was not appropriate at all, and I hope you will accept my sincere apology." As he said the word "sincere" which he thought he hadn't really meant, it gained some weight in his mind. He was sorry, even if only slightly. He had let his own anger get the better of him and had taken it out on Victor. He knew Victor deserved it, but he started to think in that moment what it would have been like if someone had done the same to him. He swallowed and waited for a response.

Victor was embarrassed. He looked around, afraid of what the other people had seen. Then his surprise turned to arrogance. He chuckled as he looked at the other workers. When his gaze returned to Bowie, he had a bit of a swagger. "Well it's about time you showed some respect."

Bowie had seen this coming a mile away. He knew Victor would take it too far. Victor was too prideful. He decided to wait it out and let Victor to stop talking.

Judging by the look of satisfaction on Victor's face, it was going to be a while.

"Mr. Swift, what you don't realize is that this is a business. We all have to work here together. When one person is upset it affects everyone around them. You are right, you were completely out of line. Did you even stop to think about how your actions affected your co-workers?"

Victor paused, waiting for Bowie to respond.

Bowie didn't know what to do. Looking around, he didn't see his actions affecting his co-workers that much at all. They knew what Victor was doing. Victor was trying to make Bowie look and feel worse than he already did. Bowie's anger began to rise, but instead of lashing out, Bowie took the sweetest revenge he could. He made it seem unimportant. "Oh, yeah." Bowie said as if it were so obvious even Victor wasn't aware. "I mean, I totally wasn't thinking about that. My bad, guys." He raised a hand in apology to the onlookers.

"You can't go through life talking to your superiors like that. You'll never get ahead that way." Victor started in again.

"Totally." Bowie agreed.

"If you're going to set an example to your peers and co-workers you need to learn how to behave. I don't know who promoted you in the first place, but you might want to take a serious look at your career path and ask yourself if you can handle it. As it stands, you'll be lucky if you aren't terminated. I've already filed my report and it's out of my hands."

That was a blow. Bowie had originally earned his promotion because he had worked hard and knew the job. He wasn't just someone's favorite. He'd earned it. The comment bit at him a little, and he forced a smile, determined to keep his composure. If he lashed out or said anything wrong, Victor would win. He couldn't have that. He had done the right thing by apologizing. He wouldn't sabotage that effort now.

"Don't you worry. I'm on it." He said, almost a little too cheesily. "I came here to apologize for a reason. I was in the wrong and I'm sorry. I'll let you get back to your work. I know it's quitting time soon."

He turned to go and saw Amy there, peering around the corner giving him a thumbs up. He had only managed to take a few steps when Victor stopped him.

"Aren't you forgetting something, Mr. Swift?"

He turned back around to Victor, who was smiling and trying to look good intentioned, though it was clear he was reveling in his own self-satisfaction.

"Aren't you going to apologize to everyone? Remember, what affects one affects the whole."

"Yeah. I already did. My bad." He raised an apologetic hand with half the enthusiasm he had before.

Victor didn't let it go. "'My bad' doesn't cut it. Morale has suffered as a consequence of your actions. You owe them more than just a 'my bad'."

Bowie almost laughed. It was so pathetic. Victor wanted him to hurt more, to rub it in, he could tell, but the way he was going about doing it was so childish. He shrugged and gave a look to the nearest of his co-workers. "We cool?"

His co-worker nodded, so he turned his gaze to the next. "We good?" Then the next, this time saying nothing, and so on and so on until he'd made eye contact with everyone. Their reactions were all the same. It was clear they didn't think it was an issue at all.

"See. We're good." He turned around, satisfied with his resolve and started to leave.

A slow clapping echoed through the building over the hard concrete.

Bowie turned around, thinking it was Victor. Everyone else looked as well, thinking is was a co-worker making an ill-conceived attempt at lightening the mood. However, nobody recognized the clapper. Except Bowie.

"Bravo, bravo." Scratcher yawned. "I honestly didn't think you had it in you." He said with a sarcastic grin.

Bowie was about to respond but Victor cut in.

"This area is for employees only. I'm going to have to ask you to leave." The overweight manager said as politely as he could manage.

"I'm afraid I can't do that. I have business here." Scratcher stopped clapping and stood up away from the racking. "There's something I want."

"And what is that?" Victor asked.

"He's after me." Bowie took a few steps forward to try to present himself as a target. He didn't want to get anyone else involved, but now it was too late. The only thing he could hope for was to contain the potential danger to his co-workers.

Victor raised an eyebrow.

"Wrong, but nice try. I'm not after you." Scratcher smiled. "I'm after him." He said, lifting a finger toward Victor.

Victor took charge and started walking toward Scratcher. "What do you want?"

"I just need you to come with me." He said.

"I'm afraid you'll need to be a little more specific." Victor insisted. He was almost within arm's reach of the Hellion.

Bowie couldn't let him get any closer. "Wait!" He shouted. Desperately, he looked around for anything that would help.

Victor turned his head toward Bowie and waited for an explanation but Bowie didn't have one. He gave

Bowie a funny look before turning back to the stranger to ask him who he was.

"Bowie!" Amy called out.

He turned to her just in time to see her toss the nail gun. He snatched it from the air turned and popped a shot off. The nail nearly hit Victor's arm as he was reaching to shake Scratcher's hand. It missed and buried itself in Scratcher's ribs. The wound hissed and spewed black as Scratcher recoiled.

Victor hadn't noticed scratcher's wound and his face was crimson with anger as he turned on Bowie and shouted "What the hell is wrong with you?!" He didn't have time to launch into a tirade. Before another moment passed, Scratcher's jaw split open and he roared an unearthly rasping roar at Bowie.

Everyone panicked. People ran from the area, some screaming in terror, and made a break for the doors.

Victor's attention snapped back around and his eyes grew wide in horror. He had only enough time to take a single step backward before Scratcher rushed forward and used him as a springboard to launch himself into the air at Bowie.

Bowie stepped back and started shooting. The Hellion swatted the nails away with his claws as he leaped through the air. Bowie didn't land a single shot as Scratcher landed. He charged but at the last second shifted his weight to duck under Amy's swinging machete. He came crashing down clumsily and thrashed wildly to keep his assailants from attacking.

In that time, Bowie and Amy retreated back to the corner of the racking. Bowie thought about unloading his clip at the creature but the way he was swatting them aside was unreal. He couldn't afford to run out of ammunition. On the other hand, it might buy some time for his co-workers to escape. He aimed the gun and started popping off shots.

Scratcher didn't have any choice but to keep his distance and dodge the attacks.

"We need to get everyone out of here!" He shouted.

"Where's Victor?" Amy asked when she realized he had disappeared.

"I don't know, but we need to think of something fast. I'm gonna run out of nails."

Before he'd even finished his sentence, Scratcher had darted out of the line of fire and hidden himself behind a row of tall steel shelving stacked high with pallets.

"He didn't come here for you. That's what he said. We need to find Victor." Amy said, keeping an eye on where she'd last seen the Hellion.

"Do we really want to save him?" Bowie thought out loud.

"Do you want them to keep hunting you?"

"Good point." Bowie sighed. Deep down he knew it was the right thing to do but he disliked the thought of doing it. "C'mon." He chased after Scratcher.

Amy followed close behind and as they rounded the corner, Scratcher released his claws from the racking and dropped onto her. His weight knocked her flat and drove the air out of her lungs as she hit the concrete hard. Breathlessly she managed to flail the machete to try to get him off of her but her swings went wide.

Bowie turned when he heard her fall and managed to fire twice before Scratcher leaped off of her and out of the aisle. He rushed to her side. She was winded and moving stiffly but she appeared otherwise unharmed. He stood by as she got up, keeping a watchful eye out. They both heard a door slam and the muffled sound of groaning metal coming from the corner of the warehouse.

"Crap. He went to the office." Bowie realized.

"What?"

"Victor." Bowie knew that if he'd heard it, the Hellion had as well. Victor was trying to barricade himself in his office.

"Are you okay?" He asked.

She coughed, still catching her breath but nodded. Bowie ran toward the office with Amy following behind, but when they got there it was too late. Victor had closed the steel door but Scratcher had avoided it entirely. Instead he'd punched right through the drywall and tore open a hole large enough to get through. They could hear the sounds of struggle from the other side as furniture was turned over and papers flew everywhere. Bowie ducked in through the hole.

Scratcher had his arms wrapped around Victor, his clawed hands digging into the plump manager's face. Victor's eyes were wide with terror but he made no attempts to struggle.

Bowie aimed the gun but Scratcher used Victor as a shield. Amy stood close by but she was at a loss. Neither of them knew what to do.

"Get out of the way or I'll kill him." The Hellion threatened. He seemed desperate.

"If you were going to kill him you would have done it already." Bowie countered. He knew he was standing on shaky ground, calling Scratcher's bluff. It was clear the Hellion wanted Victor but he had no idea why.

Scratcher narrowed his eyes at Bowie. "Get out of my way." He took a few steps to the side, skirting the outside wall of the now devastated office. He moved slowly, getting closer and closer to the hole he'd ripped in the wall.

Bowie kept the gun trained on him but he didn't dare move to block the Hellion's movements. If he did, there'd be no telling what the creature would do. If he moved in closer to Victor, the Hellion could easily drop him and attack at close range. If he tried to take a shot, he'd risk hitting Victor in the process. He was out of options.

Amy moved out of the room and stood in front of the hole in the drywall ready to swing the machete.

Scratcher's muscles tensed and he sprang at the door with Victor in his arms.

Bowie tried to get out of the way but got knocked into the door-frame. He rebounded off the jamb and slipped on some loose papers that sent him crashing to the ground. He tried to take aim and fire off a shot but it was too late.

Amy took her swing but Scratcher was a blur and her swing went wide. Scratcher escaped with Victor in tow.

She quickly helped Bowie off the ground and together they made for the front as fast as they could. When they burst out of the warehouse into the open air, they saw Scratcher with Victor heading toward the center of the parking lot. Before they could get close the ground opened up. Scratcher leaped into a massive sinkhole and plummeted down into darkness still clutching Victor.

Bowie and Amy came to a screeching halt at the lip of the sinkhole. Bowie clutched at his sides and threw the nail gun at the asphalt. "Shit!" He cursed through clenched teeth.

Amy gazed down into the hole with wide eyes.

They stood there for a moment, neither one saying a word. It seemed so quiet.

Eventually, Bowie spoke up. "Don't think about it. We're safe for now. That's what matters."

She looked at him for some small token of hope. "What about Victor?"

He shook his head and bit his lip. "There's nothing we can do for him right now. I don't know. Look, you need to get some rest and have some time to sort all this out. You've been through a lot."

Amy moved to him and put a gentle hand on his arm. "What about you?"

He shrugged and gave a weak half-smile. "I've already done my best to sort through what I can. There's just so much I don't understand about all this, so there's not much point in thinking about it."

"Yeah, but look at you. You're walking like an old man. I think you could use some rest too."

He nodded.

"Do you think they'll be back for you?"

He gave it some thought. "It's hard to say for sure, but my gut says no. I think they're up to something else."

"Okay." Amy sighed. "I think I'm gonna go home. I doubt I'll be able to sleep but I'll try." She turned to head to her car but only managed a few steps before she hesitated. "Actually," she corrected herself, "I don't suppose I could crash with you?"

Bowie raised an eyebrow.

"You know… If those things come back... Well, I'd feel better if I knew there was someone in the other room. You know?" She explained, stepping a little closer.

Bowie tilted his head in a nod. He followed her to her car and she drove him to his apartment. She helped him to his bed, leaving the bedroom door open and soon fell asleep on his couch.

In the middle of the night, as she lay staring up at the ceiling in the dark, recounting everything that had happened, she spoke up and asked Bowie if he was asleep.

His voice broke the silence from his bedroom. "No."

"This isn't real, is it?" She asked.

There was a pause.

"Yeah. It's real."

She curled up a little more. "Is it over?"

"No." He said quietly. "It's not over."

She contemplated what that meant for a while. "What are we going to do?" She asked.

That question had been running through his mind ever since he'd laid down. He hadn't slept a wink since they'd turned out the lights. It was possible that Scratcher meant to kill or torture Victor, but in his gut, he knew that there was more to it than that. The Hellion had wanted him for something. Why else would they have followed Bowie and Amy to the sewage plant? They could have killed Amy outright but they hadn't. They'd captured her. It wasn't about killing. They needed one of them alive for something. These thoughts ran rampant in his mind until at long last Bowie took in a deep breath and let out a long sigh. "First, we're going to get some sleep." He said. "Then we... well..." His voice trailed off. He knew what was next. Arsen had shown him the kind of man he needed to become. He just dreaded doing it. "In the morning we're going to figure out how to save Victor."

Amy nodded to herself, thinking the same thing. "He deserves what he got though, doesn't he?"

"Yup."

"And we're going to save him anyway?"

Bowie didn't answer right away. He recognized the truth and it hurt. "Yup. We have to. It's the right thing to do."

"Even though he's a terrible person?"

"He's still a person." That was the last thing Bowie said before he turned over to sleep.

Amy lay awake for a while, her aching eyes staring up at the ceiling until at last the gentle weight of sleep fell upon her.

PART III

XIV

In the devouring shadows of night, the cold air ripped sharply across Bowie's face as he cut through the heavy gale. His hot breath was torn away as he peddled furiously. Around him trees swelled and the air swam with leaves and bark as the winds grew in intensity. His lungs were on fire as he pressed hard against the unrelenting gale, struggling to keep his balance against the storm. Amy lagged hard behind him, almost unable to keep up, her hair flying behind like a wild mare's tail.

They pressed onward against a nameless deadline. Every second they wasted was another second Victor's life was in danger.

"Why are we using bikes again?" Amy yelled after him. Her voice barely reached him over the howling storm.

"Your car would get towed. This area is limited access. Plus, we won't be able to use your car once we get there!" He shouted back. "We're almost there. It's just a little further!"

"What?" She yelled, unable to hear him over the howling wind. "Couldn't we wait until the storm passes?"

"There's no time. You were there. You saw what happened. If we don't hurry, he'll die!"

"How can we be sure?"

"What?" Bowie came screeching to a stop, sending up a shower of gravel.

Amy caught up with him and hit the brakes hard. "If that thing wanted to kill him, wouldn't it have already done it?"

"I don't know. I'm not sure why it took him, but I doubt it's for anything good. Come on! You and I both know there's a good chance he'll get killed."

"Do we have to?" Amy asked.

"What! Of course, we do! We're the only ones who can."

"No." Amy said loudly, lifting her finger to point over his shoulder. "I mean, do we have to get through them?"

Bowie turned to look and his face turned white. Ahead of them down the gravel road, just before the gate to the sewage plant, stood a dozen men and women, unmoved by the wind, staring blankly into the storm. He was unsure whether they'd seen him or not., dimly lit by pale light from the plant.

"Come on. Let's go back!" Amy said. "There's got to be another way."

The figures took notice and started heading toward them.

Bowie cursed to himself and whipped his bike around. "Yeah. Let's get out of here. We'll head back to my place until we come up with a better plan."

Amy nodded and followed Bowie as he left the sewage plant. She wasn't any happier about retreating than he was but it was just the two of them against a dozen or more Eidolon. She kept pace as best she could with Bowie until, after a long period of hard peddling, they arrived as his apartment. She racked her bike on the back of her Taurus and followed him inside where they were greeted by a peaceful silence from the wind outside.

Bowie leaned his bike up against the living room wall and tossed his jacket on the chair in the dining area. He felt a little embarrassed about the sparse furnishings in his apartment but he invited Amy to make herself at home.

"We need to figure out a better plan," Amy said as she flopped down on the sofa. "Those things were just waiting for us."

He took a seat next to her. "Those were Eidolon. Just like the ones at work."

"And those are the mindless ones that we can't hurt?" She asked, glancing over at him curiously.

"Right. We have to use iron or steel or we're powerless against them."

"Scary. I can't believe you're so comfortable with this." She laughed.

Bowie looked at her funny. "Comfortable?"

"Well, yeah. You just seem to take all of this like it's normal. Doesn't this stuff freak you out?"

Bowie raised his eyebrows and nodded to himself in agreement. "Yeah... Huh. I guess it's just that I've come to terms with it. After actually going to Otherside, everything else seems like just the surface of weirdness to me. It still freaks me out. I just feel like I have an enemy to face, that's all. Honestly, I feel out of my element just as much as you do, I think. I'm just trying to stay focused on what we need to do."

Amy nodded in understanding. "Yeah, I guess I just wish I knew as much as you do. I've never seen Otherside." She paused. "So, what is the plan? How are we going to get Victor? I thought the sewage plant was the only way to get there."

Bowie shrugged and leaned up against the kitchen counter. "It's the only way I know of. Halloran brought me there specifically when he took me to Otherside. There must be something about that location that makes it special. I just don't know what."

She nodded. "Alright. So, maybe we can find somewhere else that is similar that might have whatever it is we need to go there."

"Maybe..." Bowie said with some skepticism. "I just don't know. I'm so worn out right now, I'm not thinking well. What do you think?"

Amy didn't say anything for a few moments. She was just as clueless as he was. "I think maybe we should try to tackle this tomorrow. Get some sleep, you know? We didn't get any sleep and it will be morning soon. We just spent the night biking to the sewage plant against the wind. We need to regroup and come up with a better plan."

"Yeah. I hear you. You wanna crash here again? I don't mind, but I know this place isn't exactly comfortable."

Amy laughed a little. "Yeah. You're not lying. Sorry, but this place is a bachelor pad in all the wrong ways."

Bowie couldn't help but smile. "Yeah. It's kind of a dump."

"I think I'm going to head home and get some sleep there." She yawned.

"Will you be alright on your own? There's always a chance we'll have to deal with more Eidolon."

"I think I'll be okay tonight. I'll be careful. Having my own pillow beneath my head will help me clear my mind. Don't worry. I'll sleep with the machete nearby." She winked at him.

He gave a half smile and chuckled. "Alright. Just watch out. Don't turn your back on anyone. I'm still not sure how the Eidolon get here or where they come from. If you run across any just run and get somewhere safe. Call me and I'll come get you."

"Deal," she agreed. "You take care of yourself too. We'll think of something. Don't worry."

He tried his best to smile and they parted ways. The night was quiet and the apartment felt empty after that. Bowie lay awake staring at the ceiling, trying hard to figure out how they were going to get to Otherside. He ran through the scenario over and over again in his mind.

He imagined every way getting through all of those Eidolon at the sewage plant could possibly go wrong. Every time he ran it through his head, he knew that the two of them would probably get killed if they tried. Bowie had to come up with another way to get there. He thought about the spell that Halloran had used to get him there in the first place. The mirror and the brass ring and the blood... all of those things were important. They were too specific not to be. However, he wasn't convinced that the sewage plant was the only way. There was something about the location, he was sure.

He went over what he knew about Otherside. To him, it was like another plane of existence, dependent upon his own. Everything there was a reflection of life in the real world. A twisted reflection, but a reflection nonetheless. Almost like the world represented in metaphor. Everything he'd seen had to do with the life energy and the atmosphere of things. He tried for a while to think of a place in Echo City that had the energy and atmosphere of a gateway but nothing leaped to mind. Even the sewage plant didn't have that kind of gateway vibe to him. Then he started questioning if he really needed something that represented a gateway at all. He speculated well into the night, coming no closer to a solution. It wasn't until he started drifting off to sleep that he wondered if it had more to do with the surrounding environment at the sewage plant. Maybe it was all the trees and life around the plant. Maybe it was the water. Maybe...

At last his thoughts faded into meandering dreams and Bowie fell into a deep sleep.

The next morning was slow. A faded sunrise lit the sky in dismal grays and orange. Bowie woke around 10:30 and stumbled through his morning routine, his mind foggy and his senses dull. The day promised to be just what it seemed it had always been: cold and empty. Bowie barely noticed when his cell phone went off and he dug through a pile of clothes in his bedroom to find the muffled device. He managed to reach it just before it went to voicemail and answered.

"I think I figured it out. I'll pick you up in twenty minutes." Amy said over the line.

"Huh? What?" He said groggily.

"I figured it out! I have an idea where we can go to get to Otherside. I'm coming over to pick you up."

"Oh. Okay." Bowie said as he yawned.

He quickly downed his breakfast and got dressed, grabbing a few items for the journey. It wasn't long before Amy knocked on his door and soon they were both headed downtown.

"So, where are we going?" Bowie asked from the passenger seat after they'd been driving for a few minutes.

"So. You know what we were saying yesterday? About how there might be a different place we could try to get to Otherside?"

"Yeah. I spent all night thinking about it." He rubbed his eyes.

"Me too. And I was thinking, maybe it has to do more with the energy around the place, kind of like Feng Shui or something. You know, the energy of the surroundings affects the space itself."

"Yeah. I was wondering about the same thing."

"Well, it got me thinking. The sewage plant has a lot of trees and plants growing around it, so we need to be somewhere that there's a lot of plants. There's also a lot of water."

"Yeah. Yeah!" Bowie started to get a little excited. "I think you're right!"

"Well, we need to go someplace where there's a lot of trees and a lot of water. It's also fairly isolated out there, so it needs to be someplace where there isn't a lot of human presence, you know?"

"I get where you're going, but I couldn't come up with a good place in town. Did you think of somewhere?"

She gave his shoulder a playful slap. "Duh! You got to give me more credit than that! I know the perfect place. Do you know about Bates Island?"

"Sounds familiar. I don't know anything about it though."

"It's that island just off the main highway. You have to walk across a bridge from Wye Park, kind of where that music shop is. It's right in the middle of the river."

"You mean over by that run-down apartment that had the shooting last year?"

Amy shivered. "Yeah. I know. It's not the best neighborhood. But the island is nice. It's a natural reserve. Deb from work says she takes her pit bull there sometimes for a jog. It's the only place I could think of in town."

Bowie couldn't help but agree. "Yeah. I'm just not too familiar with the area is all. But you're right. I think we should definitely try it." He was staring out the window, taking mental note of the neighborhoods they passed as they drove on. An old brick building caught his eye and made him wonder. "What's that?"

"Huh?" Amy said, glancing over to see where Bowie was looking. "Oh. That. That's the old courthouse. I think they moved down to eleventh street after that whole thing twenty years ago. It was empty for a while but I think they are using it for an office building or something now."

"What happened twenty years ago?"

She paused. "Ummm... Hmmmm... I think it was something to do with a bunch of racist judges. They were sentencing Hispanics unfairly and letting white guys off the hook for crimes against Hispanics. I was pretty young when it was happening so I don't remember everything."

"They got caught, I take it."

"Yeah. If I remember right, there was a big trial all over the news about some white guy who raped a Mexican guy's daughter and the judge let him walk. That kind of B.S."

"Jeez."

"Yeah... After they uncovered all of the people involved there was a massive reopening of convicted cases and they reduced the sentences of a whole bunch of people and let several people out of prison. After they convicted the judges, they decided that the courthouse was too stained so they closed it down and opened up another one about a year later. My mom was hired on as a stenographer when they opened, so I got to hear a lot about it. I remember a lot of tension between my mom and my dad because there was a lot of pressure on her from the city after that."

"No kidding. Wow."

"Yeah. This neighborhood has gone downhill since then. There's a lot of graffiti and tweakers in the area."

Bowie noticed a couple of guys leaning against a wall down a graffitied alleyway, staring vacantly up at the sky. "I see what you mean. This whole town has been going downhill. You know?"

Amy shrugged. "Yeah. I guess so. I don't know. There's a lot of good stuff here too."

Bowie laughed a little.

"What? There is."

"Like what?" He gave her a half grin.

"Like that coffee shop down the street from Fleischer, or that Thai restaurant that shows local rock bands on Fridays. You know they're redoing the uptown now?"

Bowie was surprised. "No kidding? That place has needed it bad for I don't even know how long. I thought all of those shops were closed these days."

"Yeah. A bunch of them did. But new businesses are moving in and there's a couple of pretty cool stores there now."

"You ever been to that little bar next to the teriyaki place?" Bowie asked.

"The Crier?"

"No. Those guys are probably going to go out of business. That place has been like totally empty since Jack's reopened. The other one. Not Ray's Golden Lion. Just down the way from it."

"Oh. Yeah. I know the one you're talking about. Something or other Bar and Grill, right?"

"Yeah. That's the place."

Amy smiled a little. "Isn't that just a run-down hole in the wall?"

He laughed. "Yeah. It's a dive bar, but that's half the fun. That place is always busy, even though it's really small."

"We should go sometime after all this is over." She suggested.

"Yeah. That sounds good."

Amy suddenly noted the street they were approaching. "Okay. We're going to have to park over there, I think. That's where the park is. We can walk from there." She turned left and pulled off into a small gravel parking lot, keeping her distance from the few vehicles that were parked there. Nearby, swing sets stood cold and empty surrounded by dying grass and tufts of snow.

"Okay. Sounds good." He waited until she had parked before he asked, "you sure you're ready?"

"It'll be fine. I'm a part of this just as much as you are. Come on. Let's go."

"Hold on. We can't just go right now. We need to wait until later."

"What? Why?" She asked, confused. "Don't we need to save Vic? He could get killed if we don't hurry."

"Yeah. I get that but it's too dangerous right now. There's rules to this. We need to wait until later."

"How much later?" She asked with a little irritation.

"I don't know. Probably around sunset. That will give us the most time to get where we need to without worrying about the Hellion. I remember the Hellion keep to themselves during the night. We need to give ourselves as much evening light as possible."

"Alright. So, what do we do until then?"

Bowie nodded and looked down at the clock. "Well. We need to get supplies. This isn't going to be an in and out trip. I have no idea how long we're going to be there. Let's go grab some food and maybe get some for the road. We could be there for a long time and last time all I had was a soda."

She laughed at him.

"What? That's all I had. I was starving to death, I swear."

Amy just shook her head at him.

"Look. I have an idea of what we're going to need. Let's come back later when we're stocked up."

Amy agreed and they both decided to hit up a big box store for supplies and food. Bowie packed both his and Amy's backpacks while she grabbed hot pizza at the front of the store. Once they'd downed some food and got their gear in order they headed back to the island. Once they'd parked, Bowie took a flashlight out of his pack and checked it to make sure it was properly working.

"I feel kind of stupid for having a nail gun in here." Amy noted.

"Yeah. I'm not too keen on it either, but what else are we going to do. We don't have the time to get a permit for a firearm. It's not like I own a gun or anything already. This is the next best thing and it's a lot cheaper. I just wish it wasn't so damned heavy."

"Yeah. It's not very easy to use, either. We forgot to get a holster for them."

Bowie looked down at the nailgun he'd "borrowed" from Fleischer. It was unwieldy to say the least. "Look. Just keep in in your pack. Hopefully, we won't need them." He said as he stuffed his flashlight in his jacket pocket and zipped up his pack. "Come on. Let's go. I think it's late enough now."

Bates island was a piece of land that shot out into the wide river that ran through Echo City's center. It jutted out at an angle for about a mile and formed a triangular shape only half a mile wide. It was overrun with dense bitterbrush, black cottonwood trees and large swaths of tall grasses, reeds and overgrown bushes that appeared faded and brown in the dead of winter. The dull orange glow of the setting sun behind the clouds highlighted the bare branches of the trees.

The island stood off from the mainland by about a hundred yards and was connected by little more than a small levee overgrown with foliage. Down a short hill, a dirt path led across the thin strip of land and into the main part of the island. A chain link fence had been erected, complete with barbed wire along the top, to keep out intruders, though a gap about ten inches wide was visible between the two gate panels. About a yard in front of the gate stood an old rusted steel arm gate and in front of that, a large sign that read "Due to unsafe conditions: Bates Island is CLOSED to public access until further notice".

Amy stopped short of the sign as they approached and took a look around while Bowie continued past her.

"Shouldn't we stop?"

Bowie turned and looked up at her from down the path. "What do you mean?"

She pointed at the sign. "It's closed."

He shrugged. "What are they going to do, arrest us?"

Amy noticed a few of the other signs. "You have a point. I think it's just for the winter, to be honest. I guess it's still recovering from the fire."

"There was a fire?" Bowie asked.

"Yeah. In two thousand one. The whole thing went up. You can hardly tell now."

Bowie noted some graffiti on the back on one of the signs near the gate. "And now it's off limits during the winter?"

"Yeah." Amy said. "Maybe they want it to recover before they let people in."

"We don't have much of a choice. We have to try. If it doesn't work, we'll leave as soon as we can, okay?"

"Yeah. Okay." She said hesitantly.

"Come on. Let's get over to the island before someone notices." He said.

They headed down the small hill and slipped through the fence. As they were walking down the path to the main part of the island, Bowie noticed the large piled up shards of ice washed against the shore. It made him even more aware of the chill in the air as they walked across.

At first the island seemed pleasant enough. They walked down the faded path through tunnels in the dense brush. A gentle breeze quietly wafted through the dead branches making the tall grasses sway. As they got further and further down the path the brush opened up into small fields with little more than undergrowth sprouting up. Standing here and there along the path and through the fields were the gnarled remains of blackened trees, still twisted and toppled by the rampant fires. Bowie wondered aloud, "Are you sure this is a good place?"

Amy shrugged. "You have any better ideas?"

Bowie noted a bedsheet suspended in the branches of a cluster of bent trees and signs of habitation strewn about the ground. "I don't know. It just… seems a little off?"

The Island was quiet. Few birds were still in the area and the brush was quiet. As they neared the far point of the island, and a small clearing designated as a picnic spot, the wreckage of the fires was highly apparent. The grass clearing swept down to the river's edge and a wide shoreline. A tree lay to one side of the shore like a fallen soldier, left abandoned through the years. Water lapped the shoreline uneasily as the wind picked up.

Amy and Bowie stopped and looked at each other.

"What do you think?" Amy asked.

Bowie took notice of a "No Littering" sign that had long succumbed to rust and graffiti. "I don't know. I mean… Looks okay to me. Just… It feels off somehow. Maybe I'm just on edge. I'd say we should give it a shot."

"Okay. Sounds good." Amy agreed as she breathed out a puff of steam.

Bowie started digging around in his backpack. "Now we have to do the ritual."

"Ritual?"

"This is what Hal had me do last time. He had me collect all of this junk before I went to the sewage plant." He pulled the brass coupling out. "Did you bring the compact, like I asked?"

She nodded and fished the makeup mirror out of her pocket. "Is this really what we need?"

"We need a mirror and a brass ring. This is the best I could do for a brass ring." He held the fitting up in his hand. He motioned for Amy to hand him the mirror and set it on the shore, placing the fitting on top of the glass. "Sorry about this. I'll owe you a new one."

Amy winced as she watched Bowie pound his fist on the brass fitting, shattering the glass beneath. "I never knew you hated makeup so much."

Bowie gave her a wry smile as he drew the knife from its sheathe at his hip. He paused and stared down at the mirror. "Are you sure you're ready for this?" He looked up at her.

She smirked and wrinkled her brow. "Yeah. I mean... Are we doing this or not?"

Bowie suddenly felt heavy. "Once we go there, there's no turning back. If we get stuck there without our duplicates we can't return."

"Wait. What? What do you mean?"

"I mean," he sighed, "That the only way to come back is if our other self sends us back. If Varela dies, or Arsen, we'll be stuck there."

"If our other self dies, won't we die?"

"No... That's not how it works. I don't really understand it that well myself, but that's what Hal told me. If they die, we keep going. If we die, they die. It's kind of a weird one-way street."

"So, it's not a true reflection of our world then, like you told me?"

"Basically. It's like a warped twisted version. There are similarities, but it's like someone made a demented version of our world where the rules are just different. It's... it's weird."

Amy considered what he'd said, swallowed and nodded. "We're not doing this for us. We're doing this for Vic."

"Oh, god... Why did you have to say it like that? Do we really have to?"

"Quit whining." Amy said with a grin. "We're saving someone's life."

"Even though he's a douche bag?" Bowie said with a look of mock disgust.

"Even though he's a douche bag."

Bowie nodded and held out the knife, ready to cut his hand. After a moment had passed, Amy asked "Are you ready?"

He didn't respond right away. He stared down into the middle of the brass ring, lost in a moment of thought before he answered quietly. "Not really."

She gave a puzzled expression. "Why not?"

He looked at her again and stood up. "I... I don't know if I can go back. You don't know the things I've seen."

She waited for him to say more but he remained silent. "You're scared, aren't you." She tried to put a comforting hand on his shoulder.

He stepped away and walked a few paces. "Of course, I'm scared. I'm terrified. Who wouldn't be? Those things can shred a man into ribbons. I watched them and the Effigies fighting each other. It was..." His voice trailed off as he was swept off into the memory. "Arsen... I know what Varela said but even so I don't really know if he's alive. And if he isn't, I'll be trapped in that nightmare."

"Hey! Bowie." She said sharply.

He snapped out of it.

"Bowie, if you don't want to go do this, then don't. We don't have to do this. You're right. Victor doesn't deserve you risking your life to save him." She moved over to him, grabbed him by the elbow, looked him straight in the eye and told him "We don't have to go."

Something in her gaze, something in the way she looked at him cut right through everything he was feeling and hit something raw and exposed. When he looked back at her he felt the truth with sudden clarity.

"I have to. I have to do this."

"We don't have to." She insisted, putting both hands on his shoulders.

"Yes, we do," he said forcefully, "because if I don't, I won't be able to live with myself. Vic is a douche bag, but that's not what this is about. This is about doing what's right, because that's the only thing keeping people like us from becoming people like him. I'm going to go but you don't have to do this with me. This whole thing is my responsibility. I won't think less of you for staying here. It may not be safe, but it's a hell of a lot safer than where we're going."

She shook her head. "No. I want to go with you. We're doing this together. Okay?" She said as their eyes met.

He nodded and put his hand on hers. "Alright. But after this there's no going back."

She shrugged. "We can't go back to before all this happened anyway. In for a penny in for a pound, right?"

He chuckled. "Something like that."

"So, let's do this before we change our minds."

He walked back over where he'd left the mirror. "Alright. Hold out your hand."

She held it out for him and he made a small cut on the edge of her palm. He did the same for himself. "We need to let it drip into the middle of the ring. Once it goes through it will take us there."

"Got it." She held her hand next to his and they both knelt down near the mirror. "I'm ready when you are."

"On three." He said.

She nodded.

"Hold on and buckle up." He said with a half-smile as he sheathed his knife.

They clasped their good hands together and let a few drops fall silently in through the brass ring.

XV

The earth warped and contorted and soon the world they knew fell away. In its place Otherside whipped around them like a hurricane. Bowie took a step and had to steady himself before he lost his balance. Amy retched and felt on all fours, unable to keep her composure. She collapsed to the side, unconscious for a few moments. Once Bowie had regained his footing, he regretted everything. Signs of struggle and war covered the landscape as he saw the shattered bodies of Effigies and the unnatural remains of Hellion skeletons bleached and slowly sinking beneath the sand and dirt.

He waited for Amy to come to. When she awoke, he put a hand on her back and helped her to her feet and tried not to point out the remnants of bodies littering the ground like stones.

"It worked," said Bowie. "Are you okay." He saw Amy's pale expression. "Unsettling, isn't it?"

Amy glared at him.

"Sorry. I know it's unnerving. You'll get used to it in a little while." He said.

"Is it always this bad coming here?"

Bowie thought on it for a moment. "Actually, this time wasn't as bad for me for some reason. Last time I passed out."

Amy rubbed at her temples. "Yeah. I know the feeling. Why is everything so shifty?" She asked.

"I don't know," he shrugged, "that's just the way this place is." He gave Amy a minute to get her bearings and look around. "Pretty twisted, huh?"

She nodded. "The trees and plants are all broken, but not really. It looks like everything is blowing around but there's no wind. It's really weird." She glanced at their feet. "What happened to the mirror and the brass ring?"

Bowie looked down and was surprised to find they were both gone. The last time he'd come through, he and Halloran had headed off immediately. He'd completely forgotten about the mirror. "Huh. No idea. Hal said that there aren't any reflections in Otherside. Maybe mirrors just can't exist here."

"There aren't any reflections here? That's pretty strange."

He nodded as he started to lead her away from the shore. "Everything here is pretty strange."

"Well, if there's no reflections then that explains the mirror. But what about the brass thing you had? It doesn't have a reflective surface." She pointed out as she followed him.

"That's true. I hadn't thought of that. I don't know. Come on. We need to get moving. It's a long way back to the Federal Building and I don't want to get caught out here all alone."

"The Federal Building?" She gave him an odd look.

"It's like a fort or something here. There are allies there. They can help us. Keep your eyes open. If we see anyone, they may be able to help us," he said. "If you see anything moving tell me."

"Everything is moving." She said dryly.

Bowie was grateful she hadn't noticed the carnage at the shore but as they continued on it was clear that a massive battle had been waged on the island. It wasn't long before Amy noticed the strange shapes of bodies blending into the scenery.

"What happened here?" She asked as she held on tightly to his arm. "There's people."

"It's a war. There's a war going on between both sides." He explained. "That's all I really know. Try not to think too hard about it. There's a lot going on here that isn't like the real world."

As they got closer to where the gate should have been across the bridge, Amy started to see just how different Otherside really was.

The gate was gone entirely and along the slope up to the parking lot a dozen effigy bodies lay broken and mangled. Their crystalline parts shattered and crushed, strewn over the ground like glass. Their clothes were muddied and torn and they looked like they'd been there for quite some time. There were signs of struggle everywhere and a crude flag had been erected in the frozen mud from a torn piece of faded blue material attached to a broken branch.

Amy looked up toward the parking lot where she saw the carcasses of massive beasts rotting on the gravel. She rushed up the slope to get a better look. "What the hell happened to my car?" She asked, staring at the large furry corpse laying on the gravel. She got little more than a shrug from Bowie who didn't seem the least bit surprised.

She turned her attention to the rest of the city, but what she saw looked more to her like ruins than a city.

Steel beams and columns stood erect among low and unfinished cinder block walls on concrete foundations scattered around the business park. To her surprise the parking lots and streets were relatively intact, though poorly maintained. The asphalt was cracked and broken in places, bare in others, revealing weeds and dark soil.

"Come on. We still have a long way to go." Bowie's said to grab her attention.

She looked over to where she had parked. A frown formed on her face as she stared at the carcass of her little Ford. Bowie paid it no mind and walked past it.

"What happened to this place?" She asked as she followed him across the parking lot and down the road.

"This is just what it looks like," he began. "You should see the neighborhoods. They're... freaky. A bunch of Eidolon just standing around like mannequins."

"Does it look like this?" She asked, indicating the businesses.

"Kind of. Yeah. You'll get to see it once we get a bit closer to the Federal building."

"Ah. Okay. How far is it, do you think?"

"By foot? I think it's about an hour and a half, maybe a little more. It all depends on if the roads between here and there are still intact. It's hard to say."

"Have you walked that far before?"

He gave her a funny look. "No. I looked it up on my phone before we left."

"Oh. I just thought... Since you take the bus and walk everywhere..."

He laughed and shook his head. "I do walk a lot, but not that far. Most of what I need I can get around my neighborhood."

"Sorry. Haha. I guess you're right." She noticed his knife on his hip and decided to rummage around in her backpack to retrieve her machete. "Do you think we'll run into the Hellion before we get there?" She tried to hide the tremble in her voice.

Bowie swallowed and focused on the road ahead. "I really hope not. If we do, we're screwed." He saw the beginnings of fear in her expression as Amy followed by his side. He hadn't meant to sound so negative. "I'm sure we'll be fine. We just need to be careful. If we see any before we get there we should probably run. They can track us by smell, so hiding won't do us a whole lot of good."

"What should we do if we get separated?"

He stopped, put his hands on her shoulders and looked her straight in the eye. "If that happens, you need to promise me you'll run. Run and don't stop, no matter what. You got that?"

"Yeah." She answered back, returning his gaze.

"Promise me."

"I got it. I promise." She said more forcefully.

He let her go and they continued down the road. "Good. I don't know what's going to happen but I don't want you to get hurt. You know?"

"Yeah. I know."

There was an awkward silence as they walked. Soon they had gone past the business park and took a turn up an on-ramp. Amy's nerves were on edge so she spoke just to break the tension. "What road is this anyway?"

"This is the highway. I want to say two-sixty or something like that. They call this area the Wye."

"Yeah. That's it. It's a long highway."

"It's also wide open." He noted.

"Then why are we going this way? We're kind of exposed, aren't we?"

Bowie agreed. "Yeah but there isn't much in the way of houses or buildings between here and there. I don't know about the Hellion, but the Eidolon mostly keep to the residential areas and main streets, I think. The Effigies have their camps and holdouts. I'm hoping the Hellion are the same way. If this really is a messed-up version of our world, then they're roaming around the neighborhoods and won't come near the highway."

Amy nodded. "That makes sense."

As they walked together down the highway the road seemed empty and expansive. Both of them had traveled the road numerous times but there was something about being on foot instead of in a car that made the road appear larger than normal. It was a six-lane highway, three lanes to a side separated by a double set of concrete forms. They walked on the right-hand side close to where a bike path had been paved and was separate from the road by a barrier on one side.

"What happens once we get into the north part of town?" She asked after they had been walking for a while.

"What do you mean?" He asked.

"Well... you said that you think the Hellion stay in the neighborhoods. The highway ends once it hits G Way. There's a whole neighborhood on the left side of the road. It's like another mile or two before the Federal Building, right?"

Bowie hadn't thought of that. "You're right. Hmmmm..." He didn't like how close they were going to come to one of the older, more run-down neighborhoods. "There's all of those businesses to the right and there's a pretty steep hill going down on that side of the road. We can probably just keep below the slope. That'll put the road between us and the neighborhoods and keep us out of sight for the most part. That's probably the best we can do. At some point we're going to have to cross the road and get to the Federal building. We can stick to the park by the river until we get to the boat launch. That's our best bet."

Amy agreed and they continued in silence. In the distance they could see the overpass that marked where the highway turned into G Way, though it was shrouded in a thin mist. As they crossed over a bend in the river that cut underneath the highway it started becoming increasingly difficult to see the north part of the city.

"What's up with all of the fog?" She asked.

"I don't know." Bowie said quietly. He was looking around intently, listening for something.

"What's up?"

"Shhh..." He held up his hand for Amy to be quiet.

She frowned at him but kept quiet. She listened as well but when she didn't hear anything she asked "what is it?"

He held up his hand again and focused across the road on the quarry tucked in the corner where the freeway passed over two-sixty heading west.

Far across the way, on the other side where a small parking lot lay beside a gravel quarry, shadows gathered and moved. Bowie knew the area. In their world there was graffiti on the concrete barriers lining the parking lot and he had seen groups of people congregating there on the few occasions he'd passed that way. Here he could see only black splashes of unknowable substance splattered on the concrete. The figures mingled near the barriers, crowding and leaning over something that Bowie couldn't identify at that distance. He was too far away to be certain but his gut told him they were Hellion.

"What is it?" Amy asked quietly as Bowie crouched down and motioned for her to do the same.

"We need to go back." He whispered.

She huddled down with him. "What? Why? What is it?"

He couldn't tell if they had been seen but he didn't want to take any chances. He swallowed and started backing away, never taking his eyes off of the figures in the distance. "Those are what I was afraid of. You remember Mouth? That freaky guy from the sewage plant?"

Amy nodded, her face growing pale.

"Well, there's three of them over there and I can't say for certain but I think they're eating something."

Amy followed Bowie's example and they continued backing away until the Hellion were no longer visible through the fog. Once Bowie felt they were at a safe distance they turned and started walking back the way they had come.

"How are we going to get around them?" Amy asked, digging in her pack for her nail gun.

Bowie grumbled to himself and thought for a moment. "Well... We could try to crawl across without getting seen. I don't know if they'd smell us though. The water is far too cold to swim across and I think they'd hear us. I mean, just listen.

It didn't take long for Amy to realize just how awfully quiet the air was. The familiar rumble of traffic and construction was gone. Nature made not a sound. It was silent, like the aftermath of a nuclear blast.

"Damn," she cursed. "So now what?"

"I don't know. We could go the long way around on Riverwood but that would take us through some of the neighborhoods."

"Do we need to avoid the neighborhoods?"

He sighed. "I guess not. Hal didn't seem to feel much danger when we had to go through a couple of big neighborhoods. We just had to get there before sunrise. Maybe it'll be okay. This was just the fastest way."

"Wait... If it's so dangerous, why are we going during the day?" Amy asked with growing concern.

"To be fair, you wanted to head out first thing in the morning." Bowie reminded her. "That's why I wanted to get supplies and wait until sunset."

Amy was starting to get mad. "I thought you told me the other night that the Hellion like to come out during the day."

"I did," he said, "but that's just what the Effigies told me. I don't know where they go the rest of the time. I figured if we went at sunset, giving ourselves time to get to the tower, the Hellion would be congregating near the Effigy's base trying to break in instead of prowling around. It would keep them distracted enough that we could move behind them without being noticed. That's why I had us wait. If we got to the building by the time the sun went down, we would have more night time to find Victor."

"Okay, but how were you planning to get past them? If they leave the tower at sunset, they'll be heading elsewhere, probably right toward us."

"You're right. I don't know." Bowie massaged his temples. "Maybe we can hide somewhere out of the way until we're sure the coast is clear. What do you think?" Bowie asked.

Amy thought on it before shaking her head. "I think I'm kind of hungry. I think we should go somewhere out of sight and eat something. It'll be easier to figure out what we're going to do on a full stomach."

Bowie couldn't help but agree. He was also getting pretty hungry. They slid down a gravel slope off the road and down to a half-built concrete building not too far away. Once they were hidden behind one of the partial walls, they tossed their packs down and Bowie began digging through his gear for some food.

"What's this?" She asked when he produced what looked like a candy bar.

He tossed her the bar and pulled out another one for himself. "It's a meal replacement bar."

"You brought candy bars?"

He laughed and tore into his. "Meal replacement bar. That thing's got like five hundred calories and a ton of protein."

"It's chocolate." She pointed out.

"What?"

"It's a chocolate bar." She insisted.

"Meal replacement bar." He corrected.

"…That tastes like chocolate." She added.

"Look. It's got a lot of energy in it. I packed a bunch in your backpack too." He noticed the expression on her face. "What?"

"I don't know. Don't you think there's something else that would have been better?" She replied.

He shrugged and tore off the wrapping. "I wasn't sure how long we were going to be gone. We needed something lightweight with lots of calories that wouldn't take up that much space. MRE's are *way* too big and heavy and we'd need a ton of water. These are lightweight, high in calories, and don't take up much space. It seemed like a good idea."

She continued giving him the same look.

"What? My dad had a lot of military history. He was kind of a survivalist. This is the kind of thing he would have done if he was in our situation."

Bowie chowed down while he watched Amy prodding her own. After he'd swallowed a few bites he said "It won't kill you. I promise."

"What happened to your dad?" Amy asked him.

Bowie was a little surprised. "What do you mean?"

"You said he *was* a survivalist."

He nodded and looked down at the ground for a moment. "He died a while ago. Same with my mom," he told her.

"Oh. I'm sorry." She said. "I didn't know."

He shrugged and took another bite. When he finished chewing, he explained, "They were both killed in a car crash when I was seventeen years old. It was my senior year. It was all over the news back then."

Amy felt bad that she had brought it up. "I'm sorry for your loss. I'm sure it wasn't easy for you."

"Yeah." He said dryly. After he'd taken a few more bites he looked to the bar Amy was holding. "You haven't touched yours." He said to change the subject.

Amy wasn't too keen to try it but she decided she was too hungry to care. After a few bites she shrugged. "It's not terrible." She admitted. "But if we have to be here for very long, I'm going to get really sick of eating chocolate bars."

He was about to correct her but she spoke for him. "I know, I know. Meal replacement bar. Sheesh."

He laughed a little. "Well, at least we're fed. And we have plenty more so if we have to stay here for a while, we'll be okay."

"Pretty strange first date, wouldn't you say?" She joked.

It was his turn to give her a funny look.

"What?" She said, her mouth still partially full. She swallowed and explained. "I was just kidding. We haven't really spent that much time together and here we are roughing it in the most messed up place in existence. I'm just saying."

"You're just saying?" He repeated, a mocking expression on his face.

She gave him a playful punch in the arm followed by her best pout. "Shut up. This is stressful." They laughed together and finished eating while Bowie dug through his pack for a map of Echo City.

"I was thinking we can use this to get a better lay of the land. I know not everything is the same but from what I've seen the streets are still intact for the most part." He laid it out in front of them and pointed to a place on the map he'd already circled. "That's where we're going. If we get lost or separated, that's where we need to meet."

"Alright. So, what if we can't make it to the federal building?"

Bowie nodded. "If we can't get some help from the Effigies that would be a problem. There's no way the two of us can find Victor in a city this big. It could take weeks or even months looking through every neighborhood and every building in Echo. Other Echo." He corrected himself. "Man, this is a weird place..." He muttered.

She laughed. "Yeah. I get this weird vibe here too. It's like I know this place but at the same time its empty. And not just because there's nobody here. Like, it's got no soul or something. Or it's just different from what we normally feel about a place. You know what I mean?"

He shrugged. "I think so. It feels like that to me too. Like it's just a shell. Like the feeling you get when you see a mannequin and you know it's not real but it still gives you that feeling."

"Man, I hate those things," she sighed. "I used to work in the mall not too far from Bates Island and at night when we were doing our rounds and closing up, I would freak out when I saw someone standing in one of the shops. Because the shops were all closed. And then I would realize it was just a mannequin. They give me the creeps."

"Nice." Bowie smiled.

She gave him another playful punch in the arm. "Butt-head. I'm serious. Those things are creepy."

"Yeah, they're pretty creepy." He noticed something nearby and gripped his knife suddenly. "Speaking of creepy."

Through a gap in the wall they could see two figures approaching. They looked just like normal people, save for the sunken pits where their eyes should have been. One was a bearded man in his forties and behind him a younger looking blond woman, maybe in her early twenties. They walked slowly; their paces lackluster. As they came around the corner and entered into the shell of the building, they took no notice of Bowie and Amy squatting in the corner.

"Holy shit! What the hell are those? What do we do?" She snatched up her machete and held it at the ready.

Bowie held up a hand to calm her. "Take it easy. They're just Eidolon."

"Eidolon? Weren't those the things that tried to kill us in Fleischer?"

"Yeah. Same things. Just keep an eye on them. I doubt they're going to try anything."

"What? What do you mean? They tried to kill us!" She hissed.

"Yeah." Bowie couldn't help but agree but he did his best to put her at ease. "They're kind of mindless. Think of them like cows. They just kind of go about their business."

She grabbed his arm and squeezed hard. "Tried. To. Kill. Us." She repeated.

"The only reason they were trying to kill us was because they were being controlled by someone else. You remember Mouth?"

Her skin went cold for a moment. "Yeah." She whispered dryly.

"He was probably the one controlling them. If they're not being controlled, they just wander about the city until night when they return to their homes and just stand there. Whoever these people are in the real world, they're probably just stopping by whatever business this is late in the evening. The Hellion don't have any reason to control them right now. I doubt they know we're here."

"Are you telling me that some people are like that?" She asked, pointing to the mindless Eidolon that were now just standing staring into the distance at something.

"Like what? People just going through the motions in life? Yeah. There's lots of people like that. It's not ideal but it's what they're like in this place."

Amy let it sink in for a minute. "How can anyone be like that? Don't they care?" She asked.

"Maybe at one point they did. I don't think we're born wanting that kind of life. Hell, my Effigy tried to kill me before he let himself turn into one of those things. I can't even say I really blame him."

"It's such a shame." She remarked sadly.

Bowie considered what she said and for a moment wasn't so sure he agreed. "You know. I'm starting to wonder about that a little. I mean, it's not like they're doing any harm. They just want to go about their lives. Maybe they're content to do just that, you know? I mean, not everyone struggles and fights to improve their lives or devotes themselves to helping others. Some people just want to get home to their families and be happy about it, you know?"

"How many of them do you think there are?" She asked.

He shrugged and guessed "I think they make up a large part of the population here but I get the impression that it didn't use to be that way. Hal was talking about it. I think there used to be more Effigies but because of their war with the Hellion their numbers have decreased. Remember, this place isn't like ours. The two are connected but it's like almost a one-way connection."

"Doesn't sound like our friends are doing too well here." She said with a note of sadness in her voice.

"Doesn't sound like we're doing too well in our own world." He added.

Their eyes met and for a moment, though they both remained quiet. After a few minutes the Eidolon left and they were alone again. They finished eating and packed up their supplies.

"What's the plan, Stan?" She asked once they were ready to go.

He gave it some thought. "You were right. Eating something really helped. I think we're better off the way we were going. The sun is going down soon and they might be going back to wherever they come from. That goes for the entire city. If we go the long way it will be a lot longer before we can cross the river which will put us out in the open. I'd rather not spend that much time exposed. If we keep low and move quietly, we should be able to get across the bridge without being spotted. With any luck they'll be too focused on getting home to notice us."

"You really think that's the best plan?" She questioned.

"Look. To be honest, I'm pretty freaked out about this whole thing. But my gut says that's our best bet. We don't need to avoid the neighborhoods at night. At least I don't think so. But we're going to need to make as much use of the night as we can to find Victor. That means we need to get there as quickly as possible. At some point we're going to have to take a risk. We'll burn through a good hour or more to take the long route and I don't really know those neighborhoods that well. I figure we're both pretty familiar with the area, since we both work in this part of the city. What do you think?"

She shook her head. "I'm not really sure. I don't know anything about this place but you've at least been here before. If your gut says we should go this way, I'll trust you. You just need to make sure that *you* think this is the best plan."

He gave a brief nod and thought on it for a few more moments. "Let's give it a shot. I think once we get past the bridge, we will be okay. We can skirt down around to the river to keep out of sight once we get that far. Just keep low and stay near me. We'll go slowly. Alright?"

Amy held out an arm for Bowie to clasp hands. He took it and they locked grips.

"Alright." She agreed, with a note of softness in her voice.

"All for one?" He asked.

She gave him a mocking look. "Seriously?"

"What? Three Musketeers, man. Three Musketeers."

"Geez..." She let go, shook her head and led the way out of the building and back to the road.

This time in crossing the river they kept to the narrow bike path to the right of the road, separated by a concrete barrier. Once they were far enough to see the graffitied parking lot across the way they ducked down into a walking crouch. The going was slow and after several minutes both of them felt an aching in their knees from the awkward position. Bowie stopped momentarily and stretched one leg out to the side to its full extent, then the other leg. Amy did as well. They had made it about halfway across the bridge by that point.

After a few more steps Bowie noticed a lone figure coming across the bridge on the path toward them. It was an Eidolon jogger, dressed in under armor, meandering down the path at a quick pace. He was heading right down the center of the path.

"Crap." Bowie cursed under his breath.

"What is it?" Amy asked from behind him.

He leaned to one side to give her a better view and pointed.

"Oh, crap. What do we do?" She whispered.

"It probably won't even notice us. We just need to get out of its way. Follow my lead."

Bowie and Amy continued forward until the Eidolon was only a little way off. At that point Bowie took his nailgun out of his backpack, moved to the side of the path and pressed his body against the concrete barrier, flattening himself against it as best he could to make room. Amy did the same.

It came closer and closer. As it moved it seemed to become aware of something. Its paces slowed and soon it was simply walking. Its empty eye sockets started scanning around. It was only a few feet from Bowie. He could smell the scent of sweat coming from the it. It took another step forward, then another, like it was sniffing around for what it could not see with its eyes.

What is it doing? Bowie wondered. Amy stared at it, her eyes wide with fear, wondering the same thing.

It had only just passed Bowie when suddenly it stopped in its tracks in front of Amy.

Bowie began to wonder. Was it aware of their presence? Was someone else looking through its eyes? His pulse began racing and he slowly reached for his knife. His fingers flipped the leather loop away from the handle and he inched it from its sheathe.

Amy was terrified. She stared uneasily at the creature. Its head moved slowly as it tilted its gaze, looking closer and closer to where she lay. She froze, tense, afraid to move. Her position was awkward. She was holding herself off the ground with just one arm while her back leaned against the high slope of the concrete. Her arm began to tremble from the strain so she adjusted the angle of her hand a little. When she did her back shifted and dropped slightly, brushing the concrete.

The Eidolon's gaze snapped to her and she stared into its dark soulless sockets. The emptiness seemed to recede back into eternity through its skull and drew her in deeper and deeper as in their eyes locked.

Suddenly, sharp razor claws shot out over the barrier and pierced the Eidolon in the chest, wrenching back and ripping the Eidolon over the concrete barrier. Savage snarls and gurgled gnashing sounds erupted from the other side of the barrier as Amy stared wide eyed at Bowie with a face of pure terror.

He could see the scream hiding behind her eyes as she stared at him, pale and motionless. Bowie stared back, pleading with his eyes for her to keep silent, hoping that the Hellion tearing into its prey on the other side wouldn't find them.

He couldn't tell the exact number but he thought he heard at least two, maybe tearing into the Eidolon's flesh. With careless brutality the Hellion tossed the body between each other, tearing it to pieces. The upper half of the body crashed down, snapping over the top of the barrier right above Amy's head, staring her in the face. Its limbs dangling lifelessly from the corpse.

Black ichor splattered down from open gashes on the body, speckling Amy's face. Amy's free hand went straight to her mouth and her eyes went even wider as she stifled her own scream.

Bowie could only watch as fear tore through her. If she made a noise it was all over. There was no way the two of them could take on the Hellion by themselves. *Please don't scream!* He pleaded in his mind. *Don't scream, Amy. Whatever you do, just don't scream!*

The torso was dragged back over the barrier and Bowie and Amy heard the disturbing sounds of carnage. Amy's chest heaved, her pulse racing wild as adrenaline ran through her veins and she gripped her nailgun hard.

After another half minute, they heard primal grunts and snarls and then suddenly clawed steps racing across the asphalt.

Cautiously, Bowie took up a normal crouch and peeked an eye above the barrier.

The Hellion were gone.

Bowie immediately went to Amy who was shaking, still seeing the soulless eyes of the Eidolon staring at her from its mutilated corpse. He took her head in his hands and tried hard to get her to look at him.

"Amy. Amy, it's okay. It's over. They're gone. It's over." He told her. "It's okay. It's okay."

Something about his voice broke her from her terror and she clung to him, tears springing from her eyes and she wrapped her arms around his neck, burying her face in his shoulder. Bowie held her for as long as she needed as she cried unintelligible words into his coat. It took a minute or so but eventually she was able to stop her tears and get a grip on herself.

"I'm okay." She told him, still trembling. "I'm okay. Oh my God..." She told him, wiping her eyes.

"It's alright. We're okay now. You're going to be okay." He said as comfortingly as he could. He was starting to question if he'd made the right decision to go across the bridge. They were alive, sure, but he felt terrible.

"Come on." She said, her expression growing hard as she swallowed her emotions. "We can't just stay here. We need to get going."

Bowie was glad to agree and they quickly scurried the rest of the way down the path, following the bike trail toward the river until it veered left under a partially collapsed overpass to the north part of Echo City.

The trail took them to a large, well-manicured grass park that bordered a small marina. The trail continued past several restaurants and hotels for about a mile, until at last it had a view of the river through the foliage as it ran into Grady Park.

As they passed behind several trees in view of the docks up ahead, Amy unshouldered her backpack. "Let's stop." She said abruptly. She knelt down and dug through her things, putting her nailgun away and taking out her machete. She became aware that Bowie was watching and wasn't buying her act.

He could tell she was still completely shaken. She looked up at him and wanted to say something to make the moment less awkward but she couldn't find the right words.

Bowie broke the silence with a comforting smile and said, "yeah. Let's take a break. I think we could both use a minute. We're pretty far away from the rest of town and we have the river on one side so it'll be okay. I don't think we'll attract any attention down here." He took off his own backpack and set it down next to hers to put his nailgun away as well.

"How can you be so calm about this?" She asked as she folded her arms around herself to keep out the cold.

"I guess I've just accepted it." He said in a low voice. When she didn't say anything else, he continued,

"That was pretty scary back there. I thought we were screwed."

"Yeah." She said quietly.

"What happened to the machete girl at the check stands?" He asked, giving Amy his best attempt at a smile.

She looked down at the ground, avoiding his gaze. "What are you talking about?"

He moved closer and put a hand on her shoulder. "Back in Fleischer you grabbed a weapon and were ready to fight. What happened to that?"

His voice sounded encouraging but Amy could tell that he was just playing strong to try to cheer her up. She knew he meant well, however, and that was enough for the moment. "I guess it just got more real. I came here because of you… well… I mean… I guess I just…" She struggled to find the right words though she tried her best to hide her feelings. "At first it was like some kind of crazy zombie movie come to life. Like a living fantasy. It was one thing when we were dealing with normal looking people in a store and fighting them. It was cool because it was just you and me and now… I guess… After that fight at the sewage plant, things are... different. We could die here."

Bowie nodded. "I'm sorry. I never wanted you to get into this."

"I came here because of you. Because I wanted..." Her face flushed and she stopped herself. "I guess it was pretty stupid, huh?"

Bowie was at a loss for what to say. Amy wasn't talking openly but she was saying a lot and he didn't know how to react. "Hey. It's okay. It's not stupid." He tried to comfort her.

She rushed into his arms and held him. After a moment she loosened her grip. "I guess this isn't a game, huh?" She said, feeling foolish.

"No." Bowie shook his head. "This is my fault. I shouldn't have brought you into this."

"Hey!" She said sharply, "this is my fight as much as it is yours."

He gave her a look of skepticism.

"What? It is. I mean, look. I am the only person who has any idea what the hell is going on. That day I found you on the side of the road. That was when I stuck my neck into all this. And now, with someone's life on the line and me being the only one you can count on, it's become my fight. You know?"

Bowie didn't have much to say. He still felt terrible but Amy was determined. Who was he to stand in the way? He took his hand off her shoulder and grabbed his backpack. "Alright. Come on. We still have a bit to go before we reach the park. From there we can cut across to the main roads and get to the federal building. Do you still need a minute?"

Amy checked herself mentally and agreed to follow. "No. Let's just get there. I can rest when we're somewhere safe."

They pressed on down the trail. Bowie thought he could see the outline of the federal building in the distance, though the sky grew darker by the minute. They managed to reach the edge of Grady Park by the time night had enveloped the city. The darkness gave him a small sense of relief. "We'll be there soon. I think we'll be safe now. The sun just set." He said to reassure Amy.

"Good. I could use some good news. How far-"

Amy was cut short as they both heard the sounds of panting and footsteps pounding across the grass fields. Ahead, four ravenous Hellion were charging through the sparse trees in their direction from the east, their claws tearing up dirt and grass.

"Run!" Bowie shouted as he broke into a sprint, dashing along the trail headed north. Amy didn't miss a moment and rushed after him. There was enough distance between them that the Hellion had to swing around to change their direction.

Bowie and Amy ran for all they were worth but the Hellion were rapidly closing the distance. Bowie knew that if the Hellion caught them there was little chance they'd survive. They had to keep them to one side. If they got surrounded, they were done for. He saw some stone benches up ahead just off the path. He didn't have time to look behind to see where Amy was, but hoped she saw what he was going to do. With a great leap he cleared the stone bench and landed, still running. Pain shot through his leg and he let out a groan through clenched teeth as he sped on.

Amy was close behind. She could hear the ravenous breath of a Hellion close on her heels. The creature reached out to tear at her back but she jumped just in time to clear the bench. The Hellion crashed right into it, flipping over the top and smashing its face hard into the ground. The other Hellion trampled right over the top of it in hot pursuit.

Bowie reached another set of stone benches and tried the same thing with Amy right behind but the Hellion were ready for it and dodged around the benches, coming up alongside their quarry.

Up ahead was a round wading pool that was normally surrounded by chain link. The fence was gone and the water dark and putrid with rotting leaves and a foul stench. Bowie tried to buy himself some time by running along the water's edge as close as he could to force his pursuers to go around. But the Hellion ignored the pool and vaulted over its edge to the other side, bowling into Bowie and sending him crashing to the ground. He struggled frantically to get up but the other two Hellion closed in on him.

For an instant he glimpsed Amy behind the creatures, a horrified stare on her face, frozen. In that moment there was no time to think, no time to act. The only thing Bowie could do was scream, "RUN!!!"

When Bowie had cleared the second set of benches, Amy had veered left to split the pack between herself and Bowie but the Hellion chased after him instead and ignored her. By the time she turned to look over her shoulder it was too late. He was on the ground and the Hellion were descending on him like jackals. He reached toward her and screamed. She didn't hear his words, only saw the motion of his lips. It took a moment to register what he'd said before she ran as fast as she could. She had to escape. Soon she heard snarling behind her but from the wrong direction.

The Hellion that had tripped over the stone bench and been trampled had recovered. While its companions attacked Bowie, it focused on her with renewed vigor.

The Hellion was too fast. It would overtake her in just a few seconds, so Amy ran for the only thing she could see that might protect her.

In front of her was the playground Grady Park was famous for. The massive, bark-lined pit boasted large concrete and wooden forms to create forts, tunnels and all sorts of diversions for the amusement of children. In Otherside it was warped and twisted into a massive tangle of distorted, split-wood pieces amid floating concrete chunks in odd and mangled shapes.

She ran for all she was worth, ducking under stone and timbers, dragging her knees over bark, putting as much mass between her and the creature as she could. The Hellion snapped and bit at her heals, just inches away, scrambling through the jungle of mutilated playground.

It reached out and grabbed Amy by the ankle as she moved deeper in. She let out a cry and pulled away as hard as she could. The tight grip ripped her shoe from her foot and she fell forward into a corner where the cement made a wall on three sides beyond a cross-work of broken logs. The space was tight and Amy pressed herself against the wall to avoid the snatching claws of the Hellion. When it reached in, pushing its shoulder through to reach further, she lashed out with her machete and scored a long slice down its forearm. The Hellion shrieked in pain as it withdrew, trying with its other arm to reach her.

"Back off!" She screamed at the creature as it swiped at her again. This time she clipped the fingers from its clawed hand.

It shrieked in agony, spitting and crying out, its eyes filled with rage as it snarled and snapped, clutching its arms and dismembered hand against its grotesque body. It withdrew a few feet, black blood drizzling from its wounds as it paced back and forth deciding what to do next.

Come on, Amy thought angrily, *just try to get through so I can cut your head off.*

Then, to her surprise, it spoke, its voice filled with vehemence. "You can't stay in there forever. Eventually you'll have to leave, and when you do, I will come for you!"

Needles of ice ran up her spine as it spoke and Amy said nothing. She just kept her weapon ready and pushed herself against the concrete.

It looked back over its shoulder and then returned its gaze to her, smiling viciously. "No matter. We've got ourselves a better prize."

Amy peered past the Hellion through a gap in the tangled playground. Bowie was thrashing around wildly as the Hellion battered and struck at him, pinning him down in the wading pool.

"Bowie!" She cried out.

In a few seconds, Bowie disappeared beneath the surface of the shallow pool. He was under for several moments. She was almost relieved when one of the Hellion grabbed him by the leg and pulled him out. The monster left the pool and continued over the grass dragging his limp body along by the leg as the other Hellion followed close behind, laughing and grinning.

"So, you see, you worthless bitch? Your time will come." The Hellion sneered and left, a black trail of fluid trickling behind it.

After they were out of sight, Amy collapsed in her concrete hollow, numb tears rolling down her cheeks.

XVI

She didn't know how long she sat there, clutching her machete. It seemed like hours. When her tears dried, she wondered to herself if time passed at the same rate in Otherside as in her own world. She tried to focus her thoughts on things like this as much as she could to keep what she'd seen from passing before her eyes over and over again. Eventually, when she could no longer occupy her mind with speculation, the images flooded through her again. She tried to be strong, but the stark reality seemed to her an impossible nightmare. She was alone. She tried to tell herself that Bowie was still alive, that the Hellion hadn't killed him, but that hope was dangling by a thread and it was a struggle for her to keep that thread from snapping in her mind.

They'd knocked him unconscious, possibly drowned him and dragged him away. She could not help but wonder why. They ate the Eidolon. Would they eat him too? Were they taking his body away to feast upon it later? The thought sent chills down her spine. However, she knew she wasn't going to get anywhere trying to figure out what happened to him. Whatever the Hellion were going to do to him, it wasn't good.

"Pull yourself together." She told herself. "Come on, Amy."

Drowning in her own despair wasn't going to accomplish anything. If Bowie was alive, she was the only one who could help him. But there was no way she'd be able to save him on her own. She was impossibly outmatched against the Hellion. If it was just her against one of them maybe she would stand a chance but there were at least four of them, maybe more wherever they were going. If she waded in to that den of jackals she'd be torn to pieces. She needed help.

Amy took a deep breath and pushed herself up from the ground. She weaved her way free of the tangled playground and stood out in the cold open air. The federal building was just two blocks away. She had to make it there, she resolved. "One step at a time."

She breathed in and took her first step. Then another and another. Before she knew it, the federal building stood clearly in front of her, rising high above the surrounding structures. She could see the concrete barricades and the signs of a great struggle all around her. The footing was difficult and she did her best to avoid the black puddles splattered over the ground. When she finally reached the front entrance, she looked around, unsure what to do next.

The stone door to the fortress was shut tight and there was no one in sight. The area was quiet and empty. The cold air bit against her skin as Amy listened for anything that might indicate the presence of one of the Effigies Bowie had told her about. She smirked as she thought to herself that maybe she should knock. After all, it was a door.

She shrugged and lifted a hand to rap her knuckles against the stone. Her knuckles missed by a hairsbreadth as the door opened suddenly. On the other side stood a figure that at once she felt she knew yet didn't recognize. She was beautiful and fierce, with eyes like an eagle, sharp and unyielding. Her features were graceful, yet they held a hard quality. Crystalline hair flowed elegantly down to her neck, save for a few chips and cracks. Amy didn't recognize her face right away, but there was no mistaking the small scar through her eyebrow.

She stepped back a pace as Varela spoke, her voice sharp. "Come inside."

Amy didn't question her and followed through the fortress doors. She found the interior both familiar and disturbing, just as Bowie had at first. She noted the differences in the architecture, which were few, as she walked through the hallways and up the stairs. Varela led her past a set of double doors to a room in the corner next to a fire exit. The door was in place just as it should have been but Amy noticed that there was no knob. The door swung open freely and beyond the small chamber was sparsely decorated with furniture made more for functionality than decoration. The walls were decked with feathers and tapestries unbefitting the stark, business-like decor of the rest of the building.

"Strange." Amy said as she entered.

"What?" Her counterpart asked.

"Oh. Sorry. No, it's fine. I was just thinking how odd this room is compared to the rest of the building."

"Is there a problem?" Varela asked, her expression serious.

Amy waved her hands in protest. "No, no. It's fine. Actually, what I meant was that it's different from everything but it feels kind of... I don't know..." She thought about it for a moment. "It feels like if I had these things this is how I would decorate too. It's weird."

Varela nodded in agreement. "You and I are perhaps more alike than you might think."

Amy shrugged and wrapped her arms around herself, not sure of what to say next.

"I know this is all pretty strange but I know you quite well. I could tell the instant you came to Otherside. What are you doing here? You couldn't have come here on your own."

"I didn't. I came here with Bowie." Amy explained.

Varela nodded. "I wondered. Arsen's counterpart is certainly bold."

"We came here to try to rescue his boss."

"His boss?"

Amy sighed. "He's this total douche-stick named Vic. We decided we had to save him, even though he doesn't really deserve it. One of those things got him in our world. The Hellion?"

"The Hellion?" Varela said, alarmed.

"Yeah. They showed up and one came to the warehouse and took him." The look on Varela's face made Amy uneasy. "What?"

"The Hellion keep to Otherside. They've never known of or had any reason to go to your realm. When we fought those two in your world, that was the first time we'd ever heard of one manifesting there. Come," she ordered. "We need to inform the others about what happened." Varela made to leave.

"Hold on." Amy insisted. "I need... I just need to sit down for a while. There's too much going on."

Varela nodded and offered Amy the only chair in the room. Once she was seated Varela took a seat on the bed. "What happened? You're troubled."

"You really get straight to the point, don't you?" Amy noted.

"We don't have the luxury of beating around the bush. This war has been going on far too long for that."

Amy explained as best she could what had happened since they'd arrived. She told Varela about the Hellion and about Bowie, recounting the events at the wading pool. It was hard for her, but she got through it.

When her story was over, Varela nodded and said, "It sounds like we need to form a search party and track the Hellion to wherever they took him."

"Do you think he's still alive?" Amy asked.

"Yes." Varela said with certainty. "If they wanted to kill him, they would have. The Hellion are cunning and devious. They wanted him alive, for whatever reason. That gives us some time."

Amy took in a deep breath and tried to calm her nerves. She noticed Varela staring at her and couldn't help but acknowledge the Effigy's calm demeanor. "How do you do it?" She asked her counterpart.

"Do what?" Varela answered.

"This. You're so calm and in control. I don't get it. How can you be so strong through all of this?"

Varela was caught off guard and a little surprised at the question. "I don't understand. What don't you get?"

It was Amy's turn to be confused. "What do you mean?"

Varela stood up and walked over to Amy, placing a hand on her shoulder. "Otherside is a reflection of your world. I cannot be anything other than you, even if we don't exactly look the same. If you see strength in me, you are only seeing it in yourself."

"What? No. That's not... I am not strong. I'm a freaking mess. I mean, look at me!" She insisted.

Varela shook her head. "And yet you are here. You risked your life in coming here. You did what you had to in order to get past the Hellion and when you were faced with a moral choice you chose to do what few others would and came here in spite of the risk." Her hand gripped Amy's shoulder firmly as she looked her counterpart in the eye. "You have strength. The sooner you realize it, the better."

The Effigy's words were hard but truthful. Amy wasn't sure she was right but she could sense confidence in her counterpart and for the time being it was enough.

"So, are you ready to tell the others? The longer we wait, the longer your friend will be in danger."

Amy swallowed her misgivings and nodded. "Yeah… Yeah, let's go."

They left the room and continued through the fortress to find the others. As they passed through the halls Amy peered in an open doorway and caught a glimpse of the strange old man who had helped her and Bowie during their fight with Mouth. He appeared to be tinkering with his grinding organ on a table in the dim glow of candle light. She nearly stopped to investigate but when she saw that Varela was already halfway down the hall, she quickly caught up with her escort and asked if they could go back to speak to the old man.

"That crazy old man? No. We shouldn't disturb him." Varela said shortly. "He's been through quite a lot in the last few days. The Hellion have grown bold and he's been protecting the gates in Arsen's absence."

"Arsen. That's Bowie's Effigy, isn't it?" Amy asked.

"Yes."

"I'm sorry. This all seems really weird still."

"Why are you apologizing?" Varela asked. "Most of your kind don't even know we exist. No one expects this to come naturally to you. In here." She ducked through a doorway into a long room where numerous Effigies gathered.

The Effigies were all shapes and sizes, and many of them seemed vaguely familiar to one degree or another, though Amy could not say why. There were at least a dozen and not one of them looked the same as another, save for the tribal robes each wore.

They were standing over a large table with maps drawn out over the surface. At one end of the table a wooden carving of the federal building stood, though its top had been shaped like that of a Native American eagle totem. At the other end of the map a bronze dagger had been stuck. Charcoal had been marked in X's in places and a few areas were circled with red.

When Amy entered, a few directed their attention her way, though many discussed things among themselves while pointing and peering at the map. She immediately caught the attention of one Effigy in particular who approached her and introduced himself.

"Welcome. We are glad you are safe. My name is Reuel. Please, do not be shy. We have a lot to discuss."

Amy held out a hand and Reuel happily shook it.

"She didn't come alone." Varela informed him. "The one from before is here as well, though he's been taken by the enemy."

Reuel's expression was grave but he tried to smile to lighten the tension. "Don't worry. We won't let them keep him for long."

"Do you remember which direction they headed?" Varela asked Amy.

"I think so." Amy gave it some serious thought. "I can probably show you. He wasn't taken far from here."

"How long ago was it?" Reuel asked.

She struggled to answer. "I don't... I'm not sure. Maybe an hour? I can't... I didn't-"

Varela cut in on her behalf. "She's still shaken up by it. I don't think it was long ago."

"Then there could still be a trail to follow. We'll have to move quickly."

One of the other Effigies cut in, a male with sharp features and a crystalline goatee pointing down from his chin wickedly. "Do you think this might be our chance?"

Reuel rubbed his shoulder absently with his hand. "I hope so but our top priority should be a rescue."

"Chance for what?" Amy asked.

Some of the other Effigies cut into the conversation as well.

"If we're going on another expedition, we need to formulate a plan. We can't afford another surprise ambush," said one.

"We need to move now," said another, "before the lad is killed. Weren't you listening? They've taken one of the humans."

"We can't go off on these kinds of expeditions!" Said a third, "the last attack took a heavy toll. We need to concentrate our efforts on defending the tower!"

The conversation quickly grew out of hand and soon there were half a dozen voices bickering back and forth about what needed to be done next. Civil conversation gave way to chaos as more and more they argued and soon they were shouting at one another.

Receding into the background, Amy tried hard to shut out the voices. She had no idea what they were so upset about and the more she listened, the less sense it made. One man spoke up about the impending war while another shouted him down, a woman with wild-looking hair insisted that they needed to abandon the tower before it was too late, and someone else began to panic about the state of the fortifications. Their voices raised to such a fevered pitch that for a moment Amy was certain violence would erupt.

Suddenly, Reuel let out an unearthly bellow that shook the very room. "SILENCE!"

The room went still, the effigies frozen in place, staring in disbelief at his outburst.

"Quiet down." He continued, "we are not going to accomplish anything by arguing. We all have a lot going on but we need to focus on what is most important. Now," he paused for a moment to let that sink in, "there is a human in our world who has been captured. His life is in our hands. We are all well aware that we cannot afford to send out a full rescue party." He looked around at all present, not sure if they fully understood the importance of the situation. "This human is Arsen's counterpart and if the human dies, so does Arsen."

The other Effigies shifted uncomfortably. "The Hellion have retreated for the night. This is our best opportunity to make our move. We have until the sun rises to find Bowie and bring him back."

"You said it yourself," an Effigy with a wide face and short crystalline hair cut in, "we cannot afford to lessen our defenses. The Hellion attacks have grown more aggressive and it has been days since we've had relief. When the Hellion return, we need to be ready for them!"

"We will be ready for them." Reuel cut him off before he could continue. "That's why we're only going to send a few. Varela will take two volunteers to locate the human and bring him home."

"That's too many!" The short haired Effigy insisted. "We cannot-"

"We cannot win a defensive war!" Reuel bellowed at an impossible volume.

The room went silent.

The gravity of his words hit home and it was clear by their faces that it was on everyone's minds. For a moment, Reuel almost regretted what he'd said, but now that he had said it the room had changed. Those who were arguing looked to one another in understanding

"We are going to rescue the human," he said looking about the room, "that's what separates us from them. Now, I need two volunteers."

No one stepped forward immediately. They shuffled uncomfortably, some still unsure of the wisdom of his plan. Reuel was about to pick someone on his own when a couple of Effigies stepped forward.

"We'll bring him back." The first one said. He was a shorter effigy with close cut hair and Hispanic features.

The second one, a woman in her late forties with an athletic frame, agreed. "We'll be back before the sun rises."

Reuel nodded his approval, feeling somewhat relieved. "See to it that you do. I don't want any casualties out there. Watch each other's backs and play it safe, alright?"

They gave him a nod and stepped out of the room with Varela. Some of the others, mostly those who had opposed the rescue attempt, stepped out of the room as well to hold more private conversations in other areas of the fortress.

Glad to finally have an opportunity to speak with him, Amy pulled Reuel aside and asked "I thought you guys were supposed to be the best part of humanity. What just happened?"

Reuel didn't understand. "What do you mean?"

"That. All the shouting and arguing. Nobody wanting to help. Aren't Effigies supposed to be good people?"

He laughed a little. "We may be Effigies but we aren't perfect. Just because we try to do the right thing doesn't mean we always agree. Everyone here is trying to do what they think is the right. Some of the others are concerned that we could lose the fortress and that is of paramount importance for our survival. However, we also have an obligation to help those in need. This is one of those times when the right answer isn't simple. I just hope three will be enough to save your friend."

Amy hoped it would be enough too. "I appreciate that. Thank you."

"Don't mention it," Reuel shrugged with a smile. "He's my friend too."

"Do you know him?" She asked.

He took her gently by the shoulder to guide her out the door to meet with Varela. "We fought the Hellion together the last time he was here. I would count him as a friend any day."

Amy was reminded of something. "I have to ask. I've been wondering. Where is Arsen? It seems like everyone is worried that he's gone."

Reuel's expression became more serious and he lost himself in thought for a moment before he gave her an answer. "Arsen left the fortress several days ago. He didn't tell anyone why, though I think he might have decided to try to find one of the Hellion nests on his own. You probably saw the map in there. We've been trying to pinpoint their nests so we can make a counterattack but they've been attacking us so frequently we haven't had much time to fortify our own defenses, let alone search the area."

"If he were here to help them would it make that much of a difference?" She asked.

He nodded, "Arsen is different. He's got a fire in his soul that won't stop burning, you know? Everyone has their own abilities, their own talents and skills. Varela is an incredible archer, for example." Reuel gestured toward Amy's counterpart just down the hallway. "Some of us even have abilities beyond physical skills, like Halloran."

"You mean that weird organ thing?" She remembered how Hal had used it at the sewage plant.

"Exactly." He continued, "Arsen can wield flames as easily as you and I breathe. His abilities make him a strong presence on the battlefield and allow him to hold off the Hellion far better than most of us can. With him gone, we all have to shoulder more to defend this place. Do you understand?"

She nodded. "I think so. This is all still really weird to me. But I think I get it."

He gave her a reassuring hug around the shoulders. "Good. I am glad to hear it."

When he let go, she asked curiously, "So, what kind of ability do you have?"

"Hah!" He laughed. "You certainly ask a lot of questions."

She smiled back, "what can I say? I'm just curious. So? What can you do? What is your gift?"

He looked a little embarrassed and then gave Amy a mischievous look. "I'm sure you'll figure it out."

She gave him a look and sighed. "Alright, fine." She conceded.

"Are you ready to go?" Varela called from down the hall.

Amy took in a deep breath to summon her courage. "Wish us luck." She told Reuel. "And thank you."

"You're welcome." He replied. "Bring your friend home. For both of us."

Amy smiled and left Reuel to join Varela and the others. She turned to look back at him as they left down the stairwell and waved goodbye.

Varela and her squad set out into the night at a rapid pace with Amy in the lead. She led them to the rancid wading pool and from there they fanned out in the direction that Bowie had been dragged away. It wasn't long before Varela found a trail through the grass.

"Over here. There's blood." She motioned for the others to join her. "We need to move quickly. Grayden, I want you to keep a lookout behind us. Luaine, I need you to watch our flanks."

The two effigies nodded and took up their positions.

"And Amy," Varela added, "I need you to stay close to me. If we get into trouble it will be better if we stick together."

Amy didn't like being given orders but under the circumstances she was relieved to have someone looking out for her. She noted that Luaine carried a spear with a bronze tip and elegant carvings along the wooden handle, and the short Effigy, Grayden, sported a pair of bronze swords sheathed at his hips. Amy hoped that they wouldn't need them. She did her best to keep up her courage as she followed along.

They moved quickly through the park until they reached the streets. From there it was a fair while before Varela was able to establish another trail to follow.

"It's difficult to follow but they were definitely headed in this direction. My guess is they headed south over the river. There's a bridge in that direction." Varela pointed. "Come. Follow me."

Varela took off down the road and the others followed close behind. By the time they reached the underpass and the bridge beyond Amy was out of breath.

Varela reduced her speed. "Let's slow down for a little bit."

Amy thought for a moment she could sense a connection with her Effigy, as though Varela knew she was tired without needing to look. She also got the feeling that Varela was equally aware of her anxiety as she looked down the way at the black smear on the concrete barrier at the side of the road where the Eidolon had been devoured before.

Amy caught up with Varela and walked beside her while the other two kept pace behind. She didn't say anything but her mind was swimming with questions.

"Don't worry." Varela said quietly. "I won't tell them what happened here."

Amy couldn't help but look at her other self with surprise. There was so much she wanted to say but even then, she thought maybe she didn't need to.

"That knife stuck in the map back at the federal building, wasn't it in this direction?"

Varela nodded. "It's over that way." She pointed.

"Is it marking something?"

"It marks a rough location for a known nest. We think they may have other nests scattered throughout the city but we've never been able to confirm it."

"Oh. Okay. I kind of wondered if someone had just stuck it in the map for dramatic effect, you know?" Amy said with a half-smile.

It was Varela's turn to look a little surprised. She thought on it for a little while before she said anything. "You know, now that you mention it, I think it was a little bit of both."

They laughed together.

"When we discovered it, Reuel, Arsen and I had to fight our way out of one hell of a mess. We ran almost the entire way back. The council had denied up until then that there was an organized concentration of Hellion, let alone a base of operations. I remember bursting into that council chamber with Reuel in the lead, the biggest stupid grin on his face. He walked right up to that table while they all stood around bickering about one thing or another, stuck that knife right there and the whole room went silent. You should have seen the look on everyone's face. I'll never forget it. If I remember right, I think he said something like 'There! That's where they are. Now, don't tell me we can't strike back.' It was amazing." Varela said, still remembering like it had happened that day.

"That's awesome. He seems like a pretty good guy." Amy smiled.

Varela smirked. "He has his days."

"What about Arsen? What's he like?" Amy asked.

Varela looked off to the right, toward the graffiti where the Hellion had gathered before. She had a look of concern but she answered, "He's different than he used to be. A long time ago he was full of life, eager and rebellious. Then he started getting all weird and kept to himself more and more. Now he's... well, he's different. I don't know. You've met his counterpart. I suspect they are similar in a way, but then again, it's hard for us to really tell, you know?"

"Yeah. I guess that's true. I just wish I knew him better."

"Once we get across the bridge, we'll need to re-establish a trail." Varela said, changing the subject. "We don't know how the Hellion operate but I think I know where they might be going."

"Where?" Amy asked. Varela gave her a look and in the pit of her stomach she knew what Varela was going to say. "We're trying to find one of their nests, aren't we?" Amy asked.

Varela nodded.

"I wonder..." Amy trailed off.

"What is it?" Varela asked.

"I just... it's nothing. I was just thinking about the nests." Amy said, second guessing herself.

"Should we spread out until we can find a trail?" Luaine called out from behind.

"Yes. I think that might be the best idea. It's pretty open out here." Varela noted. "Just make sure we keep sight of each other."

"Understood." Luaine said.

Before they spread out, Amy took a moment to ask a question that had been burning in her mind since she'd met them. "I was wondering. Are you guys aware of your own counterparts? In the real world, I mean. Like, do you know what they are doing or can you see them or something?"

Varela rolled her eyes and didn't answer. Luaine laughed a little, shaking her head.

"It's not like that." Said Grayden. "We're connected, but it's like being connected by a string that's always behind you. You can feel something tugging or pulling, but you can't hear or see it. I can feel something right now but it's vague. Like... well. Hah. Right now, I'm feeling alert and anxious but my counterpart is probably giving a speech or something. I think he's anxious too, but also a little authoritarian. It's hard to explain."

Amy found that curious. "And what about you?" She asked Luaine.

"I don't know. My counterpart... she's struggling with something but she's focused and determined. I'm actually kind of glad. It's a good feeling to have, doing what we're doing right now. Your friend is in good hands."

Amy felt somewhat relieved to hear it. She was about to ask the Effigies how many times they'd fought the Hellion when they reached the other side of the bridge and Varela cut her off.

"Alright. Fan out. Look for drag marks on the side of the road or Hellion footprints."

Amy kept close as they scoured the ground for signs of the Hellion. Down the road she came across peculiar marks on the ground by an off-ramp and a patch of spiny bushes. It looked like someone had taken a pitchfork and scraped it along the gravel, leaving deep gouges. "Hey!" She shouted. "I think I found something!"

Luaine and Grayden joined her and took a look. "Claws you think?" Luaine remarked.

Varela nodded. "Look over there," she said pointing ahead up the slope. Where the off-ramp merged with the streets a scorch mark swept up and over the edge of the asphalt. "Come on." She moved over to the scorches and noted more signs along the ground. "There's scorch marks all over here. If I had to guess I would say that Arsen was fighting someone. Recently at that. Look." She pointed over to a patch of scrub. Beneath the burnt foliage scattered embers still glowed. "He must have run across Hellion here. There's a chance he might have seen your friend."

Amy felt somewhat relieved. If Arsen had come across Bowie, maybe he had already rescued him. She was about to ask Varela if she could see any more tracks that might help them locate Bowie or Arsen when she heard the skittering of gravel from the other side of the street.

"Hellion." Varela warned as two of the inhuman creatures stalked out from the trees. She nocked an arrow and took aim as Luaine and Grayden took up position on each side of her and Amy. Amy drew her nailgun from her pack and kept her machete in the other. "Up the hill. Move. Don't let them flank us." Varela commanded.

They moved together as the Hellion closed in, carefully studying their movement.

The Hellion were careful to stay just far enough away that Varela would have a hard time scoring a hit with her bow but close enough to force the Effigies to move in order to keep their distance.

"They're not usually out this time of night. Be on your guard. They're up to something."

Soon, Varela and her companions had crossed over the road and were coming to an overpass. On either side, the slope up to the road was too severe to climb. The Hellion moved in tandem, herding them beneath the concrete underpass. Varela snarled and shouted angrily. "Fall back, Luaine!"

Luaine had strayed closer to one of the Hellion, eager to protect her companions. The creature saw its opportunity and charged, keeping Luaine between itself and Varela.

Amy's Effigy saw the move and dashed to the side to get a clear shot but Luaine also sidestepped at the same time, changing the Hellion's angle of attack. Everything happened in a blur. Luaine thrust out with her spear at the creature just as it leaped past her and turned sideways to avoid the blow. Mid-flight, it reached out with its thin, ropy arm, grabbed Luaine by the neck, using its grip to swing itself around the Effigy, tearing her neck in the process.

Varela fired an arrow and let out a forceful shout. The projectile burst from the bow as though from a cannon with a resounding boom that echoed across the asphalt. The arrow pierced the Hellion's jaw clean through but did little to stop its advance. It let go of Luaine and sprang toward Amy who was completely unprepared for the sudden attack. As it smiled wickedly and reached forward to impale her, a massive downward force brought it crashing down to the ground just inches from Amy.

Grayden's swords let out a brilliant arc of light as he cleaved its head from its shoulders. He met Amy's surprised gaze briefly as the creature perished, a big smile on his face.

"Grayden, no!" Varela cried out.

It was too late. Grayden had exposed his back to the remaining Hellion. He spun with his leading arm, sword in hand, to strike the other Hellion but his attack missed. The Hellion was upon him like a ravenous wolf, ripping and tearing in a frenzy.

Varela nocked another arrow and took aim when Amy screamed, "Behind us!"

Two more Hellion dropped down from the above on the other side of the overpass, blocking any chance of escape. Amy panicked and held down the trigger as she aimed in their direction. Nails flew rapidly from the weapon as she unloaded the nail clip. The Hellion were surprised but split apart to avoid the volley. Amy tracked one of them to the left with the gun but her shots went wide. She couldn't help but keep shooting and didn't let go of the trigger until the ammunition was spent.

Varela immediately stepped back and placed herself between Amy and the other Hellion. Amy kept her back close to her counterpart, facing the third Hellion that was quickly devouring Grayden's corpse. The Hellion stared at her intently as it continued its meal. She had only brought the one clip of nails. She dropped her gun, feeling powerless. All she had was her machete.

The enemy encircled them, watching Varela warily. Varela aimed her bow at one, then the other, constantly switching targets as they eagerly awaited her shot. They were toying with her. The instant she let the arrow fly they would set upon her. She might be able to take out one of them but there would be no time to fend off the second one... and the Hellion knew it. Meanwhile, the third Hellion could continue feasting.

"We're outnumbered." Varela said quietly over her shoulder to Amy.

"What are we going to do?" Amy asked, doing her best not to vomit from the sight of the devouring creature.

"I trust you. Will you trust me?" Varela asked.

"What do you need me to do?" Amy asked, dreading her companion's reply.

"I'm going to shoot. When that happens, they're going to attack."

Amy glanced quickly over her shoulder to the other two Hellion, then back. It only took her a moment to realize what was going to happen. Varela was going to pick a target and fire. When that happened, the other Hellion would charge. She was taking a gamble that the last Hellion would be too busy eating to join the attack and was putting her faith in Amy to fend off the charging Hellion.

"Can you do it?" Varela asked, still keeping her bow trained on the Hellion as they slowly crept closer.

Amy's faith wavered and she swallowed. That brief moment seemed to stretch out before her into eternity. Was she strong enough?

"Can you do it?" Varela hissed.

Amy whispered.

"Yes."

XVII

The cold sensation of stone against flesh brought Bowie's mind from the dark of unconsciousness. He groaned immediately from the pain pulsing with each heartbeat. His body ached in countless places. The pain was more than enough to keep him on the ground as he allowed his vision to adjust to the dull glow of his surroundings.

He was in a room maybe the size of his apartment with little there but himself and the smears of blood he'd left on the ground. There was a door at one end, solid stone, with slips of light filtering through the gap beneath. After his mind caught up with the pain and he could gather his thoughts, he remembered what had happened. He remembered the filthy pool and the Hellion and Amy and the whole nightmare. He was... he was alive? It didn't make sense to him. He should be dead. Why would the Hellion keep him alive?

The stone floor was polished and slick with moisture and it took a bit of work to push himself upright. He only managed to prop himself up at an angle before his breath grew thin and he had to catch his wind. After just a moment in that position he longed for the cool floor. Sure, it felt like needles against his skin but the throbbing pain wasn't nearly as bad when he was lying down. He felt swollen in half a dozen places. With a groan he pushed himself up further until he was in a sitting position. The movement made his head spin and he struggled to keep his stomach down. It took some time but with a force of will he got himself upright and stood there, teetering, breathing heavily.

"Breathe," he told himself, "just breathe." It took a while but eventually his nausea subsided.

He took stock of his injuries, careful not to touch them and tenderly lifted his shirt to see the damage. They had beaten him severely. In the dull light he could see only dark blotches of skin like a patchwork across his torso. He cursed and put his shirt down.

Though it hurt to move, Bowie made slow, careful steps toward the door. He had to figure out where he was. The stone door was shut tight. He felt around its surface, looking for a latch or a handle or anything to help him open it. That's when he remembered the flashlight he'd put in his coat pocket. It was still there. He took it out, praying it still worked after his fall in the water. The beam flared to life and he got a good look at the door. The door was indeed solid stone, probably several inches thick. Claw marks scored its surface in savage, desperate patterns as though at some point numerous creatures had tried to escape. There was a hole bored into the stone where a knob should have been.

He leaned his back against the door to steady himself and surveyed the rest of the room.

Bowie went pale.

Countless circles were etched into the floor in patterns and arrays surrounding the bare spot where he'd lain just minutes before. Strange yet aggressive runes were carved among them that made Bowie afraid to even guess the purpose of the room. While he found these things unsettling, they paled next to the smears of black gore along the corners and the walls.

Bowie's pulse raced.

Wherever he'd ended up, he needed to get out as fast as he could. The Hellion had put him here for a reason and he wasn't about to sit around waiting to find out what that was. Kneeling down to peer through the hole in the door, he discovered a mechanism inside, dimly lit by the orange glow from the outside. Not sure quite how it worked, he pushed his weight against the door hard. The bits of brass inside jerked slightly. Bowie was sure it held the door in place but he couldn't figure out how to open it. He stuck his fingers inside and tried to manipulate the pieces. They wouldn't move.

"Damnit." He muttered as he turned and leaned against the door again to give himself a moment of rest. He had to think. He wondered what had become of his things. The knife was gone. He looked about the room for his backpack but there was nothing. He had his flashlight but it had been in his pocket. Curiously, he fished around in his other pockets to see what else had managed to stay on his person. He found his wallet and his keys, which weren't going to be of much use. Then he felt something hard on the inside of his jacket and dug his hand into the inner pocket. He hadn't remembered packing anything in his jacket except for the flashlight. When he wrapped his fingers around it, his heart leaped.

"Yes!" He whispered. He took the multi-tool pliers out of his pocked and bounced them in his hand a bit. He had stuffed them in his pocket and forgotten about them. They were still in good working order. The knife on the tool wasn't terribly big but it would do in a pinch if he needed a weapon. However, he was more concerned with the pliers. He flicked them open and knelt down with the flashlight to get a better look at the door mechanism. Gripping one of the pins with the pliers he tried to tug it to the left. It didn't move so he put more effort into it, leaning his body to give it more force. The pliers slipped and jammed against the side of the hole.

Bowie looked into the hole, hoping to find that he'd succeeded in moving the pin at least a little bit. What he found was that the pin had been sheared clean through and drops of slag speckled the inside of the hole.

"What the..." He wondered. He looked at his pliers, then again at the mechanism. He took hold of the remainder of the pin with his pliers and tried pulling again, this time the mechanism turned and the door unlatched.

"Yes!" He whispered as he pushed hard and the door gave way. It swung open with a grinding groan, opening up into a hallway of dark stone, dimly lit by torches to either side of the door.

Bowie peered out into the hall to see if anyone was watching but for the moment, he seemed to be alone. As he carefully ventured into the hall, he noticed that the torches were some kind of bone, sharpened at the bottom, with a strange, thorny cage holding an open vessel of burning oil. It made him kind of glad that he had his flashlight. Bowie made sure to twist the end of the flashlight to narrow the beam, figuring it would give him a better chance of going unnoticed if he wasn't shooting a wide beam of light everywhere.

Lacking any clue as to where he was or where he was going, Bowie picked a direction and started moving. He crept through several hallways, carefully listening for approaching footsteps, but he encountered no one. He noted that the walls were dark cut stone, unlike anything in the modern world. It was as if he were walking through the catacombs of some ancient necropolis, only he saw no bodies, just carved out hollows and cramped corridors, lined by doors that were missing handles that led to chambers he dared not explore. He had no idea what purpose this place held but he knew it couldn't be good. He found a stair carved into the stone and went up a flight of steps to more hallways and even more steps. He hadn't seen any windows or exits which gave him the distinct impression he might be underground somewhere. After a while, he began to wonder just how far down he was.

When he saw a bright light from up ahead, Bowie got excited. He thought for a moment that it might be an exit, so he moved quickly down the corridor to the corner where it veered left and stopped abruptly, stifling his breath.

He heard footsteps clicking and scraping down the hall, heading in his direction. He flicked off his flashlight and looked around for any place he could hide. There was a door just across from him down the hall a few paces so he moved as quickly and quietly as he could and tried to push it open. To his surprise, it gave way, though it groaned deeply against stone. He hoped it was quiet enough that whoever was approaching hadn't heard. He slipped inside and pushed the door closed, pressing his back against the wall and keeping as still and silent as he could. He kept his eye on the orange glow coming from the hole where the handle should have been as he flipped the knife out of the multi-tool. He closed his eyes for a moment and prayed he wouldn't have to use it. If he got attacked by the Hellion, a knife that big would be next to useless against them.

Clawed footsteps grew closer. He could hear two distinct sets of steps and could tell they were walking on all fours, like wolves. Big, nasty, hell-spawn wolves. They turned in his direction and moved closer.

Bowie held his breath and froze.

They moved closer and closer, just outside the door now.

Pass by. Bowie prayed. *Just pass by.*

They stopped.

Bowie listened.

He heard one of them sniff the air, searching for his scent. There was a low growl. Another snort of air. Claws softly scratched at the door.

Bowie gripped his weapon, ready to thrust it when the door opened.

It went quiet.

Suddenly claws scraped furiously against stone and raced down the hallway away from his chamber, further in through the tunnels from where he had come, leaving Bowie alone in the dark room.

Bowie exhaled.

They had to have smelled him. He knew it in his gut. But they had left in a hurry. He couldn't stay where he was. He had to keep moving. He managed to pry the door open again and continued moving through the corridors. The light he'd seen around the corner proved to be a large room where numerous corridors intersected, lit by dozens of dripping torches.

Circles were scrawled on the stone chamber floor, some making rings around others and some in unusual places, creating a massive array of carvings.

Bowie looked down each of the tunnels, hoping for anything that would indicate how to get out of there. When his foot set down in the center-most ring, he stopped. He suddenly found himself looking to his right down one of the corridors. There was nothing special about it, but it seemed to call out to him. He found it unnerving but he moved in that direction all the same. With each step he felt the pull grow stronger and stronger. It was as though he was being drawn toward something.

He took turns down winding halls and past doors and alcoves and kept on moving, faster and faster. Though it hurt, he started running, the stone whipping by in a blur until at last he burst into an open room and stopped.

Laying discarded in a heap against the side of the chamber was a human corpse. Dressed in worn jeans and a disheveled, drab, collared shirt, was a man long dead.

His features, dry and hollow, his hair little more than short wisps dangling lightly against his scalp.

Bowie approached the body slowly, wondering what a human corpse was doing in Otherside. As far as he knew he and Amy and now Victor were the only ones who had come to Otherside. As he leaned over the body to get a better look, he remembered that Halloran had told him he was the first visitor in a while. Which meant that Hal knew there had been someone else.

He knelt down and turned the body to get a better look at its face. The body was light and turned over easily. A brief glint caught Bowie's eye as the body flopped to the side. A pair of dog tags peeked through beneath the drab shirt and caught the light. Curiously, Bowie picked up the tags and shined his flashlight to get a better look.

The inscription read:

SWIFT
ARCHER D
218 39 3798
A POS
CATHOLIC

Bowie dropped the tags and backed away from the body. "The hell?" His mind raced with confusion. It was his grandfather! He almost couldn't process it. What was his body doing in Otherside?!

"It's no accident."

The voice from behind him made Bowie jump and spin around. His flashlight landed on the smiling face of the Hellion called Mouth. His heart missed a beat and for a moment he forgot to breathe. He could say nothing. He was paralyzed, trapped, unable to think.

The Hellion was not alone. Two others hung back in the corridor with cold stares. Mouth made no advance but sat on his haunches coolly. He eyed Bowie with great curiosity, eager to see what the human would do next.

"Welcome to Otherside," he said, "I'm glad you've finally come. As you can see, you aren't the first to arrive but we've been waiting for quite some time."

"How..." Bowie struggled to put it into words.

"How did he get here? That thing? Oh, I'm sure you can imagine," Mouth said, never once losing his eerie smile. "We made good use of him while we could."

Bowie backed away a step, gripping the pliers in his hand harder. He was cornered.

"What did you do to him?" Bowie asked.

"You mean, how did he die?" Mouth Shrugged. "He starved to death." His voice had a tone of satisfaction to it.

"What is he doing here? What did you mean 'you made good use of him'?"

Mouth laughed and the other Hellion joined in. "You're going to take his place. Isn't that wonderful? We've been waiting years for you. This is a very exciting time."

"What are you going to do?" Bowie asked, trying to buy himself a moment to think of a plan. He looked for a way around the Hellion but it was pointless. There was only one way out of the room.

"Shut up," Mouth said with sudden seriousness. He stepped forward and snatched Bowie by the same arm that held the pliers.

Mouth's grip was like iron. Bowie tried to jab him but he couldn't, nor could he pull his arm free.

Mouth leaned forward, his face just inches away from Bowie's. "Go ahead. Please. Struggle. I want to do this the hard way." The Hellion whispered.

Bowie immediately ceased. With a grunt of satisfaction, Mouth dragged him away by the arm. Bowie followed, helpless.

They led him to a wide-open chamber with crude stone pillars around its exterior. The ceiling stretched high above them and the outer walls curved around the room. In its center stood a round dais, carved in dark stone with crude marks like the ones from the other chambers. Mouth threw him to the ground on the dais and stood over him threateningly, his open rib cage bristling with excitement.

"Move from this spot and I'll tear the tendons from your legs." He threatened. Satisfied when Bowie remained still, he withdrew to the front of the dais and stepped down onto the floor below to join the other Hellion.

"Hurry. Open it." One of them said impatiently.

"We are going to wait." Mouth told him.

"For what?"

"Denegra needs to be here for this. It was his desire to see this plan all the way though, after all."

"Who cares about Den. He's a failure! Hurry up and open it! I want to see the other side."

Mouth pounced on him like a tiger, pinning him to the ground, snarling and spitting in his face. "You'll wait and shut your fucking mouth. Understand me?"

The Hellion remained quiet.

Mouth got off of him and kicked him square in the ribs before he began pacing the floor.

Bowie watched the whole exchange with fascination. He had no idea who Den was but he figured he would soon find out. He needed to find a way to escape but there was very little he could do. His weapon would be almost useless against the Hellion and in his current state there would be little chance of survival. It was clear that Mouth wanted him alive for something. He could buy himself a little time if he could just keep him talking. He pushed himself upright with a struggle and caught his captor's eye. "What are you opening?" He asked.

Mouth just laughed and smiled at him.

"Why did you even bring me here? Huh? Am I some kind of sacrifice?"

Mouth laughed even louder. "Sacrifice?! Hah! Nothing quite so trite and cliché. No. I need you just as you are, alive and breathing. You saw our previous catalyst. You're his replacement."

"For what?" Bowie asked, hoping for a more satisfying answer.

Mouth just shook his head laughing. "You really don't give up, do you?"

"What are you trying to open?" Bowie was determined to keep the conversation going.

Mouth darted toward him and smacked Bowie across the jaw with the back of his clawed hand, sending him sprawling. "Silence!"

Satisfied when Bowie laid still, Mouth stepped down from the dais once more and went to the doorway.

Another Hellion soon appeared around the corner, limping in a weird way. His hand was little more than a stump, black and crusted over. His face was unmistakable. It was Victor's. He sneered at their captive as he entered the room. Loathing dripping from his eyes as he stalked toward the dais, his gaze fixed on Bowie.

"You took your sweet time." The other Hellion commented as he entered.

Denegra paid him no mind. Mouth stepped in his way abruptly. "We're all eager to get this done and over with. Are you prepared to make the tether?"

Denegra stopped. "Of course, I am. Do I look incompetent to you?" He sneered, "I've been waiting far too long for this."

"Watch your tone." Mouth warned, his lips a manic smile that sent shivers down Bowie's spine. He leaped up onto the dais and moved over Bowie who was trying to push himself upright. The Hellion wasted no time and made a slashing strike across Bowie's back near his kidney. He cried out from the pain and slumped back down on the stone. The slice was quick and clean and blood dribbled from the wound onto the stone dais.

As the drops flowed into the runes carved in the stone, the dais began to sink and seemed to absorb the light. The air began to charge with static and Bowie could feel electricity all around him. Mouth stepped down from the dais as Bowie began to push himself upright once more. He watched the runes as they sank deeper and deeper into the stone, pulling the light with them. He got to one knee, then managed to stand up. He looked at the Hellion who stood by in awe of the spectacle. Denegra's eyes were closed, his hands raised to the ceiling, his claws seeming to caress something delicately in the air. It was as if he was gently carving something in invisible tender flesh. All the while he whispered hissing syllables into the silence of the room.

Bowie expected to feel some kind of immense pain or be violently torn apart as the ritual continued but the only sensation he received was the tingling in the air. He thought to remove himself from the dais but with the Hellion watching he was sure they'd try to stop him. He knew he didn't have the energy to resist. Slowly, the runes died down and returned to their simple state etched into the stone. When the last bits of shadow left the stone surface, Bowie felt both relieved and confused.

"What, that's it?" He laughed a little at the Hellion.

Denegra finished his incantations and relaxed his arms, lowering his gaze to meet Bowie's.

Without warning, black shards exploded from Bowie's body like a thousand quills and he screamed, his body arching in agony. Then, just as quickly as they had appeared, they withdrew into his body and were gone. The pain vanished and Bowie fell to the ground. The world swam around him and his vision blurred. He wretched and vomited there on the dais before he blacked out.

When his sight returned, the Hellion were smiling, pleased.

"It's open! Finally!" One of the Hellion proclaimed.

"And what happens if he dies? Then what?" another asked with concern.

"Relax." Mouth assured them. "If we need another one, we'll use that fat pig."

"Hey!" Denegra barked, clearly offended.

Mouth turned to him with a half-smile. "What? Did you think you weren't expendable? Just because you know the rituals doesn't make you untouchable. Don't forget that."

"Fine. Just stay out of my way." Denegra snarled. He turned and left the chamber with an air of malicious anger. The other Hellion began conversing in ugly whispers as Mouth approached the Dais. He stepped back onto the platform and leaned over Bowie with a grin.

"You see." Mouth crooned. "That wasn't so bad, was it?" He saw Bowie mouth something inaudible. He leaned a little closer. "I'm sorry. What was that?" This time he could hear only a mumble so he stepped in a little closer and leaned further. "Come again?"

"I hate it when you fuckers smile." Bowie said. With a quick strike he jammed the short knife of his multi-tool into Mouth's leg just above the ankle.

He roared in pain and wrenched his leg away, tearing the knife from Bowie's grasp. It clattered just a few feet away and Mouth stumbled back a step. With an enraged snarl he rushed at Bowie, grabbed him up by the front of his shirt with one hand and prepared to strike with his claws. He was all set to jam them into the Bowie's throat when he saw the look of defiance in the young man's eyes.

He stopped. "Nice try." Mouth said hoarsely. "You're not going to die that easily. Rest assured you will pay for that, human."

It was Bowie's turn to smile. He didn't know exactly what the Hellion had done to him but he knew that the ritual had changed him in some way. He had become something of immense value to the Hellion and he was damned if he was going to be their tool. He had stabbed his captor knowing full well how the Hellion might react.

Mouth dropped his hand and dragged Bowie from the room, down the corridor. Bowie struggled at first to free himself but he had very little left in him to resist. He was in too much pain. Mouth brought him to a nearby room much like the one he'd awoken in and tossed him inside, slamming the stone door closed.

Bowie lay sprawled where he'd landed. He had no will to move. He was exhausted. He wanted so bad to escape, to be free, but the ritual had taken so much out of him. They had done something to him. He tried to piece it together. They'd called him a tether, a catalyst. He remembered what one of them had said. They wanted to "see the other side", to open something. He had a feeling he knew what they meant. He was part of some sort of gate to his own world. The Hellion were going to use him to reach his home.

But why was his grandfather here? The question rattled around in his mind. Archer had died years ago. They'd found his home burned down but they never managed to retrieve his body. It was assumed he had been incinerated. Yet, he was here in Otherside. It was enough to make Bowie's head spin. No matter how much he tried to figure it out, the facts remained the same. Bowie was somehow connected to Otherside and his grandfather had something to do with it. The Hellion were going to use him as a gate to get to the real world and he was trapped. He'd lost the only tool he really had. It was still sitting on the dais. He had no means to escape.

He laid there for a while, feeling the weight of defeat sinking in. He started recounting everything all the way from the beginning. The mirror, the brass, the battle on Keene Road, The Eidolon and Amy. He remembered searching for his other self. Arsen had been so determined to avoid apathy and lifelessness. No. That wasn't exactly true. Bowie was determined to avoid it. In his heart of hearts, it was him deep down screaming to change his life for the better. He felt it, right down to his core. It was like a hot ember, glowing red inside.

Bowie's eyes opened wide. When the Effigies had helped him locate Arsen they'd used him as a sort of divining rod. He'd felt drawn. Did it work in reverse? If Arsen was still alive, maybe he could reach out to him. While he couldn't say for certain it would work, he had to try.

Bowie closed his eyes and directed his thoughts toward his counterpart. He focused on that burning desire within himself and the struggle the Effigy had awoken

within him. Slowly he tried to relax and let his mind go
blank.

XVIII

He woke, aching and hungry. Pushing himself from the ground, he took inventory of his injuries. He must have fallen asleep. He was still in a lot of pain but at least he was able to get up. That's when he heard a wretched scream and saw a flash of light from underneath the stone door. Something was happening in the corridor. He moved to the door and pressed his ear to it.

Another snarling scream echoed through the stone, followed by the roar of fire and a loud *boom!*

Then silence, followed by footsteps.

Bowie took a step back.

"Come on." Varela said, offering out a hand as the door swung wide. "We need to get moving. Now!"

Not sure what was happening Bowie followed as fast as he could manage. Amy was there waiting in the hall with her machete and a flashlight. "Amy!" He exclaimed.

"Bowie! Thank god! Come on. You look like hell. We need to get out of here, fast!" She rushed to his side and put his arm over her shoulder. He hobbled along with her while Varela took point.

"How did you find me?" Bowie asked.

"Yeah. Funny story..." Amy said. "Remember that old courthouse we passed?"

"Yeah."

"I had a hunch. Turns out I was right. It's the nest."

"Nest?" Bowie asked, but he never got an answer.

Two Hellion bound around the corner ahead of them. They had scarcely moved before Varela's bow thundered and the arrow pierced the first Hellion's skull and penetrated the stomach of the second, pinning both to the wall.

"Damn!" Bowie said, wide eyed.

"Oh, shut up." Varela said hotly.

They pushed through the corridors as quickly as they could, taking out what few Hellion dared venture too close. In such confined quarters Varela was a force to be reckoned with. There was nowhere to dodge in the narrow corridors from her thundering bow.

"Wait!" Bowie exclaimed just before they turned another corner. "Victor. We have to find Victor." He started hobbling back the other way.

"We can't!" Amy called after him. "We don't have enough time. They know we're here."

"We can't leave without him." Bowie insisted. "Come on." He urged. "He's got to be in one of these rooms somewhere."

"Bowie!" Amy shouted as she chased after him. "We're all going to get killed unless we get out of here. It was all we could do to get this far. If we stay, we won't make it. Come on! We need to leave. Now!"

"We can't!" Bowie shouted back. "Why did we even come here in the first place? Huh?"

"What does that have to do with losing our lives?!"

Bowie groaned. "We came here to save him! That's why we're here."

"What we agreed is that we would try to save him. We've done that and we've failed. We've run out of time." Amy pointed down the hallway and lowered her voice. "There are swarms of Hellion out there in Otherside and if we're not careful they're going to come back while we're still here. We can't save anyone if we're all dead now, can we? I mean, come on! Get real."

Bowie slowed down until she caught up and looked her right in the eye. "And what does that mean for us? Huh? We just give up because things seem impossible. Our best chance to find him is right now. If we leave, it'll be that much harder later"

"Would you just take a look at yourself?!" She said, "you're in no condition to rescue anyone. If we don't go it's a guarantee they'll come and you won't be able to defend yourself."

"It's not a guarantee." Bowie shook his head. "Listen to yourself."

"I am listening. Are you?" She was getting heated.

Bowie wasn't going to have it. "I'm not going to just give up!"

"Oh, for the love of..." Amy looked down the passage just to see if they had been discovered yet. "Why can't you just let this go and get out of here?

"Because that's not the kind of man I want to be!" Bowie roared.

"I came all this way for you! Don't you get it?" Amy roared back.

"Enough!" Varela, who had remained quiet up until then, broke her silence. Amy and Bowie were still glaring at each other. Varela took in a deep breath and sighed. "Bowie's right. We don't have time to argue about this. If we leave now, they'll reinforce this place. If they figure out we're trying to rescue Victor, they'll either move him or kill him. Is that what either of you two want?"

"See?" Bowie insisted.

"That's enough." Varela said sharply. "She's also right. You are in no condition to defend yourself. So, stay behind me and let's make this quick. We don't have much time before they find us here. Now move!"

Varela took point and led them through the wandering hallways. The complex was immense. As far as she was concerned, five minutes was pushing it. Then they would need to leave. She checked in room after room, most of which were empty. Several hid Effigy and Hellion corpses from long ago.

"Wait!" Bowie called out, pulling back from Amy who was supporting him along the way. "There." His gaze was fixed on a strange pale light emanating from beneath a door. With the help of his companions he pushed it open. On the other side was a round, crudely shaped room with a thick stone pedestal at its center. The protrusion was cut into a perfect cylinder from the stone floor beneath, with a latticework of etchings at odd angles carved into its surface. Above it, embedded in the ceiling was a crude crystal, glowing brightly with cold white light. Floating in between about three feet above the pedestal was Bowie's knife as well as an old Colt .45 revolver.

Bowie approached slowly, eyeing the device carefully. "What the hell?"

Varela stood impatiently by the door as Amy caught sight of Bowie's backpack tossed carelessly into the corner. She picked it up and held it out to Bowie.

Bowie, however, was mesmerized. "What do you think this thing is?" He asked.

"Who cares? Let's go." Amy insisted.

"Hold on. Let me at least get my knife back." He clambered up onto the pedestal and grabbed hold of his weapon, taking the pistol with him as well. The light felt cold on his flesh and for a moment he could see faint outlines in the room around him, as if he was peering into somewhere else entirely.

"Bowie! Snap out of it." Amy called out to him.

"Huh?" he said as his attention returned. "Sorry."

Once he got down, he stuffed the gun in his backpack and threw the bag over his shoulder, wincing as he did. Although he was far from fighting condition, he was glad to at least have his stuff back. He noticed that his pack felt a lot lighter, however.

"Hold on." He dug through his pack. "Shit." He hissed.

"What?" Amy asked.

"The nail-gun's not in here." Bowie said angrily. "They must have taken it."

"We don't have time to look for it, Bowie." Amy told him. "Come on. We need to go."

He shouldered the pack again and they left. They took a turn out of the room, when they heard a panicked scream from the other direction.

"Victor!" Amy recognized the voice. "Come on. Varela, this way. It might be him."

They moved in the direction of the scream, which echoed again several times and stopped before they could reach its source.

"It was down this hall. I'm sure of it."

Up ahead the hallway expanded to the left in what looked like a grotesque nest of bones and cloth, arranged near the walls like the beds of large birds. In the corner a hole sloped down into an adjoining chamber.

Amy shined her flashlight into the hole. Several yards down she saw a smooth stone floor etched much like the pedestal they'd seen before.

Someone cried out in fear at the source of the light.

"Is that him?" Bowie asked.

She shrugged. "I can't tell. I can't see anyone."

"Vic!" Bowie called down to him. There was no reply so he called out again.

They were getting nowhere so, letting Amy lead the way, they clambered down the hole. At the bottom they found Victor a sorry mess, huddled in the corner, letting out whimpers and yelping in terror.

"Vic. It's us. It's Bowie and Amy," Bowie said, stretching out a hand to help him up.

"Is... is it gone?" Victor asked, refusing to show his face from behind his folded arms.

"What?" Bowie looked around the room to see what Victor was talking about but there wasn't anything there besides them. "There's nothing here, man," he said.

"I saw it just a moment ago. It's here. The spider. It's here."

"It's gone. There's no spider." Bowie turned to look at Varela. "Are there even spiders in Otherside?" He asked.

She gave him an odd expression that he couldn't interpret.

Victor peeked over his arm warily. "Oh. Okay. Good. I thought it got me. It took my arm. See?" He held out his arm but it seemed in perfectly fine.

"Uh..." Bowie looked to Amy.

"Oh my god. Look at what time it is." Victor started staring at the floor oddly.

"Are you alright, man?" Bowie asked.

"Huh? Oh. It's you..." Victor looked less than pleased to see him.

"Listen. We need to get you out of here. Like, now." Bowie took his arm and tried to get him up. Victor's obesity made it harder for him to push himself up but he didn't resist. Bowie noticed that his clothes were torn in several places and his skin was rather pale. He gave Amy a look.

She shook her head and gave him a hand. She had no idea what was wrong with him. "Come on. You can do it."

"Are we going someplace nice now?" He asked lazily, his head hanging a little low.

"Yes. Yeah, we're going someplace nice." Bowie lied.

"That thing," Victor began, his voice suddenly much clearer, "That thing isn't coming back, is it?"

They began making their way up the slope and out of the hole.

"What thing?"

"That *thing!* That... Me! With the split-up face!" Victor trembled both with anger and fear.

"The Hellion, you mean." Varela finished for him.

"I don't know," Bowie answered. "What did it want with you?"

"It was spouting nonsense," Victor began, "It kept telling me that it wanted to make a deal. That it would give me gifts beyond my wildest imagination. Something about a pact. I don't know. I... that thing was just god damned..." His voice trailed off.

"Pact?" Amy looked to Varela.

"We can talk about this later," Varela said. "For now, keep quiet. We still have a way to go before we're free of this place, and even further before we're truly safe."

"Oh! Spiders!" Victor shook and tried to turn away as they continued down the empty hallway.

"Some place nice, Vic. Someplace nice." Bowie said to sooth him as he grabbed him by the arm. Victor calmed down and was a little more cooperative, though his eyes kept darting left and right at imaginary things, in between him bowing his head from exhaustion.

They encountered a few Hellion along the way. Varela made quick work of them in such tight quarters, her arrows leaving craters in the stone walls. Victor slowed their progress as his hallucinations continued to grow more and more vivid in short, temporary bursts, though his energy seemed to be on the wane.

The halls opened up at last into a large natural foyer with a cave entrance at one end. Light spilled into the chamber from the outside, catching swarming Hellion as they crawled around the walls in an attempt to overtake the Effigy standing at the room's center.

Arsen was in full force, blasting fire from his palms and engulfing numerous creatures in a blazing torrent. As some shrieked and retreated, thrashing around in the flames, others tried to attack from Arsen's blind side. He swept the blaze across the room and caught them before they could reach him.

"Arsen!" Varela shouted over the sounds of shrieking Hellion.

He saw them and rushed to their side, placing himself between the Hellion and the rescuers. "With me!" He shouted, indicating that they should follow. They moved as quickly as they could, helping Bowie and Victor along toward the entrance. They emerged at the bottom of a massive hole, almost like a quarry, dug into the rock at an impressive depth, the rim above them at least a thousand feet high. They trekked up the slope that spiraled around the outside wall as Arsen popped off fireballs at the Hellion that came crawling out of the pit like wretched insects. After a long while, they reached flat ground. The Hellion from the pit ceased their attack, retreating into the safety of their nest to avoid Arsen's searing assault.

"We need to keep moving." Arsen said once he crested the top. "We've bought ourselves some time but it won't be long before they come after us."

"Let's head back to the tower." Amy suggested. "We'll be safe there, right?"

"No," Varela answered back, "that would put us in more danger."

"What? Why? I thought the tower was safe."

"Varela is right," Arsen agreed. "They're expecting us to head that direction to reunite with our allies."

"We should head north. They don't usually go that way." Varela suggested, already heading that direction. The others followed her.

"What about him?" Bowie asked, indicating Victor who was looking worse by the minute.

"We'll have to get some distance first, then find some cover where we can tend to him. I'm sorry but that's the best we can do right now." Varela said.

"Okay." Bowie looked over at his manager in sympathy.

They walked for near half an hour, keeping a decent pace all things considered. They passed into a suburb filled with the hollow shells of homes and were just about to pass into the third block when Victor collapsed to the ground.

Bowie cursed and he and Arsen worked together to get him off the ground.

"He's passed out." Arsen said, checking Victor's pulse. "We need to get him off the street."

"There," Amy said, pointing out an old neighborhood convenience store just down the way. The building was mostly intact and, unlike the other buildings, had fully constructed walls to take shelter in. "We can go there."

All agreed and they moved Victor in through the swinging glass door. Inside was dim with little light coming in through the windows. To Bowie and Amy's surprise, the building very nearly represented the real world. Aisles were clearly marked on the floor, though there were no shelves, and a counter stood in the corner near the door. Even a bank of freezer doors lined the back wall. Aside from the emptiness, it brought them a little relief from the strange distortions of Otherside.

"This is Dale's Pit Stop." Bowie noted as he took a seat against the wall in the corner.

"What?" Amy asked as she helped Varela get Victor into a laying position nearby, sliding her backpack underneath his head.

"Dale's Pit Stop. We used to come here as kids. My friends and I would save up our change or beg our moms for money so we could come here and buy candy. Dale sold it by the piece so it was super cheap. That was when I was like seven or eight," he explained.

"Huh. Yeah. I didn't grow up here so I don't know," Amy shrugged.

"Yeah. No worries. At least I have a good idea where we are now. How is Vic?"

"Unconscious." Varela said gravely. "He's very pale."

"What did they do to him?" Bowie asked.

"It's hard to say." Arsen answered. "We've never had any survivors return from a Hellion nest. Heck, we're the first to find it and get away."

"We haven't gotten away yet." Varela reminded him.

Bowie let out a sigh and slumped his back against the wall, glad to have a breather for a moment. His thoughts drifted away as the group sat nearby tending to Victor and he remembered all the time's he'd wanted to punch that son of a bitch in the nose. He deserved what he got in a lot of ways and yet here they all were, risking their lives to save him. He shook his head and thought back to that heated conversation in Vic's office. It was sheer insanity, he thought. He wondered where he'd be if he had never learned of this strange and twisted world. Would he have even had that conversation in the office, or would he have kept his mouth shut and taken the abuse? Bowie laughed to himself. Confronting Victor for the first time had been a tremendous release, like releasing a pressurized steam valve. He ran the conversation through his head as he glanced over at their obese patient, lying helpless and pale on the floor.

"Wait." Bowie said suddenly as he remembered something. There had been a small blue zipper pouch on Victor's desk during their last conversation in his office. Now that he thought about it, it had always been there, he'd just never really given it any notice.

Everyone turned their attention to him.

"He's diabetic." He realized aloud, digging through his backpack.

Amy gave him a quizzical look.

"He's low on blood sugar. That's why he's been hallucinating." He explained. "I doubt we'll be able to manage his levels completely, but he needs food."

"Should we even give him anything?" Amy asked with concern. "Don't we need one of those insulin shots or something?"

Bowie managed a grim smile. "We don't have any and even if we did it wouldn't help. His blood sugar is too low right now. We need to get him to eat something. If we can get his blood sugar up, we can at least get away from here long enough to get him back to the real world. Then we can get him to a hospital."

Amy shook her head and stood up, taking a step back so Bowie could try to feed Victor one of the meal bars they'd brought. After a few attempts it was clear that Victor was not going to be able to chew anything. "Hold on. We need to get him something he can drink."

Amy dug through her pack. "What about this?" She produced a small can of apple juice.

Bowie took it from her gratefully and popped the tab. "Oh my god. This is perfect. Help me get him to drink it."

Amy tilted Victor's head back while Bowie tried to gently pour it in his mouth.

"If we were just talking about survival, I'd be giving you so much crap for packing these," Bowie teased, "but I'm glad you did."

"Gee, thanks." Amy rolled her eyes.

"You may have just saved his life. I'm not trying to complain. What made you want to pack these?" He asked.

"We used to take these with us when my family went camping. They're smaller cans than normal so I figured they'd be better for traveling. I remember loving these when I was a kid." She explained.

Victor's pallor began to improve and Bowie asked him if he thought he could eat a bite. Victor nodded and Bowie began to feed him.

"Man. If you'd told me I'd be hand feeding this guy three days ago I wouldn't have believed you. When we get back to the real world let's pretend this didn't happen, okay?" Bowie said to Amy.

"I've been thinking about that," she said. "Didn't you tell me that only your other self can send you back?"

"Yeah." Bowie nodded.

"Well... isn't his other self one of them?"

Bowie paused. She was right.

"So how are we going to get him back?"

Bowie looked to Arsen for an answer but the Effigy could only shrug.

"You can't send him back?" He asked.

Arsen shook his head. "One thing at a time. Let's focus on getting somewhere safe. We can figure out what to do about Victor then."

Amy was determined. "Varela, when you send someone back, do you open up a gate or something?"

Varela rolled her eyes. "It's not that simple. It's more like folding someone out of our world."

Both Bowie and Amy waited for a better explanation.

"Think of it like a piece of fabric that lines your world." Arsen explained. "You fold two parts of the cloth together around an object to create a kind of bubble in the fabric. In that way you aren't in your own world, you're inside the fabric. We just kind of pull the fabric tight, which pops you back into your own world."

"That's a gross oversimplification." Varela sighed.

"The bubble you exist in is only really big enough for you. It's not like we can squeeze someone else in there. Especially not him." Arsen thumbed over toward Victor.

"So, what do we do, then? Try to talk Victor's Hellion..."

"Den." Bowie filled in.

"... Talk Den into sending him back?"

Arsen looked to Bowie and Varela with half a shrug. "Yeah. I guess."

Bowie raised an eyebrow. "How the hell are we going to do that?"

Varela laughed. "Easy. We get the two of them together and then we threaten to kill your version. The

Hellion wouldn't risk his own life through his counterpart. We just have to make it convincing."

"Ooh. That's a little dark, isn't it?" Bowie asked.

"I kind of like it." Amy admitted. "At least we have some kind of a plan. Problem is we need to get Vic's Hellion isolated."

"Well, the first step is getting him mobile," Bowie said. "Once he's on his feet we can keep heading north and put some distance between us and them." His stomach growled and he dug through his pack for another meal bar. "You hungry?" He asked Amy.

She shook her head. Her appetite hadn't been much since the incident at the wading pool. She noticed Victor beginning to improve as he ate so she focused her attention on him and helped him sit upright. "How are you feeling? Any better?" She asked.

Victor nodded but said nothing. It was clear he wasn't interested in any sort of conversation at the moment.

"They called me a tether. Any idea what that means?" Bowie asked suddenly. The rest looked at him curiously. When no one offered an answer, he continued. "They took me to a weird room and performed some kind of ritual on me. I think they were trying to open up a gate of some kind. I remember them saying they needed me alive and they were all getting impatient."

"What do you think?" Arsen asked.

"It made me think that they're trying to get to our world somehow and they need one of us to do it." Bowie suggested.

"Well, crap." Amy said. "Is that even possible?"

"There's too many questions." Varela said. "It would take far too long for you to understand the ways of our kind and there's even less we know about the Hellion and their rituals. We can speculate later. How is he doing? Can he walk?" She looked impatiently at Amy and Victor.

Amy nodded and helped Victor to his feet, letting him take the rest of the meal bar for himself in case he needed more to eat. "So, what's the move?" She asked as she took Vic's arm over her shoulder.

"We head north and cross the river," Varela said. "If we can make it past the far shore, I know a place we can go, past the timber plain, where we'll be safe. Let's get moving before we get discovered."

Arsen took the lead alongside Bowie, followed by Amy and Victor who were moving at a snail's pace, and Varela who brought up the rear as they set out. It was slow going and every moment was an agonizing reminder that they were being pursued. They traveled in silence, each keeping a watchful eye. For Arsen and Varela it seemed like business as usual. For Amy and Bowie, it was endless paranoia, seeing shadows and movement around every corner. It was exhausting.

Victor improved considerably and was able to walk under his own power for some time, though it was clear they would need to keep an eye on him in case his condition worsened. His presence made the rest of them quite uncomfortable. After a long while, without making eye contact with anyone, he said quietly "Thank you."

For a moment, Bowie didn't recognize that Victor had even spoken. It just seemed a foreign noise to him. He turned and looked at his manager, who looked down at the ground in shame.

"What?"

"Thank you." Victor mumbled again, this time with a hint of anger.

Bowie almost asked him again but he decided instead to just be grateful that Victor had said anything at all, let alone a thank you. "We're not out yet," he said.

"You can thank us when we get home." He walked on for a few moments before he said over his shoulder, "You're welcome."

That was perhaps the first time Bowie had ever seen a reason to treat Victor like a human being.

After an arduous walk, they had nearly reached the river. By then Victor seemed to have most of his strength. Amy continued helping him along anyway, keeping an eye on him.

Arsen and Bowie walked side by side in silence, exchanging glances every once in a while. Bowie thought to say something but words escaped him. What does a man say to his own reflection? Every time they met each other's gaze he felt an innate understanding with the Effigy, as though they were in harmony. Thinking on it, he was fighting to save someone's life. He felt as though he was living for a greater purpose. Bowie laughed a little to himself and looked over at Arsen. The Effigy looked back with a smirk on his face, as though he understood the joke. They said nothing and continued ahead of the others, keeping their eyes out for trouble.

Varela brought up the rear, an arrow resting on her bow string. She kept herself relaxed with the practice of a seasoned warrior but her senses were heightened, alert for anything. As she kept watch for trouble a knot grew in the pit of her stomach. She could feel it closing in; a sense of impending doom.

"If we get into any trouble at the river, do you think you'll be able to swim?" Amy asked Victor, breaking him off another piece of the meal bar as they crossed the street and down the slope into the riverside park.

"I can try." He said quietly. "Worse comes to worse I'll float across. This insulation is good for at least something." He joked, patting his belly. No one had time to laugh, however.

"Incoming!" Varela shouted, "run!"

Amy turned to see what was happening. From the husks of empty buildings Hellion emerged, slow at first but, as soon as Amy and the rest picked up their pace, they charged. There were nine of them coursing down the slope behind them as they ran for the river.

Bowie and Arsen were just a few moments from the shore. Moving together they turned and ran parallel to the water to draw some of the Hellion away and provide support while Amy and Victor caught up. Amy pushed Victor along as best as she could but he was in no shape to run. Behind them, Varela stood her ground.

The archer drew up her bow and took careful aim as the Hellion descended. Two of them broke off from her left to circle wide and come at her from the side, while the right side of the mob ran right toward her. Stepping quickly to the side she let loose her arrow with a resounding boom! The Hellion leading the charge on the right side never stood a chance. The missile struck square in the forehead, sending it toppling end over end to the ground. Before it had even stopped moving, she had another arrow drawn tight.

Arsen and Bowie fanned out further along the shore as Varela quickly backed away from the approaching mob. A bolt of searing flame shot from the Arsen's hand and missed the center of the enemy formation. It was just enough to provoke one of the Hellion to hang back and put some distance between them. Varela took advantage of the cover fire and took a shot at the nearest Hellion on the right before continuing her retreat. The arrow ripped clean through the creature, wounding it and forcing it to slow its advance.

Victor and Amy were nearly caught up with Bowie and made a bee line for the narrow bridge that arched across the river.

"Get to the river. We'll hold them off!" Shouted Arsen. He moved up to draw the Hellion away from Victor and Amy. When Bowie moved with him, he turned and barked, "that means you too!"

Bowie hesitated.

Arsen would not have it. "Go!" He shouted.

Bowie didn't like it but he turned back and ran to regroup with Amy and Victor.

The Hellion were closing in rapidly as Varela took another shot, piercing the throbbing gullet of another enemy as she continued backing away.

"Come on!" Arsen shouted at her as the others began crossing the wooden bridge.

The bridge was slick with frost and it was all Bowie and Amy could do to keep Victor moving forward. The overweight manager stumbled and slipped, yelping as he struck the cold timbers. Amy shouted encouragement and helped Victor clamber up before he had time to slip again.

The Hellion spread out as they approached, making it more difficult for either of the Effigies to slow them.

Left with little option but to take them out one by one, Arsen conjured a white-hot fireball and immolated one of the Hellion that had circled around toward the edge of the charge. As it collapsed with screams and hisses, Arsen moved closer to the bridge waving and waiting for Varela to catch up while he provided cover fire.

Varela was too concerned with the sheer number of threats to turn and run. She picked out a target and rapidly fired two shots, one to put the creature off balance and the second to pierce its chest. It survived the shot but crumpled to the ground in agony. She continued shooting as Arsen shouted at her to retreat. She had nearly forgotten about the two Hellion who had circled left and turned her attention their way as Arsen sent a wave of fire at the remaining Hellion charging from the center. The fire was enough to catch the leg of one, causing it to scream and limp away in pain.

Varela picked off one charging from the side but in that moment when her attention was divided, the two remaining Hellion took advantage of the opening and sprinted toward her with incredible speed. Seeing that she wouldn't be able to take them on, Arsen ran to get to her side, sending up a wave of fire to protect her flank. It was enough to engulf one of them but the other darted to the side and pounced.

Varela had targeted the same Hellion engulfed in flame. She had just let fly another arrow, skewering it and sending it to the ground. There wasn't enough time to fire another shot.

The ravenous creature descended upon her, digging in its talons and tearing at her with its vicious jaws.

"NO!!!" Bowie screamed from the bridge as he looked back just in time to see Varela fall.

It was too late. The creature tore through her throat with its teeth sending black ichor everywhere.

With a primal roar, Arsen's body grew searing white and he tackled the ravenous beast. His fingers closed in on its throat and he pinned it to the ground with a face of unbridled rage. The Hellion choked and sputtered, thrashing around wildly. Its claws scratched and scraped the Effigy but still he held on and with a mighty flare reduced the creature to choking ashes. His eyes darted to the few wounded Hellion who were still standing, giving them warning not to approach. They kept their distance but looked eager for an opportunity to attack.

While they debated making an attack, Arsen caught sight of a lone figure at the top of the slope. It was hard to make out every detail but he noticed the Hellion's missing arm as it stood there watching patiently. Carefully, Arsen backed up and made for the bridge, sending bolts of fire behind him to keep the remaining Hellion back.

Bowie left Victor in Amy's care and hurried to Arsen's side to assist him. "Go back!" The Effigy bellowed as he moved onto the bridge. "We need to keep going!"

As wounded Hellion cautiously approached the bridge, Arsen took a deep breath and, with a powerful thrust of his hands, conjured a fierce flame that rapidly engulfed the structure, burning off the frost with a massive hiss.

The Hellion held back, fearful of the flames. When he was satisfied they would wait, Arsen turned and ran to catch up with his comrades.

XIX

Nobody said a word as they pressed hard to the north. They were all getting exhausted. Sometime later, long after the bridge was out of sight, they came across an irrigation ditch running parallel to the road near a suburb and Arsen motioned for them to climb down. There was no water running through it in the dead of winter so it made for an ideal place to lay low.

"Here." Arsen said once he'd gathered several clumps of weeds and tossed them into a pile. He snapped his fingers on a blade of tall grass and it caught fire. He nodded to his counterpart and Bowie busied himself collecting more bits of brush to feed the fire while Amy sat down and helped Victor take a seat nearby to warm up. Once Bowie felt he'd gathered enough brush he sat opposite them and stared into the meager glow.

Arsen kept watch, keeping his head just over the edge of the ditch to see if anyone was approaching.

"Hey," Amy began with concern, "won't they see the smoke?"

The Effigy nodded.

"They're going to find us!"

Arsen remained calm, his eyes alert as he kept watch. "I'm counting on it," he said coldly. "Take some time to rest while you can. It will be a while before the Hellion try to cross the river. We'll be long gone by then."

"Wait. What?" Amy shook her head, "I'm confused. First you say you want them to find us and then you say you want to leave?"

"Just... trust me." He replied, a little frustrated. "We need Denegra to find this camp after we leave. He'll most likely follow us on his own."

"How do you know that?"

Arsen shrugged. "Just a feeling."

There was a long and uncomfortable silence as they sat around the fire. Bowie kept his gaze on the flames, avoiding looking at Amy as best he could. The gravity of what had just happened felt like two tons of cement piled on his shoulders. He wanted to tell her that he was sorry, that everything was his fault but the words escaped him. Amy was trapped in Otherside and there was no going back. Eventually the food would run out. Eventually the Hellion or their Eidolon would catch them and it was over... Bowie swallowed and began to feel nauseous. He'd sentenced her to death.

As they sat quietly, Amy kept looking over at him, hoping he would look back, or say something of comfort, or anything at all, but he avoided her gaze and all she got was cold air biting at her skin. She swallowed and steadied herself, moving closer to the fire, trying hard to be brave.

"It's okay." She said quietly. She wiped her eyes casually, pretending it was the smoke.

Bowie looked up and their eyes met for a moment. Neither of them could find the words to say and so he swallowed and averted his gaze. He started up some conversation in the awkward silence that followed. "So, how did you know the courthouse was in the same place as the nest?"

She cleared her throat. "It was the only place I could think of. That courthouse is where one of the worst events to ever happen in Echo City took place. It was a hunch, but you told me that things are a reflection of our world. I guess it made sense."

Moments passed and the air grew warmer. The smoke began to sting his eyes so Bowie stood up and moved over to his Effigy's side. They stood together for a while saying nothing until Bowie asked, "You're planning to use Vic's connection to Denegra like the way I found you, aren't you?"

Arsen nodded.

"You think it will work?"

Arsen sighed, "no, but you do."

Bowie looked puzzled at first but nodded. "The other Hellion were threatening Denegra and, although they're using me as the 'tether', I heard them say something about killing me and using Victor instead. Den's going to want to keep Vic alive at any cost to save his own skin. If he brings the other Hellion they might not care if he gets caught in the crossfire."

"Exactly."

"You don't think it will work?" Bowie asked again.

Arsen sighed and looked his counterpart in the eye. "It's worth a shot."

"It's also a big risk," Bowie admitted.

"No way to know unless we try," Arsen said. "What about the girl?"

Bowie looked over his shoulder at Amy and turned away when her eyes met his. "I don't know what to say to her. This is all my fault."

"You were trying to do the right thing. Doesn't that count for something?"

"What's the saying? The road to hell is paved with good intentions? Whether my heart was in the right place or not, she's trapped and there's no going back. If we had just left Victor to die here none of this would have happened."

"And could you have lived with yourself if you had just let the Hellion take him?" Arsen asked.

"No. You're right. I couldn't do that. I don't think Amy could either. The regret of doing nothing would have haunted us the rest of our lives."

"The only thing necessary for evil to triumph is for good men to do nothing. And if you had left him to die," Arsen continued, "They would have used Victor as the tether and opened up a gateway to your world anyway. At least this way you know it's coming and can do something about it. If you didn't there would be no hope of containing the Hellion in Otherside."

"So, what do we do?" Bowie asked.

"Well... you aren't going to like..."

"Yeah, I know," Bowie finished for him. "If we can't get Victor and myself back to safety, then the only thing that would stop them is if all of us die. That's the only sure way to remove all possibility of them opening up a gate."

"Yup."

"But won't they try again? Won't they just project another one of themselves into our world and take someone else?"

"That's the thing, isn't it?" Arsen said. "You and Victor have counterparts. Not everyone does and in order to track someone down they would need someone who they know to have a counterpart here. The only reason you were targeted is because they knew you and I were connected. When Mouth projected into your world to hunt you down, he found Victor."

"Oh, shit. I led them right to him." Bowie realized. "What about Amy?"

"My guess," Arsen suggested, "is that without her counterpart her link to this world has been disrupted. Other than the fact that she's here, of course instead of over there. I don't know as much about this sort of thing as Halloran but I would hazard a guess that they can't use her like you or Victor anymore."

"I got you," Bowie nodded. "So, what now?"

"Now..." Arsen kept his gaze toward the river. "Now we need to get moving and put some distance between this campsite and us. Come on." He turned to Amy and Victor who were still huddled by the fire. "We need to get moving. Get him up. If we can cover enough ground, then there's a chance we can make this work. Let's go."

Victor grumbled and insisted he stay by the fire but, after some urging, they got him moving once again. They pressed on into neighborhoods neither Bowie or Amy recognized and after several miles they came across a wide-open plain with wooden timbers embedded in the soil at uniform intervals.

The Timber Plains were vast, bordered on one side by a road and on the other by massive pylons and the empty frames of storage buildings. Imbedded in the gravel, blackened timbers stretched on into the distance, each set a few feet from the next in a seemingly endless progression. To the west was a large concrete platform about three feet tall.

As they moved further into the plains, they noticed figures in the distance behind them rapidly approaching. Bowie and the others increased their pace but it was clear they wouldn't be able to make an escape in such a large open area.

"They're coming." Arsen noted.

"Damnit." Bowie cursed. "There's more than one."

"They're going to kill us all. What are we going to do?" Victor whimpered, looking around desperately for somewhere to hide.

"Don't worry, Vic. They would smell you from a mile away," Bowie said dryly. "There's nowhere you can hide. We have to stand our ground."

Amy noted, "At least there's just the two. We outnumber them."

Bowie swallowed. "In our current state, two is more than we can handle. That's Den. The other one's Mouth. I thought you said Den would come alone to better protect his other self."

Arsen nodded. "Mouth probably wouldn't let him out of his sight."

The Hellion approached to within a few yards, saying nothing. Den hobbled a little more without the use of his arm and Mouth smiled pleasantly as though enjoying an afternoon stroll. The tension was palpable as they studied one another.

"Give us the boy and we'll let you go." Denegra bargained.

Bowie wasn't going to hear it. "We're not giving up anyone. Go back to where you came from and we'll leave you in peace."

Denegra snarled.

"Please. Don't humiliate yourselves by forcing a confrontation. We would all prefer to avoid that. Just surrender this one," Mouth pointed to Bowie, "and we'll go."

Arsen gave him a cold stare.

Mouth shrugged. "Or, if that does not please you, surrender the fat one."

"Don't let them take me!" Victor pleaded with his rescuers.

"Hey! We had a deal." Denegra protested, snarling at his companion.

"I don't recall asking for your input." Mouth snarled suddenly before quickly adopting a pleasant smile once more. "Either one will suffice."

Bowie and Amy stood beside one another to shield Victor.

Mouth sighed. "Do we really need to drag this out?

"I will not allow you to harm him." Denegra objected as he took an aggressive stance.

Amy whispered to Bowie, "If we let them fight each other we'll stand a better chance against them."

While Denegra and Mouth exchanged growls and snarls, Victor quietly moved away, hoping to place himself far away from the horrifying creatures. He made it about ten feet before Mouth and Denegra noticed his movement. With a snarl, Mouth bolted to the side around Arsen and the others to get to Victor.

Darting around the other way to prevent him, Denegra made a lunge at Mouth and the two locked together, tumbling over the ground in a biting, snarling rage.

"Get away from them!" Bowie shouted at Victor, who stumbled dumbly, unsure of where to go.

"Out of the way!" Arsen barked and dashed forward, a growing inferno between his palms. Victor dove to the ground just in time as Arsen let loose a bolt of fire into the middle of Mouth and Denegra's fight.

The Hellion broke away from one another with impossible reflexes and the flame sailed clear. Without a moment's hesitation, Mouth charged Arsen, his maw wide, wild hunger burning in his eyes. Meanwhile, Denegra scrambled on the loose gravel and stood between Victor and everyone else, snarling and ready to defend his other self.

"Get to Vic!" Bowie shouted at Amy and they both moved to flank him. Bowie drew his knife and Amy her machete, following Bowie's lead. Victor was unsure what he should do and made to join Bowie only to fall backward when Denegra turned and snarled in his face.

During that brief moment when Denegra was distracted, Bowie made a dash, both hands on his knife, ready to plunge it into the creature. Denegra saw it coming and delivered a staggering kick with his elongated leg deep into Bowie's gut, sending him flying a good ten feet.

At once Amy made her move, hoping to catch the Hellion off guard. Denegra hopped back and her machete swung wide. He tried to reach in to snatch her by the throat but she slashed her weapon as quickly as she could in desperation to prevent him. She backed away a few steps, keeping her weapon in the way as best she could to keep the creature at bay but it was hopeless. The Hellion's reach was so much longer than hers that she couldn't put enough distance between them. Her only saving grace was that Denegra only had the one arm to attack with.

All the while Bowie and Amy were engaged with Denegra, Arsen and Mouth fought furiously. They exchanged attacks with wild abandon in a flurry of gravel, claws and fire. Arsen kept himself between the creature and his companions, shooting volleys of fire from his hands to keep Mouth from getting any closer.

The tenacious Hellion moved fluidly through the volleys, coolly anticipating every shot. Arsen realized the Hellion was predicting his moves and sent a large crescent of flame against Mouth's rhythm. The Hellion leaped back just in time to avoid it.

"You're not as incompetent as you seem." The Hellion jeered as he stepped back to start his charge anew. His claws dug in deep and he launched himself low at incredible speed underneath Arsen's blasts. "How delightful!"

Bowie had been stunned by the kick and gasped for air. By the time he recovered, Amy was quickly losing ground. He charged forward and took a quick swipe at Denegra's heel. The knife nicked its Achilles and it spun and roared. Bowie wasn't fast enough to escape its elongated arm and its claws ripped right across his left arm and chest leaving crimson tears in his flesh. The force of the attack sent him spinning to the ground, crying out in pain.

Amy screamed in horror and charged wildly as he went down. Surprised by the sudden fury of her attack, Denegra was pushed back, careful to avoid her relentless onslaught. As he continued his retreat, her attack lost steam and she overextended her reach to try for one last strike at the creature's chest. Denegra brought his claws down and slapped her arm out of the way. She stumbled forward and he whipped his leg around savagely to kick her in the ribs. She crumpled to the ground with a yelp of agony, her machete skittering along the ground as she lost her grip. Denegra was about to pounce on her when suddenly Bowie yelled, "stop!"

Amy had distracted Denegra just enough to give Bowie a chance to get to Victor. Out of desperation, Bowie did the one thing he knew would prevent the fight from continuing. Victor, who thought Bowie was trying to rescue him gladly allowed Bowie to place a helpful arm around him to help him get up off the ground. He was shocked when Bowie instead grabbed him by the shoulder and held the knife to his throat.

"Back off!" Bowie threatened. Denegra froze and the two became locked in a stare. Bowie had no intention of hurting Victor but it was the only thing he could do to protect Amy. In that moment he doubted his own conviction. He couldn't kill Victor just to save Amy.

Denegra could sense his hesitation and smiled cruelly. The moment seemed to stretch on endlessly as the tension mounted between them. Bowie could sense Denegra's muscles coiling, preparing to strike.

Amy began to stir from the ground, reaching out to crawl toward her weapon. Denegra noticed and hesitated, unsure whether to strike at Bowie or the girl.

Bowie pressed the knife tip against Victor's corpulent flesh. Victor went rigid, pulling as far away as he could to avoid the sharp steel.

"Go now or I kill him!" Bowie shouted, but his voice lacked conviction. Deep down he knew he couldn't do it but Victor was the only bargaining chip he had.

Meanwhile, Mouth taunted and jeered. Arsen didn't bother engaging in banter. Mouth was too fast. It was all he could do to keep up with the creature's speed. When his opponent made a sudden lunge at him, he barely had time to step back and bring up a wall of searing flame to keep Mouth back.

With a laugh, Mouth darted to the side to swipe his claws through the fire at Arsen's side.

The Effigy was only quick enough to avoid the strike by a hairsbreadth and, when he sent a bolt of fire in a counterattack, Mouth was already taking advantage of their change in position. Mouth made his move toward Bowie's exposed back.

With a twist of his hands, Arsen pointed his fingers to the sky and his fire curled around Mouth and shot skyward, creating a wall of fire between them. Snarling, Mouth turned back on Arsen as fast as he could. Arsen took advantage of his adversary's momentum and stepped sideways, winding his way around and moving his enemy with blasts of fire. When Mouth was sufficiently far away from his allies, Arsen renewed his attack and sent a great fireball straight at the creature.

Mouth was well prepared and slid underneath. No sooner had the scorching ball cleared his back than he sprang forward with blinding speed and pounced, clutching the Effigy's arms in his claws and knocking him to the ground.

"Haha!" He laughed triumphantly as he pinned Arsen to the ground. His maw spread wide eagerly as he looked down on his prey.

It was Arsen's turn to smile. "Now I got you," He said as the Hellion tightened its grip.

Mouth's expression was confusion turned to fear as Arsen's face ignited into a raging inferno. The heat was so intense that Mouth instantly started sweating. Though he had gained the upper hand he couldn't hold on any longer.

While Mouth and Arsen grappled, Denegra raised his one hand toward Bowie and began a half growling hum. Bowie only had time for a perplexed expression before something he hadn't anticipated happened.

Victor vanished.

Suddenly, he had no hostage. Denegra had sent Victor back to his own world.

Reacting as fast as he could, Bowie made a desperate charge. By then, Amy had retrieved her weapon. When she saw Bowie make a sudden attack she joined in and tried to catch Denegra's flank at the same time.

Caught in a pincer, his ankle sizzling from Bowie's knife, Denegra wouldn't be able to stop both of them. Instead he closed his eyes...

... and followed his other self.

Bowie and Amy slid to a stop where Denegra once stood.

"Shit!" Bowie cursed.

"What?! What happened?" Amy was beside herself.

"Damnit!" Bowie exclaimed, "He sent Vic back and must have gone after him."

While Bowie and Amy stood alone staring at the space where Denegra had been, Mouth abandoned his fight with Arsen and attacked.

Bowie was caught completely unprepared and cried out in agony as Mouth ran him through the back. Amy screamed at the sight of Mouth's claws showing through Bowie's gut.

Arsen didn't have time to get off the ground. Mouth's jaws were about to clamp down on the back of Bowie's neck. He did the only thing he could to save his other self. With an outstretched hand he pushed forth with his will and Mouth bit down on empty air as Bowie was shoved through the rift.

Mouth stood there for a moment, bewildered, before he realized what happened. Amy stood just feet away from him with a horrified expression. Without a moment's hesitation he grinned and leaped on her like a savage wolf. The wind was knocked from her lungs as she hit the ground and Mouth fell upon her.

Suddenly, the creature screamed and threw himself to the side, rolling on the ground in pain.

Amy was confused but soon she realized she was on fire. She yelped in fear but something wasn't right. She could hear the sizzling and smell burning flesh but it was Mouth that cried out from his burn wounds. She was unharmed, merely wreathed in glowing flames.

Arsen stood up with a wry smile and called out his foe. "Your fight is with me. Leave her alone," he commanded.

Mouth spat and his usual devious smile vanished, replaced with searing contempt. He clawed up a handful of gravel and threw it in Arsen's face viciously and charged. They tumbled in a mess of claws and flame.

It was mere moments before they broke apart again. Mouth roared angrily and dove back at his prey before Arsen could recover. He grabbed the Effigy by the collar, but before he could tear into his flesh he suddenly let go and darted to the side.

Amy's machete barely missed as she swung recklessly. She let out a primal scream, daring the Hellion to try another move.

Mouth hesitated. He seemed to realize something briefly before he smirked and fled, leaving a thin wisp of dust trailing behind him.

With a sigh of relief, Amy dropped her machete and fell to her knees, exhausted. She took in a deep breath and then let it go. The fight was over.

After a moment she asked, "Do you think he'll be back?" He didn't respond. "Arsen?"

The Effigy was almost completely absorbed, watching something unfold before him that she couldn't see.

"Arsen." She repeated his name.

"The fight isn't over yet." He said, engrossed in the images flooding his vision. His eyes followed unseen shapes and he held his breath. "Come on..." He muttered to himself.

Echo City was sharp and cold. Bowie fell onto all fours at first, breathless and disoriented. He tried hard to get his bearings. He was in a train yard. Steel rails stretched on endlessly in both directions and covered a massive expanse. Parked steel cars lay silently on the tracks blocking the road. He saw the corpulent figure of Victor clambering up onto the nearby concrete platform, fleeing for his life.

Denegra stood out in the bitter winter air. He seemed out of place now that he was free of the muted, shifting colors of Otherside. He looked every bit an unholy blight on the landscape. His exposed ribcage bristled hungrily around the gurgling gullet that begged to be filled. His elongated limbs and hunched back betrayed his animal-like intensity. The monster breathed heavily, his stumped arm and oozing leg radiating pain that made him all the more dangerous.

Bowie stood afraid, but prepared to fight to his last. Outmatched as he was, Bowie knew he was the only thing standing between Victor's wicked Hellion self and his city. His left arm clutched around his gut and in his right hand he gripped his grandfather's knife. He was exhausted. His right side was growing numb. Every labored breath put steam into the cold air.

They faced each other and said nothing. Both of them understood what had to be done. The train yard was silent and the air still. Denegra gripped the ground with his claws and Bowie dug in his feet. There was a moment when time itself seemed to grind to a stop.

The instant Denegra sprang forward Bowie made a wide arc with his knife and took a step back, causing the Hellion to hold back his attack for fear of the steel blade. However, it only bought Bowie a second. He simply wasn't as fast and before he could take another swipe the creature knocked him down with a fierce blow using its incredible reach. Bowie flailed desperately with the knife to keep Denegra's onslaught in check. He crawled backward as best he could but Denegra kept right on top of him, his jaws snapping as he leaned in, careful to avoid the singing weapon.

Denegra toyed with him, letting him crawl away a little only to catch back up again and try for another bite. When Bowie took a stab, trying to plunge the blade into Den's stomach, the Hellion swatted the blow away, knocking it out of Bowie's hand.

Bowie cried out. He was defenseless. Far away a train's horn sounded as though heralding his demise.

Denegra smiled wickedly. "Finally! I've been waiting too long for this," he growled, his eyes blazing with hunger and hatred. He took another step and stopped. There was a burning, hissing sound. He had stepped onto one of the steel rails Bowie had been crawling over. The metal began to sear against his flesh and he reared back, screaming in pain.

Bowie rolled over, grabbed the knife and with a burst of energy jammed it down through Denegra's foot, pinning it to the rail road tie. The Hellion roared in agony.

Almost too late Bowie realized that the horn had come from an approaching train bearing down right on top of them.

Denegra tried to pull his foot free but the blade held fast to the timber. He tried again and again, squealing and roaring, all the while the train's horn blared. Bowie rolled out of the way just in time, the heavy steel wheels grinding against the rails just inches away as the massive engine barreled right through Denegra.

The rail cars clattered and rolled past, lazily slowing as the train came to a stop some minutes later. Bowie lay there, catching his breath inching a few feet away and letting the railway do its work. Denegra was dead. Bowie rested his head on the cold dirt and let out a sigh of relief.

The cars eventually came to a stop and he was able to reach underneath to pry his knife loose. He clutched it to his chest and silently thanked his grandfather for leaving it to him.

The engineer came a few moments later while Bowie was pushing himself up off the ground. "Hey! You can't be here. You need to leave." The man said.

"Yeah... I know." Bowie said hoarsely as he staggered away from the train to find a way to the loading platform.

"Hey man. Are you okay?" The engineer noticed the blood soaking through Bowie's shirt.

"Yeah. I'll be fine," Bowie said, looking down to see just how bad his wound was. "I'll be fine."

The engineer helped him to the building. "Do you need me to call an ambulance? You've lost a lot of blood."

"Yeah. That might not be a bad idea." He said, feeling light-headed as he noticed someone looking back at him through the glass. It was Victor, who stared only for a moment before turning and leaving.

"Alright. Once we get you inside you need to sit down until help arrives, okay?"

Bowie nodded.

Grave concern spread over the engineer's face. "Look. I don't know who you are or what you were doing here but I won't say anything to the authorities if you'll promise to keep out next time, okay? You look like you could use a break."

"Yeah. I appreciate it. Thanks." Bowie said as they reached the door. Before he went inside, Bowie looked back at the train yard to the black smear on the tracks as it evaporated into the winter air.

An ambulance took him quickly to the hospital and they were able to patch him up. Beyond all odds, the wound had managed to miss his vital organs and although it would take a while to heal, he would eventually recover. Nobody asked him too closely what had happened, which he was grateful for and, after a night in the hospital, they sent him home.

Like the warm embrace of a summer's night, sleep took him as he lay on the familiar bed in his apartment. Even if just for the night he forgot about everything and the whole ordeal flew far from his mind.

When he awoke the next day to the gentle rays of winter sun peering through his small bedroom window, he felt relaxed for this first time in a long while. He lay in peace for a while, thinking nothing and not worrying about anything at all.

The jarring sound of his cell phone snapped him back to reality. For a moment he was afraid it was work calling but he didn't recognize the caller ID on his phone, so he answered.

"Hello, is this Mr. Bowie Swift?" Came an older man's voice from the other end.

"Uh. Yes, this is him," Bowie answered doing his best to not sound sleepy.

"Hello Bowie, this is Kyle Reddinger. I'm the general manager over at E. C. R. How are you today?"

"I'm doing alright," Bowie was a little surprised. "Uh. How are you?"

"I'm doing well. Thank you. Listen, I was going over your application and I was wondering if I could ask you a few questions. Do you have a few minutes?"

"Yeah. Sure!" Bowie replied. "Go ahead."

"I noticed you work for Fleischer and you supervise the freight team at the warehouse?"

"Yes. That's correct."

"How long have you been working there?"

"I've been there for a couple of years as a supervisor, and I was there as a freight associate for about three years before that."

"Alright. That's great," Kyle said. "Considering your leadership position, how would you feel about a non-management role?"

"Hmm..." Bowie thought about it. "Honestly, that sounds great. I like working with my team and all but I am looking for something different."

"Alright. Alright. Well, would you be interested in coming in for an interview this week?"

"That sounds great. What is the position?"

"Well, it's for a freight technician. The position involves loading and unloading and coupling and uncoupling cars. What do you think?"

"I'd be happy to interview. When can I come in?"

"Are you free Thursday at 10:00 AM?"

"Yes. I should be," Bowie said, though he wasn't sure if he was supposed to be working that day or not.

"Great. I'll see you then. Just come in to the main entrance and head down the hall, first door on the left."

"Alright. Great. Thank you."

"Thank you. I look forward to meeting with you. Have a nice day." the man said before he hung up.

Bowie smiled to himself and let out a big sigh. Maybe things would turn out alright.

"Oh crap..." Bowie thought aloud as thoughts of his own job flooded his mind. He tumbled painfully out of bed and quickly checked his calendar. He had work. Of course, he did. However, there was no way he could do his normal job in his condition. He fished through his drawer to find the note he'd asked for at the hospital.

He made a quick call and let them know he wouldn't be able to work for a week or so. They asked him to come in to fill out some paperwork. It was weird coming to the warehouse and seeing everyone. His team gave him strange looks. He wanted to say something to them but he couldn't think of what he could say. When he got to the office, he was surprised to find some unfamiliar faces. There were two older, nicely dressed gentlemen in the office with Victor who sat at his desk. One man was sitting on the corner of the desk and looked as though he had just gotten done saying something to Victor, who had a slight look of guilt on his face. The other was rifling through a filing cabinet in the corner. Bowie knocked on the door to get their attention. The two men turned, somewhat surprised, but Victor looked at him with an expression Bowie had never seen before or since. It was a subtle mix of confusion, disbelief, fear and gratitude and he wasn't sure what he should make of it.

"Hey." Bowie said, "I came to fill out some paperwork for a short-term LOA."

"Oh. Yes. Here," said the man in the corner. He handed Bowie a folder and went back to what he was doing. Bowie got the distinct impression he had interrupted something so he turned to leave. He laughed a little to himself when he saw the hole in the office wall which was still in a state of disrepair.

"You're Mr. Swift, right?" Asked the man sitting on the desk before Bowie could leave.

"Hmmm? Yeah." Bowie said, turning around.

"Do you mind if we give you a call later today to ask you a few questions?"

"Uh, sure." Bowie said.

"Great. Thank you," The man said, turning his attention back to Victor.

Bowie didn't hang around and headed back through the warehouse.

"Hey! What's up, man?!" It was Ed.

Bowie gave a huge grin as his friend came jogging up to say hello.

"Looks like you're still in one piece!" Ed commented, glad to see that Bowie was okay. "You alright? I was worried about you, man."

Bowie nodded. "Yeah, for the most part." He looked around to make sure nobody else was paying close attention before he tenderly raised his shirt to show Ed the dressings.

"Geez, man. Does it still hurt?"

"Not too bad. The pain killers are pretty good."

Ed took Bowie under his arm and led him to the side a little to get out of sight of the other workers. He indicated the gaping hole in the office. "What was all that, eh? That was some serious-"

"I know," Bowie cut him off. "Look. We can talk about it later."

"Sure. Why don't you come over and visit the family and we can talk about it over a drink, alright?"

"Sounds good man. Hey, who were those guys in there?" He thumbed over to the office.

"Oh man. Those guys. Listen, man. Victor was gone for a few days and nobody knew. They're here investigating what was going on, you know? Some serious stuff."

"You think they're going to investigate me too?" Bowie wondered.

"I doubt it man." Ed laughed.

"Why do you say that?"

"Cause I told 'em you had called me to let me know you were in the hospital the whole time."

It was Bowie's turn to laugh. "Thanks, Ed. I owe you one." He paused before he added, "what about everyone else?"

"Don't worry about it, man. I don't think they really know what happened but they like you. We all got your back."

"Cool. I appreciate it, man. Thanks."

They gave each other a fist bump before Bowie said goodbye and left. He looked to the sky as he stepped outside and took in a deep breath as he caught the first few rays of light peeking through the clouds. He wasn't sure what was going to happen in his future but things were changing. He decided right then that he was going to make the best of it, no matter how bad it got.

EPILOGUE

The sun had set by the time Bowie reached the sewage plant by flashlight. He unshouldered a heavy backpack and set it down in the gravel before taking out the brass ring and a cheap little mirror. He felt like he was growing used to the ritual already, which was a little disturbing, but he continued all the same. He made sure to grab up the bag again before he completed the process.

When the world had settled around him and he was once again in the uneasy shifting of Otherside, he was glad to see a familiar face.

Amy gave him a half-smile. "Hey."

"Hey." He said back. "You okay?"

"Yeah," she shifted uncomfortably. "How about you?" she indicated where he'd been run through.

He shrugged. "I'll be okay."

"How did your double know you'd be here?" She asked.

"Well, I guess we can kind of sense each other or something. It's a little weird, to be honest."

She nodded. "What happened with Victor and the other Victor?"

He told her what had happened and she was relieved.

"I brought you some supplies." He said, changing the subject and handing her the bag. She started digging through it. "There's enough food in there to last you a week, though nothing too amazing. And there's a lantern and some toiletries and stuff too. I'll come back in a few days and get you some other stuff. Whatever you need, okay?"

She dropped the bag and gave him a big hug. "You rock! Thank you!"

He patted her shoulder. "It's the least I can do since... well, you know…" There was an awkward silence for a moment.

"It's not your fault," she said quietly.

It took him a bit to say something. "Well... I still feel bad. We'll figure out a way to get you back home, okay? I promise. There's got to be a way."

She gave him a squeeze and then let go. "Okay."

"And Amy," he said, "thank you. For everything. If it weren't for you, I don't think I would have made it."

She smiled. "We did kick a lot of ass." She tried to look cool and offered up a fist bump.

He laughed a little and returned it.

"So," Amy said after an awkward pause, "what do we do next?"

Bowie didn't know how much further they had to go and how long it might take to fix things. He wasn't even sure it was possible when he really thought about it.

"We keep on moving forward," He said, "no matter what."

The End